Craving Jake
Return to Welcome Book 3
By
Bonnie Edwards

I0633212

Craving Jake Return to Welcome Book 3

Return to Welcome, Volume 3

Bonnie Edwards

Published by Bonnie Edwards, 2023.

This is a work of fiction. Similarities to real people, places, or events are entirely coincidental.

CRAVING JAKE RETURN TO WELCOME BOOK 3

First edition. January 20, 2023.

Copyright © 2023 Bonnie Edwards.

ISBN: 978-1989226032

Written by Bonnie Edwards.

Table of Contents

Dedication

This book is dedicated to all the volunteers and caring people
who run rescues: for people, for dogs, for cats, for turtles
Well, for anything...
Kindness wins with people like you in the world.

Chapter One

STALKING WASN'T ALWAYS a bad thing, Brianna Bowler told herself. Not when it happened by accident. Seeing Jake Morrow from afar three times in one month could be called a coincidence, couldn't it?

But this was the first time she'd seen Jake with his girlfriend. From across the street, Brianna froze in shock as they stood in front of the fire station together.

Jake had always been easy on the eyes and fifteen years hadn't changed that. Jake had black, untamed curls and deep blue eyes, and if she were close enough she'd see his spiky black eyelashes that looked like inky starbursts. Women would kill for those eyelashes. In fact, they paid swank prices for extensions that looked just like the ones Jake grew on his own. It wasn't fair.

But she was distracted from the real reason she stood numb and still at the open trunk of her mom's car.

Jake's girlfriend was petite and slim and looked like a chirpy little sprite in her skin-tight activewear cropped pants and her kicky cross-trainers. And her dark curling hair made her look like a little sister or cousin. She'd just bet the gorgeous specimen of femininity also had blue eyes.

Not to mention she looked much, much too young for him. Even from across the street and up the block Brianna could see she was a very young twenty-something. Young and fresh and pretty and perfect.

Brianna had already heard they lived together. She tried not to scowl, but Jake should be ashamed of himself. He was over thirty and this girl-child was an entire generation behind.

She shook off her dark emotions and bent to her task. And yes, her chest always clenched when she hefted bags of dog food and dumped them into a car trunk. Her eyes always smarted and her breath always caught.

Four bags later, she dusted the kibble dust off her hands and closed the trunk lid. She studiously kept her eyes away from the fire station's open front doors, where Jake and his perfect girlfriend stood, probably talking about what to have for dinner together or what shows they'd be binge-watching tonight. The ordinary stuff of lives lived together.

She didn't miss that part of a relationship, not at all. She'd left Anthony behind in Seattle and he'd been content enough to be left. Whatever they'd shared had run its course and she was free now. Single again, and not looking at Jake Morrow and his cheerful, chirpy child-sized girlfriend.

On stiff legs, she marched to the driver's side door and climbed inside the car. Slipping on her sunglasses, she sniffed as her side vision caught a quick kiss on Jake's cheek from the sprite. The woman had to go on tiptoe to do it. Fine. He liked them young and tiny. Everything Brianna wasn't. As her mom said, Brianna was statuesque, an old-fashioned word for tall and square-shouldered.

Not that it mattered. Not anymore. She was *so* over her high school crush. Had been for years.

Actually, she was glad Jake had found someone. After what happened all those years ago, it was a wonder he could find any happiness at all. She revved the motor a titch too hard in agitation.

Bowler's Dog Rescue needed a new truck, but she and her mom hadn't had time to even look at them. Until they bought a newer pickup, the rescue had to rely on her mom's ancient econobox that Brianna had learned to drive in high school.

She added the truck shopping chore to her mental list and squealed the tires as she took off. At the squeal, she winced and felt as if she'd whipped the poor old car like an old horse, poor thing.

She settled her shoulders. The squeal wasn't that bad, she thought, a mere chirp, hardly noticeable, she decided.

Brianna hated drawing attention and she feared her childish response to Little Miss Perfect had done just that. She drew a deep, calming breath and forced her hands to relax on the steering wheel. Gossip ran rampant in Welcome and her attempt at ripping up the road could be commented on.

She liked her hometown, she did. But returning to Welcome hadn't been as easy as she'd hoped. People seemed disappointed in her as if they'd expected her to set the world ablaze when she'd left. Nothing could be further from the truth.

Brianna had snagged a decent job in a field that was quickly disintegrating in a world that valued rumor and gossip over the truth. A fact-checker for a news team on a radio station, Brianna had developed mad skills and contacts, but little respect and no job security. When her mother needed help for a few weeks to recover from knee surgery, her boss had refused to give her the time off.

With her relationship stalled on neutral, she'd looked forward to coming home. Now, she wasn't so sure she was in the right place to be happy.

"I'm glad to be home in Welcome," she said to Beau, the rescue's mascot, who sat shotgun, tongue lolling out of his wide, grinning mouth. The pit bull's eyebrows shot up at the sound of her voice.

She wasn't sure who needed convincing, herself or the dog. "My mom needs my help and no one will chase me away again."

Beau groaned in agreement like he always did.

"No one," she emphasized with a glance at her rearview mirror, "including Jake Morrow and his sprite," she said with determination.

Beau farted and stuck his nose to the cracked-open window.

"I'm glad you agree," she said as she opened her window, too.

WAS BRIANNA BACK IN Welcome for good? She'd been here for at least a month. Jake Morrow watched her out of the corner of his eye as she picked up the last bag of dog food and stowed it in the back of an old car. Her mother's car if he wasn't mistaken. She must be visiting because she sure as hell wouldn't have moved back permanently.

"Thanks, Jake. I'll see you later," Theda raised her lips and caught him on the cheek before he could swing his head out of the way. He used his palm to swipe off the orange lipstick she had on this morning. Theda was messy in more ways than one.

"Sure. Let me know how the apartment hunt goes today."

Theda's wide, blue eyes moistened. "I'm baking your favorite pie today. Stop by the bakery when my shift's done and we'll bring one home."

"Sure," he replied. It was useless to point out that the pie baker was the owner, Alyce Markham. Theda's use of the truth was fluid and it came and went like the tide.

Besides, his mind was on Brianna and his gaze followed her mom's old car as it belched fumes down Main Street. Theda used his distraction to grab his jaw and raise her lips to his. Surprised, he allowed the kiss for a fraction of a second.

She took his hesitation as an invitation and wrapped her arms around his neck, pressing her body to his. He set his hands to her forearms to disengage.

She clung.

He tugged free.

And then he turned and walked into the station.

Doug Marton, his partner, waited with a sly expression on his face. "Theda still living at your place?"

"Not for long. She'll find something." Doug must have witnessed Theda's clinging kiss. "Don't bust my balls. She's a sweet girl, just slow to get the message." He never should have opened the door to her when she appeared, wet and bedraggled, six months ago, claiming she had nowhere else to go.

But Jake had always had a thing about damsels in distress and Theda had had that whole lost little girl thing down pat. It hadn't taken long for them to move beyond roommates to something more. That *something* wasn't working for Jake anymore.

"How's her job at the bakery panning out?"

"Okay. She's got regular hours now. Alyce was good to give her a chance." Jake had seen to the bakery owner's boy when he'd fallen and hit his head at school. Alyce was a good soul and had always said she owed him, like a lot of people in Welcome.

Jake was careful not to pull in favors. He didn't want people thinking of him much. They might remember things he wanted to be forgotten.

"So Theda can afford a place of her own?" Doug's comment led Jake toward the same conclusion these conversations always ended in.

"She's looking. Got a viewing today for a basement apartment."

Doug snorted and opened the back doors of the aid car. "We have to do our rig check." Paramedics were expected to check inventory every morning. Restocking supplies was mundane, but important and set Jake's mind on the coming day.

Relieved he could put thoughts of Brianna aside for the next few hours, Jake climbed in and grabbed the clipboard to start the count.

His thoughts drifted to where he didn't want to go. It rankled him that Theda was still living at his place.

Six months ago, they'd met at the scene of an accident on the highway. She'd been at the side of the road hitchhiking when in a sudden blinding cloudburst a car ran off the road. She'd barely had time to jump out of the way before the car swerved straight at where she'd been standing.

She'd had minor cuts and scrapes, a bruise on her cheek, but he'd cleaned her up and left her to the police on the scene. She hadn't needed any further medical attention and the cops would get her to where she needed to go in town.

Theda's eyes had filled with tears when he'd dealt with her injuries. Later that night, she'd showed up at the ER entrance, as if she'd been waiting for him. He frowned as he considered that second meeting.

After she'd explained she had nowhere to go and no money to take her farther down the road, he'd dropped her off at a hostel with a few bucks, and she'd sobbed with gratitude.

Not the way to start a relationship. He preferred both parties to be equals. While he'd been happy to help her out, he hadn't expected her to come around to the station looking for him over the next week. They'd shared some laughs, a meal or two that she'd brought along.

And then, out of the blue, she'd arrived at his door with her bulging backpack.

Doug had warned him then that having her stay with him would only lead to trouble. There was enough hero-worship that came with the job. No one needed it in their personal lives.

BRIANNA'S MOM, KAREN, stood on the back stoop, leaning on her cane watching her unload the car. "We should have all this delivered now," her mom commented. "No need to drive into town for supplies anymore." Gingerly, she stepped down the three steps. Her knee replacement had been a great success, but the new knee served to point out how bad the former "good" knee had become.

Another surgery loomed in her mom's future. With any luck, it would be sooner rather than later. Brianna swiped her forearm across her brow.

"But then I'd never go into town. I like meeting Shandy, or Elle or Mercy for lunch. You should come sometime." It would do her mom good to get out a bit more now that her pain had been reduced to manageable.

"The dogs need me," Karen replied with a shift of her shoulder.

"That's an old excuse. We have a lot more volunteers now and even some paid staff. All that means more freedom. You should take advantage." Beau settled at her feet and waited patiently. "Mercy did a lot of work to get her Hollywood friends to donate to the rescue. You don't have to be here every minute."

Before her mom could answer, Brianna's phone vibrated in her pocket. She held up a finger as she read a text from her oldest friend, Elle Foster. "It's Elle."

"Say hello for me."

Elle: Meet us at Clay's

Brianna: Who's us?

Elle: Me and Logan

Brianna: Give me an hour

Elle: You have half

She laughed at the last text and then raised her eyes to her mother's expectant gaze. "It looks like Elle has news. I have to shower and get over to Mercy and Clay's." Their next-door neighbors, the Fosters, had subdivided their lot so Elle and her children could live in the back half in a double-wide while Mercy and Clay lived in a house at the front of the lot.

Times had changed drastically for all the Fosters in the last year. Clay had married Mercy, a newly-discovered actress, and his former sister-in-law, and Elle had returned to Welcome and begun an ill-fated affair with her boss, Logan Hughes.

Brianna frowned.

Her mother struggled to hold back a sly grin.

Logan. Elle had said me and Logan. "What? What do you know that I don't?" she demanded of her mom.

Karen Bowler was a legend in the fine business of gossip in Welcome. She often joked that the gossip stopped with her, but everyone knew to get some you had to give some.

"You won't get me to say a word. Just go." Then Karen whistled at Beau, who rose to gaze adoringly at her. "I'll get help with these bags."

HALF AN HOUR LATER, Brianna tapped once on the French doors at the back of Clay and Mercy's home and stepped inside. A small crowd had gathered that included Mercy, Clay, their little girl, Dilly, all of Elle's children, Daniel, Liam, and his twin, Jorja, and even Elle's former mother-in-law, Susan Murdoch.

After saying hello, Brianna sidled up next to heavily-pregnant Mercy. "This is a large group. Do you know what's happening?"

"It must have something to do with Logan because they're both coming. But I thought they were through."

Brianna nodded. "Elle's been miserable and apparently, Logan's no better. At least according to my mother."

"She who has the best gossip in town."

Brianna chuckled along with her friend. "Here comes Shandy, maybe she knows." The tall blonde came straight over when she entered the house, her eyebrows raised in question. The four women had become close in recent weeks; sharing dinners, movies, and their lives. Most recently, they'd supported Elle through her breakup with Logan Hughes, local heartthrob and truly, really, a nice guy.

The couple had had good reason to end things. Logan was adopted and Elle already had three children, so the fact that Logan wanted a child of his own blood, while reasonable, was impossible for Elle. Everyone around them had been heartsick, but understanding. Still, it was hard to see dear friends suffering.

Brianna scanned the room again. "Looks like everyone is here." Even Logan's parents had slipped inside without fanfare.

"Clay's handling hosting duties," Mercy said as he poured juice for the younger children. Mercy's last month of pregnancy was weighing heavily and she took a seat on the sofa away from the crowd in the dining area. The furniture in the great room was family-friendly and inviting. The two friends followed and sat on either side of Mercy.

"May I?" Shandy asked and raised a palm toward Mercy's belly. "I miss babies," she said on a sigh.

"Of course," Mercy murmured and allowed the slow rub of Shandy's hand.

A hush came over everyone in the dining area and the three women perked up. Logan Hughes and Elle Foster stepped into the house. They each looked eagerly around the great room, looking happy.

Murmurs filled the space as people said their hellos in hushed, expectant voices.

Logan held up his hand for silence. Brianna held her breath.

Elle flushed to see the crowd looking at them. Logan threw his arm around her shoulder and she raised her face to his. "We're engaged!" They spoke in tandem, wide grins splitting their faces.

The group went wild with happy shouts amid a crush of congratulatory pats and hugs. Mercy levered herself up from the soft sofa with a little help from Brianna and Shandy.

Brianna couldn't be happier with the news and made her way to her dearest and oldest friend to congratulate her and Logan, another high school friend. Elle was three years her senior but living next door to each other had bonded them as they'd shared their love of rambling around the woods that encircled the properties.

Elle and her brother Clay had had miserable, fear-filled childhoods, but both had taken their chances on love and finally, finally, won.

Maybe that meant there was hope for Brianna. A flash of the sprite kissing Jake hit the back of her mind and Brianna shut the thought down.

There was no way Brianna would ever talk to Jake Morrow again. Not as long as he was in a relationship.

She'd made that mistake once and it had cost her friend, Tiffany Rhodes, her life.

Chapter Two

AN HOUR AFTER THE IMPROMPTU engagement announcement, Brianna, Shandy, Mercy, and Elle gathered together in the living area. Most of the guests were in the backyard playing baseball, kids against grownups. From the sound of happy laughter and good-natured catcalls, the kids were winning.

"You managed to get Logan to come to terms with not having children?" Shandy asked Elle.

"No. I'm the one who changed my mind."

Brianna gaped. "You want more?"

"With Logan, yes. He's meant to be a father and after a couple of weeks of agonizing, I realized that I'm not half-bad as a mom. I've got three well-adjusted children who have bonded with grandparents they never knew before and half-siblings and a stepmother who loves them."

Elle held up her hands. "Somehow, we've all made this work. Having Logan in my life and giving him children will only bring more love. More love can't be a wrong decision, especially with him."

"And you love him," Mercy said.

"More than I thought possible," Elle confessed. "I thought he was cute back in high school, you know."

Shandy rolled her eyes. "We all did. Logan was always the nicest, most decent guy in town."

Brianna gave an emphatic nod. "Yes, to that. So, back then, was it his age that held you back?"

Elle nodded. "Three years was a big deal back then."

Mercy shifted in her seat and stuffed a pillow behind her back. "I can't get comfortable these days." She looked at Shandy, the mother of an active almost ten-year-old boy and Elle, the mother of a teen, and seven-year-old twins. "Did this happen to you? Sitting, standing, walking, nothing seems to help."

The two mothers shared a look. "How close are you?" Shandy asked.

"Next week."

Brianna sat up and watched knowing glances pass between Shandy and Elle. "What? Is it happening?"

"It's too soon. Isn't it?" Mercy licked her lips in a nervous gesture.

"BUT IT WASN'T TOO SOON," Brianna told her mother a couple of hours later over their dinner of lasagna, salad, and fresh-baked bread. "Mercy went into the hospital half an hour ago." She felt triumphant as if she'd done something exciting just by being there when the decision was made to leave.

"Really? It'll be a few hours before we hear anything more, but tomorrow for sure," Karen said. "A new baby right next door," she said with a sly glance at Brianna. "Imagine. I should clean up your old crib in case they visit with the baby."

"I should have known you'd find a way to get a dig in." Brianna sighed. "I want a family, but I have to find a good man first."

"That's what I thought, too, but I had you on my own."

She couldn't have heard right. Of course, she knew her mom had always been on her own, but she'd never considered that it had been her choice. "Are you saying I should just get pregnant?"

"I'm saying the clock's ticking." Her mother's steady gaze unnerved her.

Brianna sputtered. "I'm only thirty-two. I have plenty of time." Maybe not as much time as the sprite who lived with Jake, but still, she was far from being over the hill. She took a drink of water to keep from saying anything more. When she put her glass down, though, it landed with a thud.

Her mother's lips turned down and suddenly Karen looked tired. Was her hair more grey than the last time Brianna had come home?

"I want you to be happy," her mother said on a sigh.

"Don't we all," Brianna responded brightly so they could move past the topic. "Speaking of happy, I got a nibble today from a company I used to be in contact with at my last job." It was a stretch to call it a nibble. It was really more like good luck with the new venture.

"You think you can make a go of this online assistant thing?" Her mother passed her the salad bowl.

"Virtual assistant," she clarified, "and yes, I think so. At first it won't be enough to live on, but eventually, I'll make it work." She had goals and a good, solid plan of how to attain them. She wanted to be free to set her own schedule, work around her life and help people from home. That way, she'd have time to pursue her other dream of writing a thriller. Just the idea of scaring the pants off her readers gave her a rush.

"You can live here for as long as you need. I'd love having you at home and you've already done wonders for the rescue. Anyone would want a mind like yours working for them." Her mom served herself a slice of lasagna. "And this place will be yours someday. It's a nice nest egg."

"Now, you're being morbid." Really, she didn't want to think of a time when she'd be alone in the world. "But thanks for the support. I'll stay until I can afford to move out. I'd prefer to be in town."

"Did you hear that Jake Morrow's girlfriend works in the bakery?"

"No, I didn't know." She loved the bakery and went in all the time and hadn't noticed the tiny brunette. But then, until today she didn't know what Jake's girlfriend looked like. A heavy stone settled inside. She hated to give up her favorite blueberry scones. And their lattes were the best in town.

"Her name's kind of old for such a young thing. Theda something. I think there was a really old-time actress with that name. I wonder if it means anything interesting?"

"I wouldn't know," Brianna hedged. Her mom could be a bloodhound about gossip sometimes. She'd grown up with a gossip-obsessed mother who could dig up dirt on anyone. Maybe that was why she'd found fact-checking so much fun. Digging for the information came naturally, except Brianna dug for the truth.

"This lasagna's great," she said with a wide innocent smile.

Her mom raised her eyebrows at the unsubtle redirect of the conversation and settled in to finish her meal, while Brianna decided she needn't give up her visits to the bakery.

She'd come home to Welcome because she wanted to live here, she wanted to settle here, have a family here, and with any luck at all, find the right man to share it all with. Here, not anywhere else, in spite of Jake Morrow.

Returning to Welcome had given two of her friends all the things Brianna wished for. Mercy had come back, gotten married and started a family, and Elle had just become engaged to Logan.

Surely, the right man was on Brianna's horizon. She just couldn't see him yet.

But he was there, she was sure of it.

"AUTUMN JANNA FOSTER," Brianna repeated into the phone, loud enough so her mother could hear the name. Elle had called with the good news about Mercy and the baby.

Karen grinned wide and clapped her hands in joy. The same joy Brianna felt. "That has a lovely ring to it. A baby sister for Dilly."

Her mom had been right, the baby had come in the wee hours of the morning and everyone involved was tired, happy, and excited. "Tell me when I can come over to help," she offered Elle, the new auntie, who was rounding up volunteers for Mercy.

The friends had had a plan, of course, but the early arrival had messed with the schedule. Brianna wondered if Autumn would always be in a hurry.

"We've got a lot going on at the office today," Elle was saying, "or I'd take Dilly with me and let her grandparents pick her up from there."

Hope and Nate Talbot had been at the hospital through the night with Mercy and Clay. Dilly had slept at Elle's place.

"And it's the twins' first day of third grade," Brianna remembered aloud. "You're needed in too many places at the same time so I'll come right now."

"Thanks, Brianna, I owe you. Shandy will bring a casserole later."

"How's Dilly with the baby?"

"She's great and her grandparents will pick her up after they get some sleep. They plan to keep Dilly for a couple of nights until Mercy gets a bit more rest."

"I'm happy to help, Dilly's a sweetie. I'll be over in twenty." Brianna hung up, drained the dregs of her first coffee of the day and gave her mom a hug in the kitchen. "A baby girl, all's well and I have to go watch Dilly."

Her mother looked teary with happiness and Brianna suffered a pang. Someday, it would be Karen's turn to be a gramma. She kept her promise silent, of course.

FIRST THING IN THE morning was too early to deal with Theda's whining, Jake thought. "Just stop, Theda. I don't want to hear it." It was cruel, but she wasn't listening. She'd wound herself up to the point where nothing but her own voice filled her ears. "We've gone over this before." Too many times to count.

"You promised, Jake," Theda whined. "You promised I could stay here for as long as I needed." She stepped up close, her breasts brushing his chest. "Remember?" Her voice went husky and he felt her hand on his crotch.

All he wanted was to get to work on time. He'd almost made it out the door, but she'd advanced on him like an avenging angel. Now he was trapped with his back to the front door and Theda leaning against him. Her fingers danced across his fly. He shook his head. "I'm out."

He opened the doorknob behind him and slipped outside. The air had turned chilly overnight. September could be mercurial. Jackets in the morning, shorts on a sunny afternoon, and chilly nights. "I'm going to work and when I get back I expect to hear that you went to see a place to rent."

She bit her lip and put on an innocent expression.

"Today, Theda."

"Good men don't go back on their promises." She pouted for a brief moment then turned on her most brilliant smile. Other men would be dazzled. "I'll see you later," she promised, and softly closed the door in his face.

Sixty minutes into Jake's day shift and a call came in from Bowler's Rescue. Karen Bowler had fallen. She wasn't elderly but had had recent knee surgery. Depending on the fall, this could be serious. He and Doug headed out and arrived at the acreage in twelve minutes.

When they jumped out of their rig, he saw Karen sitting on the bottom step of her front stoop, her head in her hands. Brianna was holding a wad of paper towels to her mother's bloody forehead.

"Jake," Brianna said, worry etched into every feature. "She fell from the top step."

"It's only three steps, Brianna," Karen groused. "Hardly the Grand Canyon. I'm fine."

"Let's see what we've got here," Doug said and covered Brianna's hand with his own so he could gently lift the wadded up paper towels.

Jake assessed Karen with his eyes. "She's pale, trembling, but her eyes are clear," he said as he shined a light to check her pupils. "Good, you're doing good." He was aware, hyper-aware, of Brianna standing just off to the side, watching everything. She smelled like sunshine and oranges, but her eyes were worn with concern. A small girl sat with her arm slung across the neck of a black and white pit bull.

The dog looked calm, but interested in whatever was happening with his people.

"Is that dog going to give us a hard time?" Doug asked.

Brianna answered. "No. He's smart and easygoing."

"Okay," Jake responded for both of them without looking at her. Was the child Brianna's? She was a pretty little thing. Jake pulled his wandering thoughts back to the matter at hand. "Did you pass out? Even for a moment?" he asked Karen.

"No, but it was mind over matter." She winced when Doug inspected her head wound. "I felt lightheaded and dizzy so I sat down."

"Anything else hurt?"

"My leg. I twisted my knee when I went down. And I think I wrenched my shoulder when I grabbed the railing trying not to fall."

"Which knee?" Brianna broke in. "She's just had a knee replacement." The child came to stand beside Brianna and took her hand. The dog followed and stood beside the girl, watching the men carefully. He cocked his head.

"Not that knee, the other one." She sounded gruff with discomfort.

Doug went to get the gurney.

"No way," Karen blustered when she saw which way this incident was heading. "I'm not going to the hospital. I have dogs to feed. Just stitch me up and let me get back to work."

"Mom, you have a head wound, a wrenched shoulder, and your knee's been twisted. If this were me, you'd expect me to go."

By the time Brianna had finished her imploring speech, Karen was on the gurney being wheeled to the back of the rig. She slid right in, still protesting.

"At least she's not trying to get off the gurney," Jake said. "Follow us. That way you'll have your car."

"I'll have to wait for Dilly's grandparents to come get her."

"They live here in Welcome?" Odd that he wouldn't have heard Brianna had a kid with a local. Something was off. He frowned.

"Nate and Hope Talbot are Mercy's parents. This is Clay's daughter, Dilly."

And then he remembered that Clay had been married to the other Talbot sister. They had a kid and then Janna had wrapped her car around a tree. He hadn't been there that night, but a tragedy like that gets all over town fast.

"Will she be okay?" the little girl asked. "I gots a new baby sister," she said with more excitement.

"I'm sure she will," Jake said gently, relieved that he hadn't just met Brianna's kid. "And I'm happy to hear about your new sister. Congratulations."

Brianna shifted and drew his attention. "I'm filling in as sitter until the Talbots come for Dilly. They'll be here pretty soon. Do you think my mother will be at the hospital for long?"

"You can count on them running tests, and with three possible injuries, most of the day, I'd say." He climbed into the rig with Karen while Doug waited to shut the doors.

"Mom, I'll be over soon."

"Good, you can see Dilly's sister while you're there, too. I want pictures."

"Sure thing. Dilly, stand back from the door."

Doug shut the left door.

"Thanks, Jake, you're a lifesaver," Brianna said as the second door slammed.

They both knew that was a lie.

Chapter Three

ON THE WAY TO THE HOSPITAL, Brianna fretted and fumed over her mom's fall. If she hadn't been with Dilly, playing hide and seek at Elle's place, she'd have been at home and her mom wouldn't have had to go out to help feed the dogs. But Mercy had needed Brianna's help. Still, guilt made her hurry.

Guilt also swarmed her heart because, without this fall, she wouldn't have seen Jake in action, either. And that would be a jumpstart to any woman's day. The bigger part of herself, the kind part, the part she usually showed the world chastised her wayward Jake thoughts.

She shouldn't have any kind of Jake thoughts, wayward or otherwise. What was wrong with her? After all these years, the first words he spoke to her were all business, professional, and caring and the other part of her, the part she never shown anyone, was disappointed.

After parking near the emergency room entrance, Brianna caught sight of a familiar pair of shoulders. Jake had broadened since high school. And he was taller. He and his partner were closing the doors of the boxy truck they drove as she walked up.

Jake turned and gave her a terse glance. "She's inside."

"Thank you." She flashed the partner a look and he took his cue to give them privacy.

"I'll be up front," he said to Jake and pivoted away. Three strides took him to the passenger's door.

"What?" Jake was surly and clearly defensive as if talking to her was the last thing in the world he wanted.

Too bad. She was here now and had something to say. If she could only think what it was. But faced with him, her thoughts scattered. At the most important moment, her wits failed her. It was just as bad as reading aloud back in high school.

"I don't know," she muttered, with a shake of her head, because she really *didn't* know what she was doing standing here, waiting for some kind of acknowledgment. Of something. Of nothing. Of them, maybe. Them, all those years ago on that one night.

She blinked into his hard gaze, her eyes filling because the them they once were would never return. "Nothing, I guess. There's nothing to say."

Jake folded his arms over his chest.

"You never should have come back." A muscle in his jaw ticked.

Her spine did a funny thing. It straightened as anger curled around it as if resentment could brace her against old pain. Old guilt.

"Well, I'm here now and I'm staying," she said tensely. "You won't drive me away a second time."

She turned and strode through the automatic doors into the emergency area lobby. Somewhere in here, she'd find her mother and all her reasons for returning to Welcome.

HOURS LATER, TIRED and spent, Brianna held open the door to the Welcome Bakery and waited for her mother to enter ahead of her. "Let's take the first booth."

"I told you it was all fine," her mom said for the fifth time. "Every test came back good."

"You'll need that new knee sooner than we thought." The images had shown more wear on the cartilage than expected.

"Good. After how well the first replacement went, I'm happy to do it again." Her mother slid into the booth. She had a small plaster and a couple of stitches near her hairline. She glanced around the bakery. "I haven't been in here in a long time. Are their scones as good as ever?"

"Blueberry's the best," Brianna responded. "I'll go put in our order. What will you have?"

"Whatever you're having will work for me, too."

Brianna rose.

"Hand me your phone, I want to look at that beautiful baby again."

Baby Autumn was beautiful and tiny and so delicate. Her little fingers had grasped Brianna's with strength and she'd stretched and sighed. Brianna had lost a piece of her heart at first glance. "Here you go." She passed her mother the phone. "I had no idea babies' heads smelled that good," Brianna said with a smile.

She walked to the display case with her mother's chuckle in her ears.

"Hello, what can I get you?"

Dread washed over her, ruining all the happiness she'd just been feeling.

Jake's sprite, here at the end of a very long and emotional day. "Two blueberry scones and two lattes." She kept her gaze on the pastries displayed. Whatever strength was needed to look into the eyes of Jake's girlfriend had slithered under the floorboards. She sidled toward the cash register to pay while Little Miss Perfect made the lattes.

With the young woman's back turned, Brianna was able to inspect her more thoroughly. She'd seen her before, of course, but without the Jake connection, it had been easier to smile at her and exchange small talk.

Brianna had no idea what the sprite would think if Brianna continued to ignore her friendly chatter. But she didn't have to give up her scone and latte habit just to avoid a woman she'd never be friends with. She could find a way to be cordial without getting too chatty.

Not that being too chatty was ever a thing for Brianna. Her natural caution and private nature had always saved her from overt too-friendly attention.

The sprite turned around and smiled brightly at her, catching Brianna mid-inspection. Wide, guileless blue eyes crinkled at the corners. "Looks like you've had a hard day. Is that your mom?" she asked with a nod toward the front booth.

"She fell."

"Oh, that's terrible. You go sit, I'm sure you're feeling stressed. I'll bring your order over for you." She rang up the bill. "You like your scones warmed up, right? With extra butter?"

Brianna smiled tightly. "That's right."

"I'll take care of that and be right over with everything."

"Okay," she said, because, really, what else could she say? There was no table service at the bakery so it was sweet of the sprite to offer. Brianna paid for their food and took a seat with her mom.

"Did you notice that nice, young, doctor?" her mom asked.

"Which one?"

Karen raised her eyebrows. "The one with the warm hands."

"How would I know if his hands were warm?"

"Well, I'm telling you they are. Nice bedside manner, too."

Brianna drummed her fingers on the tabletop in disinterest.

"Maybe you're still interested in Anthony. Any chance of that sparking to life again?"

"No."

"Okay. Are you ready to say what happened between you?"

"Nothing, really. Anthony didn't want the same things I want. Different times in our lives, I guess." Her last relationship had fizzled out just before she decided to move home. It had been serendipitous that her mom's operation had happened when it had. The decision had been easy and Anthony had looked relieved when she'd told him about it. "No harm done," she said to emphasize her lack of interest. "No hurt feelings for either of us."

"How's the book coming?"

"I'm working on my plot and doing research."

"Anything actually written yet?"

"No. There's a lot of groundwork to cover before I start." She hoped that's what was taking her so long to type the words *chapter one*. Because if it wasn't, she was very afraid she'd never be brave enough to start the book. But facing that fear was for another day.

"You were a fact-checker for a radio station. Research for a book should be a snap for you."

"Maybe you're right. I need to apply myself instead of waiting for inspiration to strike."

A shadow appeared at Brianna's shoulder as the sprite arrived with the lattes and scones on a large round tray. Her mother smiled kindly. "You're new here," she said with a large unspoken question mark dangling at the end of her statement.

"I guess," Little Miss Perfect said blandly as she set first the lattes and then the scones onto the table. "I've been here for a few months." She bit her lip, looking shy. "Did I just hear that you're a writer?"

Brianna shifted in discomfort. Her desire to write was not a secret, but it was private and rarely shared with strangers. "Not really. Not yet, anyway."

"This is Brianna, my daughter, and I'm Karen Bowler. We have the dog rescue outside town." Her mom sighed gustily as she took a sniff of her latte. "Brianna's researching a thriller or suspense novel. But she hasn't typed a word of it yet," she said with a pointed look.

"I've been busy," Brianna said with a glare at her mother that said, *back off*. She looked up at the young woman, saw interest in her gaze and went on. "I get caught up in the routine with the dogs and by the time I want to sit quietly, I'm not up to doing much creative work."

"I think she's scared," her mother said.

"Mom. Stop."

"I can understand that," the young woman said in a reassuring tone. "But if it's peace and quiet you want, why not come here early in the morning?" She tilted her head and smiled more widely. "During the breakfast rush, we don't get a lot of people sitting in the booths. Mostly it's take-out before work and stuff."

"I've never been in here at opening time." The bakery was more a late afternoon treat for her.

"If you sit in the back you'll hardly notice the rush."

Brianna sagged into the seatback, shocked into silence. Could she do it? Come here first thing in the morning and write? "I've heard some people write in coffee shops."

Her mom cackled. "What's your name?" she asked Jake's girlfriend.

"I'm Theda Levi."

"Oh? You're with Jake Morrow, right?" Her mom held out her hand to shake Theda's. "Pleased to meet you. Jake and Brianna went to school together."

Theda turned to her with wide, trusting eyes. "Did you?"

Brianna cleared her throat very quietly. "That's right. Haven't seen him in ages, though."

"Well, he works just across the road and down a couple of blocks at the fire station. He's a paramedic."

"He's the one that came out to the house this morning. Took really great care of me," her mom said chattily. She raised an eyebrow at Brianna's blatant lie.

Theda nodded and waved her hand vaguely over her shoulder. "I need to get back. Maybe I'll see you in the morning?" She gave Brianna a steady gaze.

"Maybe." The word came out weakly and Brianna wanted to kick herself.

Theda stepped away and returned to her duties.

Her mother pounced. "No maybe about it, Brianna. You've done enough for me and for the rescue. It's time to do something for yourself."

"I'll think about it," she conceded to get her mother off her back. Suddenly, her blueberry scone had lost its allure in spite of the extra butter Theda had provided. *Damn it, why did she have to be so nice?*

"I MET AN OLD FRIEND of yours today. She was with her mother in the bakery."

"Yeah? And who would that be?" But he knew before Theda said the next words.

"Brianna something?"

"Bowler," he contributed as he hefted three heavy grocery bags to the kitchen counter. Theda was on a new cooking spree. The freezer would be full of frozen meals for weeks after she was done. He used to love it when she made meals easy this way. He could grab a freezer bag full of beef stew and chow down in minutes. But now it meant she planned to stay longer.

Theda ran her fingertips down his arms, leaving tendrils of dread along the way. He shrugged her off. "Her mom said you tended to her this morning, but Brianna said she hadn't seen you in ages."

"We used to know each other, but we don't anymore." Not a direct answer, but Theda had no right to ask. "She left town and never looked back."

"Until now," she said with a mysterious smile. "I think I'd like to get to know her. She seems very interesting."

He caught her eye. "She's shy. Doesn't make friends easily."

"Really? That's odd. I love to make new friends."

"She always kept to herself." Except for Tiffany, Brianna had had few girlfriends. But, for a short time, she and Tiffany had been as close as sisters. And there'd been Elle Foster. He'd almost forgotten Elle was a good friend, too. And Leon had hung around Brianna at school. But Leon hadn't been into girls. Just Brianna. They seemed to understand each other. So many memories surfaced they were hard to track. He shut them all down.

"Brianna was a bookworm. Quiet." And smart, so smart she made his brain spark just to keep up with her.

"Funny how she denied seeing you today." It was a leading statement and just the kind of trap Theda liked to spring. Jake was used to it, but it still bugged the hell out of him.

"I didn't say we hadn't seen each other, just that we used to know each other." He walked out of the kitchen. Then he turned around and faced her from the hall. "Did you see that place today?"

She scrunched up her nose. "Too dirty."

"But it was in your price range. You can't be picky."

"You don't know what I can afford."

He snorted. He was getting nowhere with this. "I want you to move out."

"Maybe I should find a roommate? Someone nice and quiet who won't be a bother. Someone who likes me just the way I am."

"Whatever, whoever. Just go." Jake couldn't be any clearer than that. He headed outside to clean the gutters. This old house was his, so he wouldn't be the one moving out. Theda had to go.

He pulled his ladder out of the garden shed. When he had it set up against the house, he called his buddy, Justin Camden. He'd once been married to Shandy.

"Theda's still not out of here," he said by way of greeting. Justin lived in California but visited his son, Josh, as often as possible. Jake and Justin had known each other all their lives. Like brothers, except without the sibling rivalry. They shared most things and this breakup was one of them. They'd been known as the Jays because they were always together.

"So those apartments didn't work for her?"

"Apparently not. But I'm starting to wonder if she even saw them."

"Whoa. You think she's lying?" Justin had met Theda early on, but since then, she'd always had an excuse not to hang out with Justin. Jake was half-convinced she was jealous of their friendship.

"This breakup is harder for her than I thought it would be. But, I never promised her more than a good time and a place to stay 'til she got herself together." He wasn't quite sure how this all happened and he was starting to feel like a fool.

"She's working and hasn't been paying rent," Justin said. "She must have enough set aside to find a place to live."

"Maybe she doesn't like living alone." Not everyone was suited to it.

Justin chuffed a blast of air. "Theda was alone when you found her at the side of the road, like a lost cat. She was hitchhiking. A woman who does that has steel balls. She can handle living alone until the next guy rescues her."

"Hey. It wasn't like that."

Justin snorted. "Of course not."

"She's thinking of finding a roommate."

"Good luck with that," Justin commented. "She's not the warm, friendly girl she seemed at first."

"True." Even though she claimed to make friends easily, the truth was her intensity was off-putting.

Jake wasn't sure where she'd find a roommate since she'd been glued to his side for the last six months. Even now, after he'd asked her to leave, she wanted to keep tabs on everywhere he went, who his friends were, and how he spent his time off. The questions about

Brianna were typical and the very reason he was done with her. Too clingy, too controlling and if he was forced to he'd say, too creepy.

"I'll tell you one thing," Jake said. "Sleeping on the couch sucks."

"Give her a deadline and stick to it."

He'd been trying, but she skated through everything. Like today, with the groceries. He knew damned well she'd use the cooking marathon as an excuse.

"Are you coming up this weekend?"

"Of course. Josh will be ten and I can't miss it." Justin sighed. "I'm thinking of moving back. He's growing up without me and I never wanted that."

Justin was a dedicated father, but his job had taken him out of state. What had shocked everyone was his wife's refusal to leave Welcome. Shandy had opted to stay, tempers had flared and neither of them had given an inch. The family had broken.

But, to Jake, there would never be anyone for Justin but Shandy.

Oddly, an image of Brianna floated across his mind's eye. Brianna as she'd looked that night, so long ago. Prom night; before the accident that had ruined everything.

Chapter Four

SIX A.M. WAS NO TIME to be loading a laptop and notebooks into her mother's old car. Brianna's light sweater did not cut the cool September breeze, but she didn't want to go back into the house and maybe wake her mom. Karen needed to rest and heal after yesterday's tumble down the steps.

Yanking open the creaky door, Brianna slid inside, turned the ignition and fiddled with the knobs looking for the heat setting. There. She buckled up and let the car creep forward down the driveway to the road. Turning right would take her to Clay and Mercy's driveway, but left meant town and her date with her laptop at the bakery.

This was insane, she thought as she made her turn and watched the first light of dawn pinken the sky. Taking Theda's suggestion seemed wrong because it had come from her, but right because it made perfect sense.

All Brianna knew was that something had to change to get this book started. Doing the same thing and expecting different results was the definition of insanity. At least, that was the saying and Brianna was tired of researching and thinking and researching some more without ever typing a word of her story.

So it wasn't insane to go to the bakery, find a quiet booth and open a file with a title. Today was the day.

Fifteen minutes later, she dragged in a deep breath, opened the door to the Welcome Bakery and slipped inside. She took her place behind four other people and waited for her turn. Her laptop felt heavy, dragging down her enthusiasm and determination. Maybe she should leave before she made a fool of herself.

Writing in public? She hated doing anything in public. Her stories were the most private thing about her, she mused as she moved up in the line. Writing was a peek into her heart and soul and who would want to open themselves up like that in a bakery during the morning rush?

She shifted the weight of her purse and laptop and moved up another spot.

There was no one here that she could talk with about other things; ordinary things. No one to pretend with that she was on her way somewhere and stopped to grab a quick breakfast. She couldn't even fake a reason for being here. Thank goodness the other customers had places to be so there was little small talk and no questions asked of her.

Suddenly, Brianna was first in line, staring across the display case into Theda's wide and welcoming smile. "You came! I'm so glad you made it," she said brightly with a keen eye on her laptop.

"I'm not so sure I'm glad about it," Brianna muttered.

"It'll be great, you'll see," the sprite assured her. "You can take your laptop to any table, but I think the one in the back will be quiet enough."

"Thanks, Theda. I'll do that." She made her choice from the display of tempting savories and sweet treats. "I'll take a cheese scone for a change," she said, feeling more comfortable every minute.

This would work. A quick glance behind her showed again that the customers at this time of day were not chatty and were focused more on getting out of the bakery with coffee and food in hand.

The smell of baking was heavier at this time of the morning. The air was full of the scent of baked bread. Later she'd smell pies: cream, fruit, and even some savory pies. She breathed deep, took her laptop to the back booth and then returned for her coffee and scone. Two bites and two sips later, she lifted the laptop lid.

She opened her word processing program.

She cleared her throat and squared her shoulders. Then, just for good measure, she stretched her arms with her fingers linked. Giving her hands a good shake she looked at the blank screen.

The blinking cursor danced and wobbled like a bobblehead on a dashboard.

She'd driven all the way into town for this?

No, not for this. *For this*, she thought and typed the first title that sprang into her mind. *The Stalker.* Not at all what she wanted for a title, but she had to have something on the page. Next, she typed *By Brianna Bowler* and on the next page she typed *Chapter One.*

And still the cursor blinked.

She centered the three lines.

Ignoring the blinking light mocking her, she took a quick look at some of her research notes on the psychology of stalking and stalkers. She was tempted to do some more reading.

No, it was time to write. Time to get the words on the page. Time to not be a slacker.

But research was what she was good at, what she loved to do.

Brianna knew that last part was a lie. She enjoyed fact-checking and digging for the truth, but she loved storytelling more. Her short stories had given her hours of pure creative joy and she wanted, more than anything, to create a longer, more complex story.

Before she could type another word, Theda strolled over with a cloth in her hand. She wiped the table across from Brianna's and gave her another of her wide smiles. "How's it going?"

"It's not." Brianna blew a raspberry at the screen. "This is supposed to be a thriller, but I can't even come up with an opening line."

"A thriller, huh? Wow. So is it about a murder?"

"Not really. Well, sort of." She wasn't sure she could pull this off. A whole book. It just seemed so long and demanding, with a huge scope. *But hadn't she just convinced herself she wanted to write something longer?* "It's about a woman who decides to kill her stalker. I think."

Theda looked shocked and then her eyes narrowed. "Sometimes women have to take matters into their own hands," she said with a slow nod of understanding. She clenched the cloth in a grip that reddened her fingers and whitened her knuckles.

Briana thought about her comment. *If the police weren't able to help much or dismissed the character's claims about being followed and subtly threatened, would that be reason enough to take the law into her own hands? Hmm.* "You're right, sometimes we do have to be pro-active."

What if the stalker had killed a friend of the heroine's and she knew all the steps the stalker had taken. The early signs. The signs that her friend had ignored, the signs the police told her meant nothing. She backed away from those thoughts.

"I'm not sure I can do it," she muttered. Doubt crept through Brianna's mind on tiny spider feet. Inwardly, she shivered.

"No, no," Theda said in a firm, instructive tone. "Don't think that. Of course, you can. You've written stuff before, right?"

"Short stories. I've won a few contests. But they were light and funny and this is much darker." And longer and more complex. Just more. More of herself would have to go into the story. "I'm not sure I want to show my own darkness on the page." She said it more to herself, but Theda heard her and softly smiled.

But it wasn't a kind smile. Brianna couldn't tell what sort of smile it was. Dark? Avid? Private, she decided. It was a private smile that spoke of Theda's secrets.

Theda blinked and her expression brightened, as quickly as flipping a light switch. "But darkness can be overcome. People can change and move toward the sunnier side of life, right?"

"I guess." Had this conversation turned philosophical?

"Then that's what you should write; a story about a woman who's seen the dark side, but wants to get past it. Wants to be happy."

Brianna nodded. "I'll think about that." And she would. Maybe Theda had a point. Most strong stories start with a point of change in the protagonist's life. Maybe she could start where the heroine decides to stop cowering and hiding from her unknown stalker. She pursed her lips and leaned over the keyboard as if getting physically closer would make this easier.

A customer came in and Theda walked away with a small wave, leaving Brianna's mind in turmoil. She liked the idea of a woman struggling to get help. A woman who had no choice but to move forward by taking charge. But did it have to be so dark? Did she have to struggle alone?

What if she met a man...

An hour later, Theda wandered over again. "How are you doing now? I saw you typing like crazy."

Brianna closed the laptop lid, suddenly shy about the words she'd strung together. "None of it is any good, but it's something. They say writing is rewriting anyway, so whatever I write now will be changed a lot before I'm through." She'd started with the heroine's friend's funeral. The heroine, for now named XYZ had noticed a stranger at the back of the service. A stranger who caught her eye and smiled silkily at her.

"Mind if I sit?" Theda was saying. "It's my break."

The other customers had drifted away and when she checked the time, Brianna saw that most people would be at work by now. Theda would have time to relax for a few minutes.

Brianna slid her laptop to the side and waved Theda into the seat opposite. "I have to thank you for suggesting I come here. You were right, it's quiet and I have nothing on my mind but my story. No dogs to feed and no volunteers to organize. No sad stories to hear about abused dogs."

Theda frowned. "I guess you hear some awful things."

At Brianna's nod, Theda went on, "People often do terrible things. It's not always their fault."

Dog abuse and neglect were always people's fault, but Theda seemed to be talking more to herself than to Brianna. The sprite's face brightened with a new thought.

"I guess you can always put the worst ones in a book and give them what they deserve," Theda said with a dark smirk.

"I hadn't thought of that." The idea had merit if only to give her the satisfaction of totally harmless revenge on animal abusers. "I'd like to buy you a coffee to thank you for getting me here."

"No need." Theda reddened in the cheeks.

"Please, you've already been on your feet for hours, so my treat." Theda looked so sweet. Sort of forlorn and Brianna wondered what her life had been like before she came to Welcome. "I'll be right back. How do you take it?"

"Black is fine. Thanks."

When she returned with two mugs, Theda smiled and thanked her again. "I'm dying to know what you're writing."

Brianna settled into her seat, uncomfortable with Theda's curiosity. "I'm not ready to show it to anyone yet. It's mostly random thoughts." Her face warmed under the other woman's scrutiny. "I haven't even strung things together yet."

"Did you leave a man behind when you came back to Welcome?"

Brianna blinked at the sudden change of topic. It seemed Theda's mind skipped lightly from one thing to the next without a discernible pattern.

"Not really," Brianna said quietly. "I wanted to come home, and he was happy enough to be left, so no hard feelings."

"In my experience, there are always hard feelings. Men want to walk all over me, it seems." She looked over the rim of her mug at

Brianna, eyes sparking with old anger. "But I don't let them. I've learned to respect myself so they'd better, too."

A chill slipped between her shoulder blades as Brianna thought about Jake. "But you're with Jake now. He's always been a good guy."

Theda grinned, showing her teeth. "Jake," she said with satisfaction. "He loves me. We'll be getting engaged anytime now."

"That's great," Brianna replied with a smile of her own. She hoped it looked genuine, but she couldn't be sure.

"Maybe you should try to make it up with that guy you left. Bring some spark back with you when you go home? You could do some new sexy stuff. Try something you haven't before." Theda leaned across the table. "I could give you some pointers in that direction," she whispered huskily. "Jake's a wild man and has taught me a lot."

Brianna couldn't think of anything she wanted to hear less about. Jake's sexual prowess was the worst topic ever. "I bet he has," she murmured weakly. "He's quite a bit older than you, right?"

"I'm older than I look," Theda said as she leaned back. "And I'm tougher than I seem." She drained the last of her coffee and stood. "Back to work for me. See you here tomorrow?"

JAKE TOOK THE RAMP off I-5 and headed toward downtown Welcome. He'd had dinner with Doug and his kids. A single dad, Doug had developed some mad skills with a wok and always made extra. More and more, Jake was showing up at Doug's place hungry. It was a great way to avoid Theda.

Up ahead, he caught the familiar red-blue glow from the lights of first responders on the roadside. He slowed to a stop and pulled in a safe distance behind them. After donning a reflective vest he grabbed out of his backseat, he ran up to see if they needed an extra pair of hands. He kept the vest handy because even going into his truck bed could be dangerous on a dark night. "What have you got?"

"Hi, Jake. Thanks, but we're all set." The paramedic, a new guy, closed the back of his rig and headed for the driver's door. They drove off and left Jake with the police who had contained the scene. Flares lit the side of the damaged vehicle in a red glow.

A cry from the underbrush beside him caught Jake's attention. He advanced slowly in the direction of the sound, not wanting to send whatever was in there running off.

A pup, he saw. Very young. Thick, fuzzy fur and a round belly. Only weeks old. Had it been in the car? He gently scooped the fuzzy little guy up into the crook of his arm and walked with it toward the first cop he saw. They knew each other from other scenes. "Hey, Gary."

"Hiya Jake. What've you got there?"

"Was this pup in the vehicle?" He held the squirmy bundle out so Gary could get a better look at it.

"Could've been. I saw a bag of kibble in the backseat. Lucky you found him."

"Yeah, were they locals?"

"Yes. Live over on Maple."

Jake nodded, thinking fast. "Let them know I've taken the pup out to Bowler's Rescue. They'll keep him until the owners can come to get him."

Gary directed a car around the accident scene. "Will do. And thanks. I don't need the hassle of dealing with a dog on the scene."

Bowler's Rescue, Jake thought. Brianna would take good care of the fur ball who was now determined to lick the bristles off his chin.

BRIANNA TOSSED A LAST scoop of food into Beau's dish. Her back ached, her shoulders had tightened and her brain had turned to mush as she'd used the last feeding time of the day to muse about the next scene in her book.

In her mind, she'd discovered a hero for her heroine and she wasn't quite sure what to do with him. But did a woman who was planning a murder deserve to fall in love? Wouldn't she be focused on her own problems to the exclusion of everything else? Everything good and happy? Hmm. Clearly, she had more thinking to do.

This book was supposed to be female-centric and a male lead had seemed unnecessary. It didn't sit well with Brianna that this guy had shown up. Her subconscious must be out of whack. Brianna's heroine was supposed to deal with the stalker on her own.

She'd never expected a hero to show up, but once she started writing the idea of the heroine being totally alone had seemed wrong. Here she was, with a heroine and a hero. Maybe she could demote the guy to sidekick. Yes, that was it. He'd be a neighbor, someone removed from XYZ's inner turmoil. When the heroine talked with him, she'd be reminded of what normal felt like.

She still hadn't named her heroine. XYZ didn't count. She thought of several names: Jordyn, Katie, Faye, Teri, but none of them fit this type of story. They sounded like romance heroines and this book was *not* a romance. Definitely not. She didn't care how hot the sidekick was.

The soft crunch of tires rolling to a stop caught her mid-thought and, with a last pat on Beau's head, she turned to see Jake Morrow stepping out of a pickup. In his arms was a furry bundle of black and white fluff. Beau beelined to the newcomers while Brianna took a deep breath and swiped her gloved hand across her forehead.

Not that a breath and a swipe would help her reaction to seeing Jake. Nothing ever helped with that.

"This dog was fine with people when I saw to your mom yesterday, but how is he with dogs?" Jake warily held the pup high and close to his chest.

"Beau is our resident greeter and all-around welcoming committee. We use him to help socialize new dogs and help calm them. You're in more danger of drowning in dog spit than being bitten. And so is the pup."

Beau sat at attention inches from Jake's knees, his hind end barely reaching the ground because of his excited wriggling. He opened his mouth and bellowed "harrooow" three times while Jake looked confused.

"Give up and let him sniff the pup," she instructed.

Jake tilted his head in doubt but lowered the pup to within snuffling range. Beau nosed at it gently and then his tongue came out for a full wash. Jake laughed, smiling at the antics. The pup wriggled and whined.

Jake grinned and chuckled.

Brianna found her feet moving toward his deep-throated laugh and remembered how long-ago Jake had been. It pained her, the memory. In his teens, he'd been happy-go-lucky, easy to be around and open to adventure. Now, there was darkness hanging over him. He'd matured. Seen things in his job that must give him nightmares, but still, he drew her.

But long ago, he'd been kind to her, the quiet nerdy girl that had a hard time speaking to strangers and standing up in class. Jake Morrow had always been kind.

Until he'd driven her away.

Chapter Five

BRINGING THE PUP OUT here when Brianna was home was a mistake. She'd obviously been working with the dogs. She had a smudge near her temple, her lush red hair was falling out of a clip she had on top of her head and whatever lipstick she'd had on earlier had disappeared. He knew she favored soft pinkish brown for her lips.

Strange thing for a man to know, he thought. Her lipstick color drove him mad because it toned down the natural pink lushness of her mouth.

Her freckles had never looked more interesting. He wanted to kiss every freckle that danced across her nose.

Damn him for noticing.

Stupid to come out without checking first that she was somewhere, anywhere, else.

Never mind that he had no way to know when she'd be in town and not at the dog rescue. Brianna approached him and the pup while the black and white pit bull snuffled and wiggled in welcome at his feet. She'd said to trust the larger dog so, trusting her judgment, he set the pup on the ground.

The pit bull immediately lay on its side to let the pup sniff him. It was an amazing show of trust and confidence. The pup squatted for a pee and then nuzzled at the pit bull's lips. A pink tongue came out and soaked the pup's face, forcing the pup to sit.

"I've never seen anything like this."

"Beau's very intuitive and understands the differences between pups, full-grown dogs, children, and the elderly. He treats them all according to their needs." She kept her eyes down toward the dogs and away from him. *Fair enough*. He couldn't blame her after his treatment of her earlier at the emergency entrance to the hospital.

"Usually the dogs I run across at work are confused or scared," he said. "They're aware of physical distress in their humans and react in different ways. Some run off, some become defensive and protective over their owners. You never know what you'll get." He bent over and ruffled the pup's ears. "But this guy is too young to have bonded with the owners yet." He still held that unique puppy scent.

Beau sat up on his haunches while the pup stretched up in an attempt to gnaw on his ears. Beau swung his head slowly and set the pup on his back in a gentle warning. Beau's tongue lolled and his mouth opened in a grin.

"Where did you find him?" She darted a gaze his way, then settled it on the pup again.

Following Brianna's lead, Jake kept his eyes on the dogs. Then he told her about coming upon the accident and hearing the pup cry from the underbrush. "I couldn't leave him there and the cops will tell the owners where I brought him. Can you keep him a few days?"

"Of course, no problem," she replied briskly.

He heard dismissal in her tone and he deserved it. He'd been cruel earlier at the entrance to the ER. Brianna had trouble opening up when she was stressed and he'd bullied her into shutting up even tighter when she'd wanted to talk. Not his finest moment.

"I should have been more patient with you at the ER entrance," he admitted as she squatted beside the dogs. "You needed to talk and I didn't want to hear it. I'm sorry for reacting that way."

"Oh." She settled on her heels and tucked in her chin. He recognized the pose. Brianna was gathering her thoughts.

He focused on the dogs to give her the time she needed. The pup alternated between worrying at Beau's ear and sniffing Brianna's hands. The furball overbalanced more than once and landed on his butt with his round, soft belly making him look like a hairy Buddha.

"How's your mother?" he asked after a long moment. "Feeling better?"

She looked up at him, one corner of her lips tilted in a half-smile. "She's fine for now. Thanks for taking care of her. Her forehead has a couple of stitches, but she had no concussion. Her knee is worse than we thought. Not because of the twist. Just wear and tear."

"And her shoulder?"

"It's fine. One of the nurses suggested an Epsom salts bath and for once, she took the advice."

"Come here," he said and took a step backward toward his truck door. "Sit with me in the truck and we'll talk." He wasn't sure she'd do it. "Please."

When she lifted the pup into her arms, he knew he had her.

He followed her around the front of his truck and opened the passenger door for her. She smelled of dogs and kibble and sunshine and he hated that he noticed the sunshine.

After closing the door he trotted back around to his side, taking a glance at the back of the house. He saw a curtain twitch so he held up his hand in a wave. "I think your mom saw you get into the truck," he said as he climbed into the cab.

"Great," she muttered. "Now I'll have to suffer all her questions."

"You wanted to talk earlier and I cut you off. I'm sorry," he repeated and ran his fingers through his hair. "I know you've been home a while and I just—I don't know—I didn't want to face you. After what I did."

"What you did? Do you mean kissing me? And then blaming me for that kiss? Or telling me you never wanted to see me again and I had to leave town?" Her expression went soft and earnest and undid him.

Too many questions at once. Brianna had changed. The younger version wouldn't have dared ask so many things at the same time. She wouldn't have demanded answers.

Like a dog sniffing ammonia, he backed off.

Fast.

"Do you have to talk about all that?" he asked in as even a tone as he could muster. "Can't we just move on?"

"Move on to where?" she asked.

But he knew it was a rhetorical question because they had nowhere to go and she knew it. She slumped against the passenger door looking defeated.

"Maybe I do need to talk about it," she whispered.

He said nothing in response. Just waited.

Holding the pup close to her chest, she stared at the floor. Her chin absently brushed against the top of the pup's head. He looked blissed out by the casual affection. She cleared her throat. "Sure," she said, more strongly. "Let's just be people we used to know who haven't seen each other in a long time."

"Years," he said, relieved. "How have you been?"

"Pretty good," she said without looking at him. *Just as well*, he thought. "I had an interesting job in Seattle. I gave it up to come home when my mom needed help." The pup settled in her arms and closed his eyes as she stroked his ears and the side of his jaw with delicate, gentle fingers. His body reacted to the sight of the rhythmic strokes. He looked out the side window.

"Did you get married? I haven't heard much." He'd steered clear of his classmates over the years; more than steered clear. He'd deliberately cut them out of his life.

Justin had clung to their friendship like a barnacle. He was the only one he still hung out with. Thank God, or he'd be a crotchety old loner.

The old friends who still lived in Welcome gave up on him years ago because he'd driven them away. They probably figured him for an ass, but the truth was he found their pitying stares and their curious glances overwhelming. He couldn't bear their pity.

"Not married, no." Brianna's voice pulled him away from his thoughts. "You?"

"I'm living with someone," he said, although it wasn't said out of loyalty to Theda, but out of fear. Fear that this warm feeling for Brianna could blossom the way it did once before, so he used his live-in ex-girlfriend as a shield. He wasn't proud of it, but, there it was. Not only was he an ass to his old friends, but he was also a coward with Brianna.

He took a chance and watched her profile. She had a perfect nose that turned up just a bit at the end. She'd tucked a strand of loose hair behind her ear, exposing the shell and three diamond studs.

Brianna sighed and glanced at him, her eyes wide and innocent. That glance caught on his and they stared at each other. "I know about your girlfriend," she said softly. "I've met Theda. She seems nice. Kind. She suggested I come into the bakery during the morning rush to write."

He hated that they'd met. This was so messed up and could go all kinds of wrong. But whatever disaster loomed for him, he deserved it. His stunned brain focused on the only thing it could.

"You're still writing?" In school, she'd been shy when she'd been called upon to read a story she'd written. That was what made him notice her in the first place. Before that she'd been part of the blur of quiet girls who blended with the background. Brianna had come into sharper focus when he'd dated Tiffany.

Tiffany had called Brianna her pet project and had been determined to open the quiet, shy girl to new experiences. Tiffany had claimed Brianna wasn't really a friend, but more like an experiment. But Brianna hadn't caved in easily to the kind of experiences Tiffany wanted to expose her to, like drinking and trying pot. Brianna had had a strong code of behavior she never broke until he'd made her break it.

Tiffany had risen to Brianna's unspoken challenge and had become sweeter, kinder, and more interested in Brianna all the time.

Brianna turned her face to look out the side window, and the movement brought Jake back into the present. "I write short stories mostly. But, I'm playing around with a novel. The bakery is a good place for me to work."

"You should write a novel," he said with enthusiasm. "You'd be great at whatever you write. What's it about?"

"I'm not sure. Really, it's not much. I'm just noodling around with characters and situations for now, but Theda was right, the bakery worked out this morning. When I'm at home, I think about all I need to do with the dogs and volunteers and my energy for the book is gone before I get to it."

Theda had a way about her, a friendliness that made people think they were safe in her company. Her open, friendly face is what had drawn him; that and her hopeless situation. He understood Brianna trusting her. He got it, but he hated it, too.

"Ack!" Brianna scrambled to get the door open, while she held the pup in the air. "He's going to poop."

Next thing Jake knew she was out the door and the pup had been gently placed on the ground. "Did you get out in time?" he asked between guffaws.

"Yes. Whew, that was close." She chuckled low in her throat and looked over her shoulder at him and for a too-brief moment, he saw the girl she used to be and it caught at his heart. Brianna was one of the most beautiful women he'd ever seen. It wasn't her pretty features or the gentle lustrous waves in her red hair, or her curves. It was her soul. Brianna's beauty went soul-deep and made him yearn.

Yes, she was the most beautiful woman in his life.

Always would be.

Which was all the more reason to stay clear.

"So you'll be at the bakery most mornings?" Damn him for asking.

She shrugged and dug inside her pocket. She brought out a doggie pick-up bag. As she stooped to collect the pup's deposit she said, "See you around, Jake."

It wasn't until he'd driven out to the road that he realized she hadn't answered him.

"I'M NOT SURE I CAN go back to the bakery tomorrow morning," Brianna said to Elle over dessert that evening.

"Why not write there?" Elle asked as she accepted a piece of peach pie from Karen. "You said it worked out fine. What's changed?"

Her mom pretended to be busy cutting another wedge from the pie, but Brianna saw her hand still as she waited for her reply.

"I don't know," she said vaguely, with a sidelong glance at her mother. "It's a hassle first thing in the morning."

Elle narrowed her gaze. "Really? That's all?"

Karen finally passed Brianna a slice of pie and she made busy work taking her first bite. The pie was tart and sweet, while the flaky pastry was exquisite. The baker and owner, Alyce, had won awards for her pies and deservedly so.

Talking to Jake had shaken Brianna more than she cared to admit. He was so much like the boy she remembered, but still so very different. He was bigger, filled out, but darker in his soul than she could have imagined. Of all the people she knew from school Jake was the one who should be happy.

Elle had stopped by to see how Karen was doing after her fall and they'd decided to celebrate her avoiding a near-disaster by sharing dessert.

Elle was three years older than Brianna and had the same coloring as her brother, Clay. Both black-haired and blue-eyed, the Foster siblings had been raised by indifferent, sometimes violent parents.

As a child, Brianna had had no idea what Elle was forced to deal with on a daily basis. The three-year age difference meant Brianna had learned early to confide in Elle. The trust went both ways. Actually, three ways, because Elle had forged a special bond with Karen when she'd brought Clay over to spend the night on their sofa.

At the time, Brianna hadn't been aware of the arrangement. She was glad she'd been kept in the dark because she'd been too young to understand that the Foster children had needed a safe haven.

After a few minutes, Elle returned to the conversation. "You said Theda gave you some good ideas. That has to count for something."

Karen eyed her daughter with an I-told-you-so expression that Brianna responded to with a scrunched up nose. Her mom shook her head.

Brianna sighed and admitted the bakery was a great place to write. "There was just enough noise to make me focus to block it out which meant I was able to keep my head in my story; which, by the way, is not the story I expected it to be." She wasn't sure what was going to happen next, but so far, she liked the heroine and wanted to see her happy at the end of the book.

"This is your stalker book? The thriller?"

"Yes, although I haven't done much more than establish who the heroine is." She shifted, feeling uncomfortable about some of Theda's comments. "Talking to Theda about the plot sort of creeped me out."

"Why?" Both women spoke at the same time. Karen looked concerned, but Elle was simply curious.

"It was the way she spoke about men. Even though she's with Jake, I'm not sure she likes men much. Or maybe it's people, in general, she doesn't like." Brianna hadn't mentioned her brief conversation with Jake. There was no point. They'd agreed to just be former classmates and that was how the town should see them.

Her mother made a sound in her throat and Brianna remembered Jake saying he'd waved to Karen as she'd climbed into his truck to talk. She gave her mother a look that would have stopped most women.

But not Karen Bowler. "She's not saying that Jake dropped off a pup here today and they had a chat in his pickup."

Elle raised one eyebrow at this bit of news.

Brianna shrugged it off. "We're old classmates and we just caught up a bit on our lives." But she felt heat in her cheeks.

Elle widened her gaze, reminding Brianna that her friend remembered Brianna's high school crush. "If you say so," Elle commented coolly.

"That's all it was." If she continued to think of Jake as a former classmate, as agreed, she'd be safe from the pull she felt toward him. Eventually, she'd find some other man to think about. Still, she had to get both women off the topic of Jake Morrow or they'd read too much into his brief visit and their even briefer chat in his truck.

"I guess now that you and Logan are engaged," Brianna said to change the subject, "you won't be joining the girls for dinner and movies anymore. You'll be too busy planning the wedding. Girls' night will be over for a while."

Elle grinned. "I think the arrival of baby Autumn will put a dent in girls' night, too."

"So, I guess for the short term it's me and Shandy." They liked the same food and type of movies so that would work. And Shandy was just as single as Brianna was. She frowned.

"I'll have time for evenings out with you," Elle was saying. "The wedding will be small and no way would I miss our movie nights. They keep me sane. It's still not easy living here sometimes."

"Are people still giving you grief about your past?" Karen asked with a protective tone.

"It's hard to change people's memories. Once a Foster always a Foster. And now, I think some people are ticked off that I'm marrying Logan. I hear snide remarks behind my back. Just last night, I was in the grocery store waiting to check out and I heard a mother behind me tell her daughter not to hang out with my Daniel."

"Oh no. What did you say?"

"Nothing, of course. When I was fifteen I'd have said something awful, but not now. Besides, I'm too happy about how my life is going to worry about snooty witches." She frowned. "Maybe I should have taken a peek just so I'd know the girl if I see her again, but I didn't."

"Daniel's fourteen and he's too young to—"

"Na-uh! Not too young to like girls." Elle cut her off. "We had a talk sometime back about how to know if a girl likes you and what to do about it. Not that he's ready for sex, just that he's showing interest in girls."

"Already?"

"He's fourteen and his voice has changed and he's got wispy hair on his lip. I had no choice but to talk to him."

Brianna nodded. "Also, if girls are calling and texting him, it's a sure bet they've noticed him. Especially if he's new in town."

Karen looked appalled. "Kids start this stuff so young these days."

"Exactly. I can't have him making the mistakes I made. I don't want to be a grandmother yet. Also, Daniel needs to understand what 'no' means and how to recognize a real 'yes.' I put condoms in the medicine chest. One's already gone, but I think that was just for show."

"I hope so," Karen muttered.

"As far as I know he hasn't kissed anyone yet, but I'm pretty sure I won't be hearing about it when it happens. Boys don't share that stuff. It was hard enough to get him to open up about noticing girls."

"Speaking of birth control— A smile broke across Brianna's face as she realized something— Can you imagine what you'll be hearing from the friendly folks of Welcome when *you* get pregnant?"

Elle rolled her eyes. "I know what to expect, but Logan has no idea what the people of Welcome can be like. He'll be getting pitying looks for years." She bit into her last forkful of pie and sighed with contentment as she chewed. She pushed her plate to the side.

"Maybe people will feel so sorry for him that they'll give him their business," Brianna quipped as she ate her last bite. She sipped at her tea.

Through a chuckle, Elle demonstrated. "Logan, they'll say, sell my house for me because I know how hard it is for you being stuck with Elle Foster and *all those kids*." She snorted. "Could work."

"But you want more children, right? You're not just agreeing to keep him happy?"

Her friend's face softened at the question. "Yes, I really do want Logan's babies. Logan Hughes is a deep-commitment kind of man and I want to grow old with him and raise his children. I'm good at having babies. And I'm good at raising thoughtful children. The twins and Daniel have been through a lot in the last couple of years and they've come through beautifully. I'm looking forward to adding to our family." Elle narrowed her gaze at Brianna. "But what about you? You left a guy, right?"

"We were both relieved when I moved home. I'm focused on writing my book and helping Mom. If I happen to meet someone that's great, but I'm not looking." People would quit asking about Anthony soon, she reminded herself. They couldn't help but want to know if she was hurting after the breakup.

Her mother snorted. "Don't blame me if you grow old alone. I didn't tell you to come home permanently."

Elle looked at Karen. "And what about you?" She emphasized the last word. "You could be dating. Is there anyone special in your life?"

Brianna laughed. "She's got you, Mom."

Elle gave her a look that sobered her immediately. She hadn't considered that her mom might want to meet someone. Or if her return home had interfered with a relationship. "Elle's right, Mom. You're free to date. We could set you up on a dating site. Get your profile all sparkly."

The more she considered the idea the more she liked it. And it was a good way to deflect interest in her own nonexistent love life.

"Sometimes when you're not looking is the best time to meet someone," this came from Elle, who definitely had *not* been looking for a man when Logan had swarmed her with kindness and set them on a course toward marriage and a family.

Karen guffawed. "Well, then I should be swimming in a lake full of men. You see any hanging around here?" She started to gather the abandoned dessert plates. "What would you put on my profile anyway? Brand new knee and another on the way? Yeah, that sounds attractive."

Elle and Brianna shared a look. Maybe there was someone out there for Karen. As far back as Brianna could remember her mom had been alone. Maybe that was another way she could help her mother.

That would be way more fun than looking for a date herself. How could she think of meeting someone when her mind was filled by Jake? Seeing him again had brought up too many memories, too much guilt, and too much want.

Chapter Six

"DO YOU THINK YOU'RE going to meet someone else, Mr. Big Shot?" Theda hissed at Jake as he pulled to a stop to drop her off at the bakery the next morning. When he didn't respond, she added, "Do you think anyone else will love you the way I do?" Her voice hitched on the last word. But something rang false in her tone. Jake was beginning to think Theda belonged on the stage. Her whole demeanor could change in a blink.

And it changed with more frequency every day. Back and forth, like a wildly off-beat pendulum. Someone or something had wound Theda up to a crescendo. Whatever was going on with her, he wanted no part of it.

"Open the car door and get out, Theda." He kept his voice steady and calm. If she went ballistic in full view of her place of employment, she'd be fired. He didn't want joblessness as another excuse for her not to move out.

She clicked her tongue and smiled widely as if he hadn't said a word about her getting out of his life. Everything she showed him was a lie: her remorse, her friendliness, her concern, even her joy; all fake.

The silence between them thickened and she finally opened the car door. "Fine. Remember what I said about nobody loving you, Jake. After what you did, who would?"

His guts turned icy. "What?"

"You know what you did." She slammed the door and bolted into the bakery.

He checked his rearview mirror because another vehicle pulled in behind him and all he wanted was to get away, go for a run, and disappear inside his head.

He checked his side mirror so he could pull out and saw the driver behind him exit the vehicle.

Brianna.

Damn.

She saw him and stepped up to his side of the truck. He opened his window. "You here to write?" he asked her. Brianna looked fresh and sunny and real. She never faked anything.

"I am. Have you brought Theda to work?" Her smile lit her eyes.

His chest warmed in response, melting the ice Theda had put there. He nodded because he didn't trust his tongue.

"See? We can behave like ordinary people," she said around a smile. Her brows crinkled in a question that asked for agreement.

"Like ex-classmates," he affirmed. "Good luck with the writing." He looked over his shoulder to check the road so she'd get the hint and let him escape.

"Thanks." She tucked a windblown curl behind her ear, looking seventeen again. As she rounded the front of his vehicle, he watched her like a pathetic fool. She moved quickly without looking back until she blended into the other people in line for their morning caffeine fix inside.

Run. He should go for a run to clear his head.

But what he really wanted was to follow Brianna and sit with her in a booth like any other old friend while they caught up on each other's lives.

Might as well wish for the moon, he thought as he caught sight of Theda talking to Brianna over the counter. Damn. Theda had been the one to suggest Brianna come in to write. What game was she playing? What possible interest could Theda have in Brianna?

And what the hell had Theda meant by her crack about what Jake had done? He never discussed the accident with anyone and people who knew him never did, either. But some people in Welcome loved to gossip and had long memories. Obviously, Theda had been asking around.

BRIANNA STEPPED UP to the counter after Mercy's father ordered two cheese scones to go. Nate Talbot gave her a kindly nod and shuffled down the counter to pay Alyce at the register.

Theda flashed Brianna a bright, amused smile. "If I didn't know better, I'd worry about why my boyfriend's watching you from his car." Her blue eyes were wide and guileless.

"Jake? He wished me luck with the writing," Brianna responded breezily as she studied the contents of the display case as if she'd never seen the scones and rolls and buns a hundred times before.

"He knows about that? I didn't tell him." She picked a mug off the shelf for Brianna's latte and stood dangling it by the handle. Her expression was open but curious.

Brianna smiled too widely. "Jake delivered a pup yesterday afternoon for safekeeping until the owners come for it. Apparently, they were in an accident and he happened on the puppy at the side of the road." She suddenly felt vulnerable, as if her honest reply was somehow suspect.

"Oh." Theda blinked slowly, her face relaxing. "Sounds familiar," she said with a considering tone. "That's how we met. Except we fell in love and now we're practically engaged."

"That's quite a how-we-met story." Brianna pointed out a blueberry scone in the display case this time. "I'll take that one." She couldn't quite meet Theda's eyes so she focused on digging her wallet out of her purse. *Engaged.* Jake never said a word.

In fact, he'd said very little about Theda. He should have said something about an engagement. An almost-fiancée was serious. She moved along to the cash register and handed over her payment to a smiling Alyce. She picked up her laptop and carried it to the table in the back booth and then returned for her tray laden with her scone and latte. "You're busy," she said to Theda who looked as if she wanted to deliver the food the way she did the day before. "I'll take it to the table."

As she turned with the tray, she recognized Denise Jones, a woman from her school days. Denise's eyes widened in recognition.

Brianna gave her a cool nod as she sidled by with her tray. Denise was a nasty witch and always wanted the upper hand. She'd given Elle a hard time when Elle had registered her children for school and Brianna wasn't about to forget it.

By the time Brianna had settled herself at her table, Denise had followed her and stood staring at Brianna with her take-out coffee in hand. *Great.* Nodding at the woman had been Brianna's first mistake. She never should have acknowledged her.

"Brianna Bowler, right?"

"Denise Jones," Brianna responded in a flat tone to show her disinterest. No luck, the woman still stood with an avid expression on her face.

"You and Tiffany were friends. That girl that Jake Morrow—"

"Tiffany and I were close, yes," she said brusquely as she cut off the other woman. She didn't feel the least bit guilty for being rude.

"Her family must hate him."

The Rhodes family, she blinked as their names popped into her head. Cassie and Phil, and Tyler, Tiffany's younger brother. Brianna had liked them. She'd been comfortable with them, and they with her.

"I wouldn't know." She hadn't asked Jake about Tiffany's family and never would. Pouring salt on a still-open wound wasn't her style. Brianna opened the lid of her laptop, but Denise still stood there.

Finally, Brianna looked up. "Anything else?"

"How long are you planning to be in Welcome?" Denise's beady eyes turned hard and demanding.

"I'm not sure."

"I heard about your mom's surgery," Denise said in a tone dripping with certainty. "So I guess you'll leave after she's back on her feet."

Brianna wondered what business it was of Denise's, but didn't ask. No point getting on the woman's bad side.

"You keep guessing because I haven't planned that far ahead." She made a show of craning her neck to look at the clock on the wall. "Don't you need to be at school?"

Denise tracked Brianna's gaze to the clock. "You know I work there?"

"I heard all about it from Elle Foster," she said in tight, clipped tones.

Denise's eyes widened in surprise. "Oh. You're friends with her?" She said *her* as if she'd just stepped in something brown and smelly.

Brianna gave her a hard stare. "If you have anything to say about Elle or Jake, say it to someone else. I couldn't be less interested."

"I don't know why you're being so hostile now. You were always such a nice, quiet girl."

"A pushover, you mean. Well, I'm not that girl anymore." She pulled her hands off the table to rest in her lap. No way did she want Denise to see her trembling fingers. "Now, if you'll excuse me, I want to get to work, even if you don't."

"Humph." With that, Denise Jones, mean girl extraordinaire, turned and stomped out of the bakery under the watchful eye of Theda Levi and half of the customers of the Welcome Bakery.

Brianna had mustered up the courage to see the grand exit with only half an eye. She hated being the center of attention and everyone had seen this bizarre exchange. She had no idea why Denise would want to bring up Tiffany's death or talk about her family's feelings for Jake. Of course, they'd harbor hard feelings. Jake had been driving the car the night their daughter died.

But even with only half an eye on Denise's exit, Brianna saw some of the customers hide smiles while even more gave her broad grins.

An older woman wearing wedgie sneakers, liberally studded with rhinestones, skintight jeans and a bright blue blazer over a brilliant pink blouse, and sporting a bright mop of bleached-white hair approached Brianna's table. Her face held one of the biggest grins.

"I doubt you remember me, Sweetie, but I'm Sybil and I work for Clay over at the vet clinic." She tossed her head to indicate the vague direction up the block toward the clinic.

Brianna nodded, taken aback by the attention. No customers had approached her yesterday and here she was fending off two people almost at once. "Yes, I remember you. Your son and I partnered on a lot of assignments in high school." Leon had been a sensitive boy and shy, like Brianna. They'd been good, strong friends.

"I just came over to say don't pay any attention to anything that woman says. Denise has a tongue like a razor blade. No one knows why, but she's mean," she said with a sad shake of her head, which didn't seem at all genuine. "I always wondered if something happened to make her the way she is."

"I've known her most of my life and she's always been difficult," Brianna responded, trying for a kind tone. And then Brianna remembered more about Leon. Sybil and her husband, Bud, had been disappointed in their son. He'd never been the boy they'd wanted. He'd hated team sports, and loved books and music and being in school plays.

"How's Leon?" she asked to get off the disturbing rehashing of Denise's nastiness. It was too early to let a woman like Denise ruin Brianna's day.

"Leon's married now," Sybil said happily. "It's nice of you to ask. He lives in Seattle, so we see him regularly. His husband's name is Jeremy and they're trying to adopt." Sybil's smile broadened. "I couldn't be more thrilled that he's making me a grandmother." Gleeful anticipation radiated from her face and Brianna couldn't help but answer it with a wide grin.

"I'm glad," she said, pleased to see his parents didn't find Leon so disappointing after all. "Please tell Leon to stop by the rescue sometime. I'd love to catch up and meet his husband." High school had been difficult and Leon had understood her as she understood him. "He was a favorite friend when I needed one."

"You'll see him soon, I'm sure," Sybil said and waggled her fingers in goodbye. "Off to work for that slave driver Clay Foster." But the laugh she tossed over her shoulder said she was joking.

Brianna remembered Leon coaxing her to join the drama club to help her get over her shyness, but she'd never had the strength to stand on stage. She'd preferred to keep her head down and her mind on the imaginary worlds she created.

The thought brought her back to her story and soon the noise from the front of the bakery receded and her story world came to life as she typed. This wasn't good writing, not at all. This was fast and messy and emotional and dramatic. She'd have to sharpen her dialogue and develop her characters as the story moved forward. Then she'd return to the beginning and clean out the extraneous words and do-nothing scenes.

But she loved this purely creative phase where she put one word on the page; then another. And another.

She half-expected Theda to stop by the table to continue their conversation about Jake, but even that thought drifted away. Except for the part about them being engaged. That part niggled.

Her heroine had already changed from a mousey, quiet young woman into a fiery champion and Brianna admired the new version. This was a strong, capable woman who was willing to stand up and fight for what was right. If only Brianna could find that kind of strength.

An hour later, Brianna felt the presence of a body standing next to the table. A tiny squeak alerted her to her friend, Mercy Talbot Foster, now-wife and former sister-in-law to Clay. Their romance had played out right under the gossips' noses without anyone finding out.

"Mercy! And you've brought Autumn." The baby's head was covered in the baby carrier by a soft flannel receiving blanket, but the sounds she made were adorable. "Come, sit with me."

"We don't want to disturb you." The carrier snuggled sweet Autumn close to her mother's chest. Mercy gently rubbed the baby's back and swayed to comfort the newborn.

Brianna rose. "Nonsense. Let me help you unwrap yourself so I can hold her." That said, Mercy sighed gratefully.

"A grownup to talk to in the middle of the morning," her friend said. "I can't resist."

After the grand unveiling, Brianna cuddled Autumn close, keeping her head supported while she drank in the sweetest scent from her head. "You go order, I'll keep her here."

Mercy rolled her shoulders and flashed her now world-famous smile. "Dad took Dilly to pre-school today so I'm free for a couple of hours. She's there three mornings a week. Today I decided to pick her up myself."

"Nate was in here getting coffee when I arrived."

"Dad stops on the way out to our place. He brings me a decaf cappuccino."

"Have another with me. I'm surprised to see you out on your own already."

"I'm never on my own anymore. I have a baby with me everywhere I go." Mercy's throaty laughter drifted back to Brianna as she headed toward the counter, where Theda waited, looking awestruck.

Mercy's acting career had catapulted her into household name status around the state and since she'd been heavily pregnant and now a brand-new mother, she hadn't been seen around town much.

It was possible Theda hadn't seen her before. From the star-struck expression on the younger woman's face, it was more than possible.

Mercy was kind and gracious as always while Theda served her. When she came back and sat down she slid a fresh latte across the table to Brianna. "I don't want to share caffeine with Autumn so I'm jealous of yours."

"Are you getting enough sleep?" She wouldn't say so, but dark smudges had made a home under Mercy's beautiful blue eyes.

"Oh, you mean those catnaps I fall into between feedings?" Mercy smiled lovingly at the baby and reached across the table to gently stroke her bald head. "My mom said I was bald until I was a year old. She showed me pictures. My sister, Janna, had a mop of dark brown hair when she was born."

"I'm going to suggest you go home and have one of those naps you mentioned while Dilly is at pre-school."

"I would have done, but it was Autumn's first doctor's appointment today. I booked it for pre-school hours so I can take Dilly home afterward. Everything's perfect with Autumn." But after a moment her smile faded. "What's with that Theda woman?"

Brianna's hackles rose. "She was star-struck?"

Mercy waved away the suggestion. "Not at all. She was grilling me about you and Jake Morrow. Now, that's a name from the past. I haven't thought about him in years."

"Me and Jake?" She glanced toward the counter, but Theda must have gone into the back where the baking happened. "We were friends in high school. We've chatted a bit in the last couple of days. Catching up. He's practically engaged to Theda." She twisted the end of Autumn's receiving blanket as she thought.

"Wait," Mercy said. "His name came up a few weeks ago when Elle and Logan broke up. She said you had a crush on Jake when you were kids."

"A high school crush. It was nothing and he was dating my...best friend...Tiffany at the time."

"But she was the girl who died, right?" Mercy's eyes widened as she made the connection. "You were crushing on him when the accident happened?"

Chapter Seven

BRIANNA REALIZED MERCY had connected the dots between Tiffany, Jake, and lamentably, Brianna. Mercy's question about her crushing on Jake the night Tiffany died made Brianna cringe inside. Tiffany had been her friend and Brianna had betrayed her. No one else in the bakery seemed to hear or take any notice of the women with the baby in the back booth. The other customers were intent on grabbing their take-out coffee and heading to work. That was something, at least.

Brianna smoothed her hand over the baby's head. She spoke softly. "I feel guilty enough about my crush without Theda jumping to the wrong conclusion," Brianna replied with a spike of guilt stabbing her between the eyes. "I think she may believe there's more history between Jake and me than there really is." She was on a precipice here and like real life, Brianna felt a strange pull to jump off into free fall.

Autumn stirred in Brianna's arms and her deep blue eyes peeped open. Her rosebud lips opened in a yawn as she enjoyed a tiny stretch. It was enough to break into Brianna's thoughts and she pulled back from sharing confidences she had no right to share. Nothing could come of unburdening herself.

Telling Mercy about what happened that night between her and Jake wouldn't change a thing. In fact, it could change how Mercy viewed Brianna and she cared a lot about Mercy's regard and friendship.

Her friend took a few sips of her cappuccino and smiled gently. "She'll need to nurse soon. Maybe I should go to my car." She looked over her shoulder at the lineup of shuffling customers. Several held phones. "I haven't tried to feed her in public yet."

"I'll cover you up if you need help," Brianna offered.

"I'm not shy about it, but I don't want to end up online. That's not the way I want to introduce my baby to the world. I shouldn't have left the house so soon." Autumn was only a few days old. "But with Dilly in pre-school, I took the chance to take the baby to the doctor. And then I pushed things by coming into the bakery. Plus my mom thought keeping Dilly on a schedule was best seeing as how Autumn has completely invaded Dilly's world." Mercy looked worried and disappointed.

"You have so much more to consider than the average new mom." Brianna frowned at the thought. Being famous might seem like fun, but there was a downside, too. "I'd like to think people who live here would give you your privacy, especially with the baby." Autumn sighed and closed her eyes, settling to sleep again. "Maybe you should drink up and take her home. Would you like me to pick Dilly up for you?"

"I'll call my dad, but thanks. My mom is busy rehearsing a new play or she would have picked up Dilly." She drained her cup and they shared a smile.

"This was lovely," Mercy said, with feeling. "I'm so used to being busy and keeping a tight schedule that it's weird to bend to a baby's routine. But Autumn's in charge for now and I love it. I don't miss the meetings, planning my next move, or the pace of Hollywood. Nothing happens if Autumn won't let it."

"Not even coffee with a friend," Brianna offered sympathetically.

"My dad won't like it that I came out on my own. He's quiet, but he makes his point. I wanted to get out of the house alone, so I loaded Autumn into her car seat and then into the chest carrier just to learn how."

"And you ended up here. I'm glad." Brianna responded. "Nursing in public may not be a good idea yet."

Mercy rose and with a soft kiss to Autumn's head, Brianna handed off the baby.

"About Jake, Brianna. I'm sorry I mentioned that old news."

"It's okay. He's happy and his girlfriend seems nice. It's all behind me." They said their goodbyes and when Brianna returned her attention to her story, she found the thread of her thoughts had disappeared. She made some notes and shut down for the day.

TWO DAYS LATER, JAKE opened his door to find Justin Camden standing outside. He had a duffle bag in one hand and a six-pack of beer in the other. "Got a place for me to crash?"

"Better. I've got a camper out back we can both sleep in," Jake replied. He stepped out onto the front porch and closed the door behind him for privacy. He kept his voice low. "She's on a tear about something and I'm glad you're here."

"Theda? I thought she'd be gone by now."

"So did I," he admitted. "She keeps finding reasons to stay." More like excuses, but whatever. He was stuck with her for the meantime.

"Buddy," Justin said, in commiseration, "I guess you're real glad I showed up."

"You have no idea." Jake opened the door at his back and waved his friend inside. "Take a seat, I'll grab some gear and we'll get this party started." Theda poked her head out of the kitchen to see who'd arrived. "Theda, Justin's here. He's spending the night." He looked at Justin, who was grinning like a goofball at Theda.

"Or two," Justin said. "I'll stay for the weekend if that's okay." Jake would swear Justin grinned like a maniac just to get under Theda's skin.

A sharpening in her gaze confirmed it.

"Sure thing. Stay as long as you need," Jake replied without looking to Theda for confirmation. Those days in their relationship were long over. It was Justin's son's birthday. Josh would be ten.

Theda's face went from curious to pleased in a blink. "Of course, Jake's told me all about you Justin," she said as if she hadn't met him twice before. "You two were close as brothers. Didn't people call you the Jays?"

Justin shared a *what gives* look with Jake. He shrugged at his friend. As always, Theda baffled him. What was the point in pretending she and Justin had never met? Only Theda had the answer to that.

"That's right, they did," Justin said as if there was nothing unusual in the conversation. He set his bag and six-pack of beer down. "And Jake's told me a lot about you, too."

Cue the theme from *The Twilight Zone*.

Theda flashed Jake a hurt look but masked it quickly. "I'm sorry we don't have a guest room. I've been after Jake to get one set up, but he insists on keeping his workout equipment in it instead. Will the sofa be okay for you?"

Jake read a gleam of triumph in her gaze. She'd been trying to lure him back into the bedroom for weeks. "We'll use the camper, Theda." He looked at Justin. "I'll dig out a couple of sleeping bags and we're good."

"Great," Justin said and clapped his hands together. "Still have that fire pit out back?"

Jake nodded and headed into the basement to get everything they'd need. He had no idea what Theda would say to his friend while they were alone, but it would be interesting.

Half an hour later, Justin set fire to the kindling in the fire pit and then settled into a lawn chair. He put his feet up on the surrounding rocks and settled a beer bottle on his lap.

"You've got to get her out of your house," he said as he swung his gaze to Jake's.

"You think?" Jake scoffed.

"No doubt. I think she's off. Hate to say it, but *way* off." Justin looked toward the house. "What was that bullshit about not remembering meeting me before?"

"Who knows? I've given up second-guessing her motives in anything." He sipped his beer. "What'd she say while you were alone?"

"She asked about Tiffany and hinted that she was competing with a ghost. Then she said when you get married, she didn't want to have to deal with Tiffany's memory anymore."

"Get married." Cold anger swept his chest. Every muscle tensed. "I have to get her out."

"Yep. Out. I can stay longer if you need me to."

"Maybe. I've got an idea about where she can stay for the meantime." He had connections in this town and had saved a lot of lives over the years. Countless people had offered payback and one of them was in the right position for Jake to ask. "I'm beginning to think Theda needs counseling and help. There's a pastor in town who may have a place for her. I'll try there first."

"Is that the one who runs the hostel over on Cedar Lane?"

"That's the one. He's expanded services and has opened a room for self-help groups, group counseling; all sorts of stuff. I'll go over tomorrow. Lucky for me it's my day off." Jake had attended a few overdoses in the facility and he'd been struck by the evenhandedness and lack of judgment he'd witnessed whenever he'd been on a call. Pastor Reeve was a good listener and Theda needed someone to talk to. It just couldn't be Jake.

"Then I'll stay the week just to make sure she's well out of your hair before I leave. I want to spend more time with Josh anyway.

Not that I need an excuse to stay, but Shandy's hinted I'm not here enough and she's right."

"You miss him."

"Every day. I came for his birthday and now, it's too hard to leave again."

"And Shandy?"

Justin shrugged and stared into the fire. "Shandy's the same as always."

As answers went, Justin's was as vague as they came. But Justin had very little to say about his ex-wife. What happened between them was private and his buddy had never opened up about it. Maybe Justin didn't understand it all himself.

Jake reached into the cooler that sat between them and lifted out another cold beer. "Come to breakfast at the bakery tomorrow. I'll drop Theda off for work and we can grab a booth in the back."

Chapter Eight

THREE CHAPTERS IN AND Brianna couldn't get the hero off the page. He kept turning up and being all sexy and charming and—*Jake!*—was coming straight for her. Here, in the bakery, in front of all the breakfast rush people; the people who basically ignored the hunched-over, disheveled woman staring at a screen, hands hovering over her keyboard like a hawk on a tree limb, ready to pounce on ideas and wrestle them to the ground.

Jake, dressed in jeans and a vivid red T-shirt topped by a navy blue hoodie, was coming to her booth. His gaze was direct and focused and oh-so-sexy. She shouldn't notice.

Maybe she'd superimposed her fictional hero onto the man walking toward her. That must be it.

Then she realized he wasn't alone.

"The Jays," she said in surprise as Justin Camden, Shandy's ex-husband followed Jake into the seat across the table from her. She closed her laptop with an inward sigh. It might take a moment to come back to reality, especially since her fictional hero had been about to kiss the heroine.

But those sexy thoughts were dashed when she saw Theda glare at them from behind the counter. Brianna waggled her fingers at the young woman in reassurance. Theda was the one who'd let it be known that Brianna was here for privacy and peace. But Brianna had to wonder if the other woman's scowl was meant for her or Jake. Or both.

"Brianna," Justin said happily. "Great to see you. You haven't changed since high school."

Jake sat beaming at her as if he'd just opened a gift. She made sure her responding smile encompassed them both.

"Thanks, Justin. You haven't changed much either. Are you visiting Shandy and Josh?" Josh had a birthday coming up.

"Yes, he's ten on Sunday. Wouldn't miss it." Justin leaned closer. "I hear you've become friendly with Shandy."

Brianna blinked, long and slow and flashed Jake a look of curiosity. Obviously, he'd been the one to mention her friendship with Justin's ex-wife. She tilted her head at Justin curiously. "Yes, I have."

"Does she talk about me?"

"Shandy's private." Which was a flat-out lie. Shandy was an open book about a lot of things, men included. His worried frown made her relent a little. "She's mentioned how good a dad you are."

"Is she seeing anyone?" he pressed.

Brianna flushed warm and glanced at Jake for help. Jake elbowed his buddy. "Brianna doesn't like to be put on the spot."

Justin reared his head back. "Of course. Sorry. I didn't mean to pressure you. I just have a lot to think about over the next couple of months and I wanted to get the lay of the land, so to speak."

"About Shandy's private life?"

His gaze shifted inward. "If she's seeing someone who'll have an impact on my son, yes."

"That's a question for her," Jake interceded, "not for Brianna." Then he caught and held Brianna's gaze. "He's not a possessive jerk, honest. Ask Shandy."

"Oh, I will. Have no doubt about that." She desperately wanted to get off the topic of Justin and Shandy's relationship. She wasn't in any position to comment, but it seemed to her that Justin was wrestling with a big decision and Shandy would play a role. "I'm having dinner with her tonight."

"That's right. I've got Josh to myself," Justin said. "There's a movie I want to take him to." He turned thoughtful and Brianna had to wonder if that was a good thing or a bad thing. She didn't know Justin, so him being thoughtful could mean anything. She decided to mention this conversation to Shandy.

Thankfully, Justin let the topic of Shandy go and the three-way conversation shifted to movies, books, and inevitably the book Brianna was trying to write.

"It's a thriller," Brianna responded to Jake's question. "A stalker book. Nothing new there. There are a million of them, but I thought I'd give it a try." Except that the only thrills she was seeing on the pages were emotional ones for the heroine when the hero showed up.

She mentally shrugged at the fictional turn. A writing teacher had told her once to leave things on the page in a first draft because her subconscious may know more about the story than her logical mind.

No way could she share that bit about the romancey feel of the book with the Jays. They'd laugh at her and she flashed on them as teens and how quick they were to pull pranks and have each other's backs. They'd been close as brothers. Clearly, they still were.

A few minutes later, when the breakfast rush ended, Theda sauntered over with freshly-filled coffee mugs on a tray. There were four mugs and she stood beside Brianna until Brianna shifted over to give her room. She smiled widely. "I thought you could all use a fresh cup," she said sweetly.

Jake stiffened as he caught sight of her. Justin looked wary. The men's response to seeing Theda put Brianna on edge. Something was definitely up between these three.

Theda distributed the mugs and then settled in beside Brianna and across from Justin with a deep sigh. "I'm already tired. I didn't sleep well last night."

"No?" Brianna asked to be polite.

"These two abandoned me in the house alone while *they* spent the night *together* out in the camper." The way she emphasized some of the words made the statement slightly accusatory.

The insinuation was clear. Theda was hinting that the Jays' friendship was something more.

Both men turned shocked looks on each other and then burst out laughing. Brianna froze and then turned to look at the reddening Theda. The younger woman's knuckles turned white on her mug handle and Brianna covered Theda's hand with her own because she looked ready to toss hot coffee in their faces.

Theda looked angry enough to scald them. The fury in her gaze sent a thrill of fear to Brianna's belly. For a long second the women held still while the men seemed oblivious.

Theda stiffened and glared at them. She turned rage-filled eyes toward Brianna next.

"Don't laugh at me. Don't you dare laugh at me!" She rose and walked briskly to the counter, lifted the counter lid to get behind it and then slammed the lid down, causing Alyce to jump in surprise. Theda stormed past the bakery owner into the back room, her back stiff and her shoulders squared.

Alyce frowned after her employee then looked their way, confused. Brianna gave her a weak wave to indicate the upset was over.

It all happened so fast, Brianna wasn't sure what she'd witnessed.

The men immediately sobered but continued to share a look. "It's got to be today," Jake said.

"No doubt," Justin replied.

"What are you two up to?" Brianna whispered urgently. She was horrified at what she'd just seen and these two were clearly up to something and it was all about Theda.

"I've been trying to get Theda to move out for over a month and she won't," Jake admitted in a low voice.

This couldn't be right. She gasped with surprise. "Theda said you were practically engaged," Brianna responded hollowly. She glared at a frowning Jake. "I'm not making that up. That's what she said."

"I believe you." Jake made to cover her hand on the table, but she pulled away before he could. "She's having a hard time accepting that it's over," he explained. "I never should have gotten involved with her in the first place."

"You've been trying to break up for over a month?" Brianna repeated, to clarify.

The Jays both nodded.

Jake's relationship with Theda was over. And it had been over since Brianna had first come home to Welcome. She wondered if there was a connection between her return and Jake's decision to end things. But that couldn't be right. She subsided into her seat. "Theda doesn't agree."

"We noticed," Justin said wryly. He drummed his fingers on the tabletop and gave the ceiling an intense looking over. Obviously, he wanted to stay clear of this part of the conversation. He suddenly stood and, swiping a hand through his hair, headed for the men's room without another word.

Brianna blinked at Jake. "If I were you I wouldn't drink that fresh coffee," she said as he reached for it. He pulled his hand back as if he'd seen a snake. "No telling if she put something in there you wouldn't want to drink." She had no idea where that thought had come from, but there'd been an edge to Theda that didn't bode well. Bah! She was being dramatic because of the book plot. Her head was full of revenge and dark thoughts. *And a woman planning murder.*

"This is none of my business," she continued. "If you're breaking up with her then do it privately. This drama belongs behind closed doors." There was a small part of her that was appalled that the Jays had laughed at Theda in public. "I don't think she meant to imply that you two are sleeping together."

"That's exactly what she meant. You don't know her the way I finally do. It took a couple of months, but now I know she needs help I can't give her. I'm not qualified."

"So now you're saying she's unbalanced?" She wanted to defend a woman who'd been humiliated, but the way Theda insinuated that the Jays were romantically involved had been nasty and uncalled for. The Jays were friends, had always been friends. "If Theda had grown up in Welcome she'd know better than to say what she did. She'd know your history with Justin and Shandy. And with Tiffany." *And with me.*

"I don't understand how Theda's mind works or what kind of person she is," Jake said, half to himself. "I can't tell anymore." He looked earnest as if genuinely confused by his time with Theda. "At first, she seemed in need of rescue, like a lost waif and I fell for it. I let her into my home and my life, but then, slowly, things changed and I got glimpses of a troubled woman." He blew out a breath as if a weight had lifted. He lifted a corner of his mouth in a half-smile. "I wanted to sleep out in the camper last night so I could talk Justin's ear off about all this. Now that I've started talking, I can't seem to stop."

Brianna nodded. "It's good to get things off your chest." But she was still curious. "What about this engagement she mentioned to me? You never discussed marriage?"

"It's all in her head. I've never given her any reason to think we'd get married."

"Was *she* talking about it and you didn't respond?" Sometimes women gave broad hints about expecting to share a future. "Did she look in jewelry store windows at rings? Or talk about honeymoon destinations?"

"She pulled me toward a window once and I pulled her away just as quickly. No, I never gave her any reason to believe she was the one."

Something caught in her chest but rather than ask if Jake wanted to find the one, she cleared her throat briskly. "Look, I have to go pick up dog food." She fidgeted with her notebook. "And then kick some tires at the used car lot. The rescue needs a pickup truck and it's way past time I looked."

"Thanks for listening. It means a lot."

"Sitting here with you will only make things worse." Whatever was happening between them was not her business.

Justin stepped out of the men's room, looking antsy. Jake stood to join his friend while Brianna shoved her laptop into its case and gathered her notebook and purse. She gave Jake a wan look and Justin a wave of farewell. "Take care, Justin, and have a fun time with your son." She reminded herself to have a chat with Shandy about Justin's interest in her love life.

The Jays took their leave and walked out of the bakery, leaving Brianna to follow. As she walked past the counter she realized that Theda had stayed in the back. *For the best.*

Alyce shook her head sadly as Brianna walked by. The scene in the back booth was the kind of attention Brianna hated. Heat rose in her cheeks.

Once outside, she caught sight of the men heading up the block toward their vehicles. Her mom's car was parked across the street from theirs. She set off behind them, keeping an eye on traffic so she could cross the street, but Jake slowed down and turned toward her.

As he walked backward facing her he spoke. "You want company while you kick those tires?" He shoved his hands into his jeans pockets and put on a hopeful look.

She shouldn't. She really shouldn't. But, oh, he was appealing.

As she neared him, he got even more appealing. His eyes stayed steady on hers, his shoulders looked wider than she remembered, his hair black and curly. And he looked like a man who could kick tires with the best of them.

"I don't think that's wise, do you?" She hesitated. "I mean, you have things with Theda to deal with."

"I know exactly what I'm going to do about Theda and it won't be— can't be— face-to-face."

She halted in surprise.

He stopped, too. "After what we just saw, I need to end things. For good. And up close and personal isn't the way. Believe me, I've tried."

Obviously face-to-face hadn't worked. Theda had shown little restraint and Brianna wondered what the other woman might have done if Brianna hadn't been there to stay her hand on that coffee mug. "I believe you and I understand," she murmured with a nod.

"I've got a couple of things to do first, but we could meet at the dealership." He named one of the three in town. "Say at three?"

She'd never purchased a truck before and didn't know what to look for. But she had a budget and a dire need. She looked at Jake's fancy four-by-four and knew she didn't want the truck bed to be that high. "I want something smaller than that thing you're driving."

"Now, you're just being mean." He laughed and turned back to walk forward. When he reached his truck he climbed in.

She hadn't promised to meet him, but he knew she would. Really, she'd never been able to deny Jake Morrow anything. As she drove past the bakery on the way to the pet food store, she saw Theda in the front window, watching the street. Her eyes narrowed and her lips thinned. The expression sent a chill down Brianna's spine.

Chapter Nine

AFTER PERSUADING BRIANNA to meet with him later today, Jake met Justin in front of his house. "The locksmith's coming any time now," Justin told him.

"Great. I'll go pack all her things." He opened the door with a slight feeling of dread. He was never sure what he'd find in his own home if Theda was in a snit about some slight; real or imagined. Once, he came home late because of a call and found his kitchen strewn with spaghetti and meatballs. She'd hit the walls, cabinets, appliances, and counters with the gooey mess. That had been the last straw for him.

"You're sure you want to do it this way? You don't want to deliver her yourself?" Justin followed him inside.

A quick glance told him the living area was intact. She was likely on good behavior because Justin would be a witness.

"If I deliver her she might accuse me of kidnapping or worse. She'll say anything." After the display Theda put on at the bakery, Jake couldn't trust her to behave like an adult. He could only imagine what she'd do if he tried to convince her to get into his truck after changing the locks to his house. "It could escalate into violence."

Justin frowned. "I guess you're right."

"You have no idea how quickly these dramas get out of hand. I don't want any physical stuff to play out. I know she wanted to throw hot coffee at us today. She had four mugs to toss." Theda could have scalded all of them, Brianna included.

"Yeah," Justin said. "I saw it in her eyes. Raw fury."

"So did Brianna. I'm glad she controlled the situation because Theda would've lost her job if she'd done anything more." He'd avoid

the bakery from now on. With any luck, Theda would leave
Welcome soon and he could breathe easier.

Justin ran a hand across his jaw. "She won't like this plan of yours.
Theda's a scrapper and I'm willing to bet she'll find a way to get
revenge."

"Likely, but whatever she dishes out, she'll be out of my house."
He wanted that more than anything. "When she gets home after
work, she'll find her stuff outside and new locks installed. I'll leave a
note on the door."

Theda would go to Pastor Reeve's place and work through
whatever she needed to deal with. The pastor would get her the
correct kind of help and Jake would repair the property's
falling-down fence after Theda left town. That was the deal he'd
made with the pastor and he looked forward to the day when he
could start work on the fence because that day would mark his
freedom.

With his plan, everyone would win, especially Theda. He told
himself everything was for the best as he dragged out her backpack
from under the bed and began to fill it with the few clothes she
had. The girl liked to travel light. He gathered her toiletries from the
bathroom and zipped them closed in a freezer bag. When he went
to slip them into a side pocket, he found a similar pouch filled with
pictures. He wasn't interested in spying, but he wondered if these
were family photos.

Maybe he could call someone who cared about her. She never
spoke about her past or her family, even when he'd asked early on.
She'd told him she'd been raised in Texas, but she must've worked
hard to clear away all traces of that soft drawl.

The photos were not of family, but of men posing with her.

Some had their arms draped over her shoulders. Others were
kissing her cheek. All the photos showed Theda happy and carefree.

All the men had Jake's hair coloring and a similar build. They all had blue eyes.

Theda had a type. Nothing strange there. Then he recalled a selfie they'd taken a few days after she'd moved in. The pose they struck would've been similar to all of these. He walked out to the kitchen and removed the image from under the fridge magnet. Once back in the bedroom he slid the photo in with the others.

She was young to have had all these relationships. In the earliest photos, she couldn't have been more than fourteen or fifteen and all the men had been in their early thirties.

Definitely, Jake thought, he fit the mold.

He wondered where all the other people in her life fit. There were no photos of older women or men. He couldn't find one photo of Theda as a child; not a baby picture or a Christmas photo with Santa. Nothing.

It was as if Theda hadn't existed until men began to take an interest. He shuddered to think what that meant.

Definitely, she needed help he wasn't equipped to give. As cruel as this plan seemed, sending her to the good pastor was the best Jake could do for her. He'd check with Pastor Reeve in a few days and see how Theda was getting on. Maybe there'd be good news and she'd be seeing a counselor.

The sound of male voices came to him and he quickly finished packing and joined the locksmith and Justin at the front door. "Hi, Bill, when you're done with the doors check the window latches and replace any that need replacing. That is if you've got the time. Sorry for the rush job."

"Sure, no problem, Jake. My business runs on rush jobs. If a lock's broken or jimmied people want them fixed or replaced pronto." Bill grinned. "I guess your work is much the same."

"Yes, I guess it is." He remembered then why Bill looked so familiar. "How's that baby doing?"

"Running around and talking up a storm. You did a great job bringing him into the world."

Jake shrugged. "Nah, I just caught him. He was in a hella hurry." Delivering babies was the best part of the job.

Bill laughed. "He still is. My folks call him the hurricane." The locksmith returned to the job at hand.

"I've got to write the note," Jake said to Justin, quietly. "I'll be a few minutes." Once in the kitchen he pulled out a notebook from a kitchen drawer, tore out a page and settled in to write Theda a goodbye note. It took three tries, but he finally got it right. Their months together had been good, but it was time for both of them to move on. He'd found her a decent place to stay where she'd have friends and support while she sorted out the next phase in her life. Then he finished up by writing down the address and phone number for Pastor Reeve.

It seemed cowardly to end things this way, but Theda wasn't the girl she'd presented herself to be when they'd met. He'd tried everything else he could think of to let her down gently and nothing had worked. She was off somehow. Damaged in a way that Jake couldn't fix.

Bill finished up by replacing all of the window locks and recommending a security system.

"Thanks, Bill, come back and install the best system you've got," Jake responded. Welcome wasn't a town where people worried much about added security, but it was probably a good idea, given the circumstances.

"WE COULD GET A LOT of dog crates in this one," Karen Bowler responded to Jake's question about what she liked about the pickup. The truck in question had a long box. It was only a year old and had low mileage. To Jake, it seemed perfect, but it wasn't his purchase and he didn't want to influence the women to make a decision that wouldn't suit them in the long run.

He'd been surprised and a bit disappointed when Brianna had brought her mother along on this buying expedition. Maybe being alone with him hadn't felt right and she'd needed a buffer. And since the dog rescue was Karen's it stood to reason she'd have a say in the vehicle she drove.

Karen continued with her appreciation. "And I like having that extra room behind the seats in the cab. Small kennels or bags of food and gear could go in there."

"The price is close to the top of our budget," Brianna pointed out. "Maybe we could negotiate a better deal." She sidled away out of earshot of the salesman. Jake and Karen followed her lead.

They'd spent over three hours looking at two of the largest car dealerships in town. They'd taken at least five test drives and Jake's belly was protesting that he'd skipped lunch. But he felt the women were closer to a decision with every passing moment.

Karen hadn't stopped slanting him speculative looks since he'd met them at the first dealership. She was probably wondering why he hadn't had much to say, other than to point out wear and tear on some of the trucks or offer an opinion on options when asked. But he admired Brianna's way of considering all sides of a decision so he'd kept quiet to let her think.

That, and his mind wandered to Theda and how she was handling being moved out of his home. By now, she'd be with Pastor Reeve and settled in. Was she crying and looking forlorn the way she had when she'd appeared at his front door? Or was she furious and berating him; maybe even lying about his friendship with Justin? But that was a problem for another day.

"Let's go talk money," Brianna said to her mother, quietly. "How much do you think is a good starting offer?" she asked. After Karen gave her suggestion, Brianna turned her pretty hazel eyes to him.

He suggested what he thought was a fair price, which was close to Karen's, but Brianna frowned.

"I'll start lower and see where we end up," she said with a firm nod.

He grinned. "Go for it. I'll wait out here. But take your time. There's no rush. If you can't agree tonight, we'll leave and wait for them to call you in a couple of days."

"Why would they call me if we can't make a deal now?"

"It's close to the end of the month and if the dealership needs the extra sale to boost their figures, they'll call to talk money again." And he had a feeling this vehicle had been here a while. The longer it sat on the lot, the harder it was to sell.

Brianna cocked an eyebrow at the suggestion, but after a moment she smiled. "Thanks for the tip. I will not be in a hurry and we'll leave if we can't get our price."

Karen grinned slyly. "You don't have to stay if you have somewhere else to be."

In other words, don't expect to hold Brianna's hand through this negotiation. He raised his hands in surrender. "I was hoping to take you two lovely ladies out for a bite to eat." He let the suggestion hang in the air, backing it up with a wide smile.

"Sounds lovely, Jake," Karen replied for both of them. "We'll take you up on it. Now, pull on your big-girl panties, Brianna, we have a truck to buy."

The women walked to where the salesman waited and he ushered them inside to his desk.

Anxious to hear from the pastor, Jake called him for an update. The phone was answered on the second ring. "Pastor Reeve, Jake Morrow here. How are things with Theda?"

"When you and I talked about her situation, I got the feeling she would be alone and needing friends. But she called and said she was staying elsewhere."

A chill traveled across his shoulders. "She's not there?"

"No. When I asked where she'd be staying, she wouldn't say. But she sounded happy and content with how things turned out."

"Really? Maybe I overreacted then," he said smoothly. Theda? Happy to be rejected? Not likely. "Thanks for everything, Pastor. I'd like to know where she landed so if she calls back or shows up, could you let me know? I just want to know she's okay."

"Of course, Jake. She can make use of whatever services from us she needs."

"I'll tell her that if I see her. You're a good man, Pastor."

"I do what I can, with the Lord's guidance."

"I'll be over to take a look at the fence in a couple of days." Since Theda wouldn't be staying there, he could get on with the repair immediately.

"Are you sure? I feel I didn't make good on my part of the bargain since she's not with us."

"It's a pleasure to help you out," Jake assured him and said goodbye while his mind rolled over the conversation. What the hell was Theda up to? She'd never mentioned becoming friendly with anyone in town so he couldn't see anyone taking her in.

Justin was spending the evening with his son so Jake couldn't mull it over with his buddy.

And he'd just made a date with Brianna and her mom for dinner. He looked through the window of the dealership to see Brianna and Karen still sitting at the salesman's desk. They looked deep into negotiations. He walked along the outside of the glass until he caught Brianna's eye.

She tilted her head and looked curious. He mimed that he was driving then tapped his wrist and held up all his fingers three times. She nodded.

He could easily drive past his house and get back in thirty minutes.

His phone rang and when he saw the name he answered immediately. The news wasn't good; it rarely was from Sybil and Bud. They were good neighbors, but the biggest gossips in town.

"Dammit," he muttered. "No, don't call 9-1-1. This is personal and I don't want to make it a big deal. I'll be there in a few minutes to check the damage. *Theda had gone too far.*

Chapter Ten

THIRTY MINUTES WASN'T long enough to get home, cover the broken window in the living room with a sheet of plywood, and get back to the dealership to take Brianna and Karen to dinner.

The work to temporarily cover Jake's broken window took over an hour and if his neighbor hadn't had the plywood already on the porch, it would have taken longer.

"Thanks for the help, Bud, I owe you," he said as he hammered in the last nail.

"No problem, Jake. I had the plywood in the back shed."

Bud's wife Sybil had seen the whole thing from the safety of her car when she got home from work at the vet clinic. For once living next to the most gossipy couple in Welcome could work to Jake's advantage. "I appreciate the plywood and the help installing it. And thanks for not calling the cops right away."

"I figured you'd want to get the window covered up pronto." Bud's dyed-black hair shone like plastic in the dying light as he nodded sagely. "Seems a bit extreme to bust out a window if you ask me. That young woman's only been here for a couple or three months." He cocked an eyebrow for confirmation. "I figured you might want to handle this without getting official."

"Six. She's been here for six months." Jake glanced around at the other neighbors' houses. No one seemed particularly interested in what was happening on Jake's front porch. They'd probably already heard everything from Sybil anyway. He shrugged and tried to look downtrodden. "Bad breakup, but I didn't expect this."

"Sybil says she wasn't surprised at all. She says this girl was behaving oddly in the last few days. Saying things she shouldn't at the bakery, especially today after you and Justin were there."

"That so?" But he already knew what direction Theda's mind had gone. He was disappointed that she'd decided to share her thoughts with customers, but he'd given up trying to see the logic in anything she did.

Bud nodded again as if he and Jake were men of the world and had to handle upset women all the time. Maybe Bud struggled with Sybil, but Jake hadn't had a problem with a woman in years. He'd been very, very careful to avoid overly-emotional scenes since Tiffany; because of Tiffany.

Bud cleared his throat. "Just so you know, Jake, Sybil put that girl in her place when she made her innuendos at the bakery." He shrugged. "And now that we understand Leon, we know homophobia when we see it."

Jake nodded. Bud and Sybil hadn't always understood their son, but those troubled waters had been smooth for years now.

"Leon's a good guy," Jake said, recalling the shy, quiet boy who'd been friendly with shy, quiet Brianna. "He always was."

Theda must've had an earful from Sybil in the bakery, which would only compound Theda's anger once she got home and saw her bags outside the door. The note Jake had left her hadn't had the intended result. Jake had meant to offer help and respite to the troubled woman, but the note had set her off even more.

Jake gathered his tools and lifted his small toolbox, deep in thought. Bud cleared his throat and brought Jake back to the present.

"Leon and his husband are looking to adopt now," Bud said with a grin. "Sybil's beside herself happy over it. We'll be grandparents. Never thought I'd see it, but life's gonna change for us when the dust settles."

"Congratulations." Jake gave him a friendly slap on the shoulder. "That'll be great." He changed his expression to serious. "Theda didn't say where she was going, did she?"

Bud shook his head. "Sybil stayed in her car while the girl threw rocks through the window. Thought it was safer to stay clear."

"Wise choice. I've got somewhere I have to be, but thanks for everything, Bud. You're a good neighbor." He shook Bud's hand and left. He'd have some sweeping up to do. His living room floor was littered with broken glass and the rocks Theda had used.

But cleaning up could wait while he had dinner with Brianna and Karen.

BRIANNA WAITED WITH her mother outside the door of the Welcome Bar and Grill. Jake strode toward them, his expression getting lighter with each step. Her mom slid her phone into her pocket. Finally, she'd quit texting. The phone hadn't stopped pinging since they'd left the dealership.

"I hear you have some glass to clean up," her mother said as Jake strode toward them. Until now, Brianna thought all they had to talk about was the deal she'd made for the truck they wanted. But obviously, the gossip had been flying.

"What's going on? What glass?" she asked her mom.

Welcome's gossip flew fast and furious. Between her mother and Sybil, nothing went unnoticed.

Jake drew to a stop in front of them, his happy expression muted.

"I just left my place," Jake said in response to her mother's comment. He stared at Karen. "Sybil's fast as lightning."

Her mom snorted. "No comment on Sybil, but I heard through reliable sources that your little girlfriend smashed your living room window."

Brianna gasped and wanted to skewer her mother and roast her over a fire. "If you knew that, why didn't you tell me?" She demanded before she turned to Jake. Theda had been on edge in the bakery, but this vengeful act was excessive. "If you need to go home to clean up the damage, I can help."

"No." He frowned. "You shouldn't be at my house right now."

Or ever, she thought. But the way he said "right now" made her wonder if he thought there would come a time when she could be in his home. Maybe she felt a twinge of warmth.

"Let's get inside," Jake suggested, with a glance around the parking lot. "I'd feel less like a sitting duck."

Brianna suspected he was only half-joking.

Karen opened the heavy wooden door, but Jake held it to allow the women to enter. As Brianna brushed past him, she felt the weight of his hand on her back. Stupid, the small warmth his action brought.

Once seated, the trio huddled over the table in the dining room side of the building. The other half held the bar, a long-time watering hole in Welcome. A few years ago the place had been home to the rougher part of Welcome's population. Today, families enjoyed the restaurant side while the wine and craft beer enthusiasts filled the bar side. Upscale for Welcome, but it was past time, Brianna thought.

Their server set down three menus on the table and asked if they'd like drinks. Karen and Brianna ordered a locally-produced wine while Jake wanted a craft beer.

After their drinks arrived, Brianna sat quietly and listened to Jake explain how he'd had a call from Bud about Theda breaking his window. He'd asked Bud not to call the police because he wanted to fix the damage himself and not have her charged.

"You moved her things out and changed the locks without telling her you were doing it?" Brianna asked, appalled. Not that she condoned Theda's act of revenge, but Jake's actions had been stone cold.

He looked guilty. "I know it was cowardly, but—"

Karen interjected. "No, no, no. I get why. You couldn't trust that she'd leave quietly. If she's capable of making insinuating comments about you and Justin to Sybil in the bakery and then smashing your window, what other trouble might she cause? Hmm?"

Her mother leaned back in her chair as if she'd just proven Jake's innocence in a court of law.

Brianna sat in shock at her mom's comment. "How long have you wanted her out of your home?" she asked Jake.

"Months," he admitted. "I tried hints at first. Then talk. Then demands. Today was a desperate measure. And given that she wanted to toss hot coffee in our faces earlier, I didn't want a confrontation in person." He sounded frustrated and confused.

Brianna considered what she'd seen in the bakery today. "Theda's hand was wrapped very tightly around that coffee mug handle," she said thoughtfully. Theda had barely restrained herself. "I'm certain she'd have thrown the coffee on you if I hadn't stopped her."

The look on Theda's face had been murderous and Brianna had been taken aback by the scene and the obvious insinuations the other woman had made about Justin and Jake. Everything about those moments was too much. Too ugly. Too sudden. Too threatening.

Jake nodded. "She would have tossed the coffee at all of us if not for you. I'm sure you would have been included." He gave her a grateful look.

"And now, this," Karen muttered. "If she didn't go to the shelter that Pastor Reeve runs, then where is she?"

Jake shook his head. "I don't have a clue. Bud said she stormed off down the street. No one came to pick her up."

Karen nodded. "She just left?"

Jake nodded. "She never spoke about anyone she was friendly with. And since she walked away, I have no one to call to ask her whereabouts."

"She was nice to me when we first met," Brianna said. "She had a wide, friendly smile and she was kind and interested in my book."

"It was her idea for Brianna to write there in the mornings," Karen added.

"You don't think she'd go to your place?"

Brianna shook her head. "We chatted, but I wouldn't say we were friendly enough for her to presume she could come to me." She hesitated. "Besides, I believe she's unhappy that you and I know each other."

"I think our old friendship is driving most of her bad decisions."

Karen whipped her phone out from where she'd tucked it into her bra strap. "I'll call the rescue to make sure Theda hasn't shown up out there." She had a brief conversation with a volunteer and then a moment later she disconnected. "No one's seen her. It's been a quiet day."

"There must have been someone else she knew from the bakery," Jake said. "Another customer, maybe."

The server arrived to take their orders, but they'd been so engrossed in their conversation, they hadn't decided on food. After a quick scan and Karen asking about the specials, they all chose their meal.

When they were alone again and able to talk, a man approached, cutting off what Jake had been about to say. "Karen Bowler?" the man asked.

The newcomer was a stranger to Brianna, but her mother's face split into a wide and welcoming smile. She actually rose to her feet and then hugged the man. "Duncan Starling, what a surprise," she said warmly.

Duncan Starling was only slightly taller than Karen, and he had a full head of white hair, thick and lustrous. He had it held back with a thong. His eyes were a startling shade of green, like jade and they were full of affection.

Her mother's gaze mirrored his.

"Not such a surprise, Karen. After our chats online and your invitation to stop by, I came to see you. I thought I'd have a couple of days to settle in before I called on you at your dog rescue." He told them the hotel where he was staying.

Jake tilted his head curiously at Brianna, but she could only shrug in ignorance. The man kept one arm around her mother's waist as they both beamed at each other, and then down at Brianna and Jake.

"Oh, Duncan," she responded breathlessly. "I'm so glad you came."

To Brianna, she said, "We haven't seen each other since high school." Her mother flushed. "Duncan, this is my daughter, Brianna, and our friend, Jake Morrow."

Duncan said his hellos to both Brianna and Jake, keeping his arm firmly at Karen's waist. Brianna frowned at that, but her mother either didn't see the frown or chose to ignore it.

"Duncan, we don't need to bore these two," her mom said lightly after the pleasantries were completed. "Let's move to your table."

Brianna felt her jaw unhinge as it hit the floor. Her mother, Karen Bowler, was flirting, right there in the middle of the Welcome Bar and Grill.

"We could always read each other's minds, Karen," Duncan said with a nostalgic grin. "Nothing's changed there. Let's go catch up."

"Let the server know I've changed tables, Brianna." And without another glance at her daughter, Karen practically floated across the room to a booth for two. A giggle wafted behind her.

"My mother just giggled."

"I heard," Jake deadpanned.

Chapter Eleven

"WHAT JUST HAPPENED?" Jake asked a shocked-looking Brianna. Not that he really cared, because hey, he had Brianna all to himself. But still, a man jumping all over Karen Bowler was something you didn't see every day.

Brianna blinked her green-hazel eyes and pulled herself together enough to chuckle. "I think we just saw my mom hook up with an old high school flame. The other day, Elle and I were talking about setting her up on a dating site, but we haven't got to it yet."

"Maybe she took matters into her own hands. Has she ever mentioned Duncan Starling?"

Brianna shook her head. "I don't think I know the name Starling, either. The family must have left Welcome or died off before my time."

Jake nodded. He hadn't heard the family name in town either. "So, we don't have a clue who this guy is?"

"No. Did you know anything about Theda when you started dating?" Her voice sounded normal. Curious. Polite, even. But he felt a barb of accusation.

"Point to you," he responded easily. "We never actually dated. She was at the scene of an accident I attended." He blew out a breath and ran his fingers through his hair. "I saw to her minor injuries and a few days later she showed up at my door." He'd also given her some cash to help her out in the shelter, but she went through it and landed on his doorstep.

Their food arrived, and he watched as Brianna pointed out her mother's new table. The server moved on and Brianna leveled a steady gaze at him.

"You let a strange woman move in. And that woman has now broken your living room window." The statements were bland and cool.

Brianna was pissed. She always went cool when she had her back up about something. He studiously unwrapped his cutlery from the rolled cloth napkin. Next, he took a sip of his beer. Still, she sat watching him.

Judging him for a fool.

"You're right," he said. "I was stupid." He could tell her how bedraggled and helpless Theda had looked. How she'd nibbled her lip and widened her eyes and said how broke she was. She had no family, nowhere to go, and no one to help or look out for her.

Stupid.

He'd opened the door and let her have the sofa for a few nights. Just until she got work. Just until something or someone came along.

That someone had been Jake. Now that he'd seen the photos Theda kept, he understood he'd been targeted. She'd likely wanted him at first glance. Wanted him to replace all the other men who were no more than snapshots now. He'd been a brainless fool.

He wasn't about to tell Brianna he was only one in a long line of men. Even now, he didn't want to judge Theda or badmouth her. She'd lived a life far removed from his and had made her own way, such as it was.

"It was pretty clear she couldn't depend on anyone else," he said. "Things progressed until she became possessive and I realized she wanted more from me than I can give. I expected she'd move out when she settled in with work at the bakery, but she came up with excuses why every place she saw wasn't right."

"I thought she was joking when she told me you rescued her from the side of the road the same way you rescued that pup. But it was the truth. She sees herself as being in need of rescue."

And he was a guy who loved saving people so much he'd made a career of it. A match made in Heaven as far as Theda was concerned.

"Makes for a tough life," Jake said vaguely because his thoughts raced back to that night with Tiffany and his complete helplessness in the face of her horrific injuries. The images wove in and out of his inner vision. The blood from her head wound. The way her neck dangled at an impossible angle. Her torn clothes and skin. Her pretty hair matted with mud and blood seeping everywhere.

There was nothing he could do but hold Tiffany and cry. It didn't take months of counseling to figure out that night had created the paramedic he'd become.

After a long moment of him staring down at his plate, Brianna picked up her fork and knife and sliced into her grilled pork chop. But she let him think and he was grateful. She'd always been kind and wise.

For a time, they focused on food and small talk about how Welcome seemed the same but different. There was a new subdivision being built on the outskirts of town that Logan Hughes was selling. Clay Foster had hired another vet so he had more time with his growing family.

People came and went and smiled at one or both of them. By tomorrow, everyone in Welcome would know they'd been at the Bar and Grill sharing a meal. He bet none of them realized Karen had been with them when they walked in. This would definitely look like a date.

Half his heart settled at the idea, the other half beat itself to death with an urgent need to escape. The prying eyes, the pitying looks, whether they were real or just in his head, all managed to send him into near-panic. He didn't want to make Brianna the center of gossip.

That poor girl, doesn't she realize who he is? What he'd done? In his head, he heard the whispers, the innuendo.

He should have left Welcome fifteen years ago, but some twisted part of him had wanted to stay, to punish himself by seeing those looks, hearing those nasty whispers.

"You shouldn't be seen with me," he said before he could stop the words. He washed down the rest of what he should say with a swig of beer.

"Why not?" She asked, sounding appalled. "We're old friends." She took a cue from him and sipped at her wine. "Just as we decided."

He nodded but hated that she wouldn't stand up and walk out. Theda had included her in the scene at the bakery and he worried where that might lead.

"May I tell you about the deal I made on the truck?"

He closed his eyes, gathered strength and nodded. Normal things. She wanted a normal conversation, stripped of all the baggage they shared. "Of course."

She gave him the details with a fair amount of glee in her tone. "And when it looked like the business manager would balk at my price, I reminded him I'd be willing to walk out and go to the next dealership."

"And your mom didn't speak up?"

"Of course she did. While they were digesting what I'd just said, she told them we'd seen another similar truck already. And we still had one more dealership to visit."

Admiration for the Bowler women seeped into his bones. "You two did well. Congratulations." Speaking of Karen, he wondered how she and her old friend were doing.

He turned and scanned the other tables and lit on Karen and Duncan, sitting behind him and to the right. They were directly in Brianna's line of sight, but she'd done an admirable job of not gawking. "Your mom and her friend seem chatty."

"I'm trying not to look, but it's so weird to see her like this. She's smiling and happy and flushed and seems to be hanging on everything he says. It's hard not to stare," she said straight into Jake's face. "They're finishing their meal and he's waved for the check."

"Think she'll join us again?"

She blinked at the question. "Of course she will." She leaned closer and hunched over the table toward him. "She wouldn't leave with him. Go home with him or to his hotel or...whatever." Her voice was low; tight with disapproval.

From what he'd seen *whatever* was a distinct possibility.

He waved to their server. "Would you like another glass of wine?" he asked Brianna as the server stood beside their table. She may need one.

"I'll have a coffee. Decaf if you have it."

"A fresh pot has just brewed. And for you, sir?"

"I'll have the same."

Her gaze drifted to the other table again. "Duncan's paid the bill. It looks like Mom will be joining us. Maybe we should order her a decaf, too."

He glanced over his shoulder to see Karen stand and then slip her arm through Duncan's. Her face beamed with happiness and Duncan had his face turned to Karen's with an adoring expression. Brianna seemed blind to the obvious, but he wouldn't be the one to point it out.

The couple approached the table. "Brianna, I'll be home late. Don't wait up," Karen said as she and Duncan breezed past them on the way to the exit.

Brianna stiffened in her seat, her face a study in disbelief. She opened her mouth, but no sound emerged. By the time she turned to gaze after the departing pair, they'd made the hostess's podium and disappeared around the wooden wall that hid the waiting area. "She left with him," she whispered.

Jake suspected she didn't have enough air in her lungs to be any louder. "Yes," he said. "Your mom got picked up by a guy and left with him. But, just because you don't know Duncan, doesn't mean she doesn't. They said they reconnected online, so they knew each other before. Your mother is a smart woman and has no concerns about how he'll treat her." He didn't know Karen, but from what he'd seen of her, she was level headed and knew her own mind.

Brianna stared back at him with features of stone and eyes like granite. She shuddered as if pulling her stuff together and the hard expression cleared. "Mom is smart. And she's cautious." She bit her lip. "He seemed nice, right?"

"Right. She was happy to see him and I'm betting you'll get to know him pretty quick."

"I'd better."

He smiled at her, acutely aware that years had passed. While he and Brianna had been busy living with guilt, life had happened for their classmates. The others had married, had children; while he and Brianna hadn't had any of those things.

She deserved all that life had to offer and more. She hadn't done anything wrong that night so long ago. He was completely to blame and he'd been a fool to make her think she shared his guilt.

He never should have driven her away. But it was too late to say any of this now. Fifteen years of life had passed her by. "You deserve every happiness, Brianna, and all the things you've missed out on."

The server approached with their coffees, but it was clear Brianna was in no mood to stay and chat. And he shouldn't be either. This whole dinner thing was a mistake. Half the town probably already knew they were here together.

"Can you bring the check, please?" she asked, which Jake took to mean she wanted to be gone. Out of sight of everyone here, and away from him.

They fell to silence, mostly because he couldn't think of anything to say to make her feel better about this Duncan her mom had left with.

When the check arrived she tried to snag it, but he was faster. "My treat. You can get it next time," he said automatically as he pulled his credit card out of his wallet. It was a figure of speech, a nothing comment, but he shouldn't have presumed. She'd be better off never seeing him again.

"There won't be a next time."

At that, he looked up and caught a defeated expression flit through her gaze.

"You know we can't," she whispered tightly. "It wouldn't be right."

"Brianna, I—."

"No." She cut him off. "We agreed. I've had time to think and I can't shake off what happened."

"I was going to say I agree with you." He exaggerated a glance around the room. "I should have known better than to invite you here tonight. People will be talking."

She made a face. "If my mother's gossip crew is on it, then everyone in town knows we were here."

Including Theda.

Chapter Twelve

BRIANNA ROSE FROM THE table in the Welcome Bar and Grill and followed Jake to the exit, her mind reeling from the turn of events. First, she'd had the shock of seeing her mom swept out of the restaurant by a stranger. Obviously, Duncan wasn't a stranger to her mother, but Brianna had never heard his name before. If Karen had once a boyfriend who could affect her like this, wouldn't she have mentioned him? Even once?

The other reason her legs felt like lead was that this reunion with Jake was over. They shared a guilty secret, he was involved in a domestic drama that she wanted no part of, and he was still mired in guilt over Tiffany's death. She might still feel guilty, but she wasn't mired.

She, Brianna Bowler, was ready to move on with her life. She doubted Jake ever would be.

The man she followed, the man with broad shoulders, healing hands, and the sexiest eyes she'd ever fallen into, would never have all the things he said he wanted for her. A spouse who loved him, children, a happy home.

Half of her ached for him. But she had to set thoughts of Jake aside. He'd made it plain he felt the same way she did. They should never see each other again.

The other half of her wanted her mother to find someone to share her life with. She and Elle had encouraged Karen to put up a profile on dating sites, but Brianna hadn't believed she actually would.

Then, apparently out of the blue, Duncan Starling had shown up on social media. Had her mother gathered her courage and reached out? Or maybe Duncan had been circling for some time. She couldn't wrap her head around it.

Elle would be shocked, too. Brianna felt like texting her, but her friend was busy with Logan and her ex-husband at parent-teacher night for Elle's twins.

Also, the news about Theda breaking Jake's window unsettled her. Theda felt she still had a claim on Jake. But Jake seemed adamant it was over. Soon, the young woman's pride would kick in and rescue her from her mistaken notions. At least, that was Brianna's hope.

Her own breakups had always been easy, like the one with Anthony. She frowned and wondered if her breakups were easy because her heart had never been truly involved.

Brianna turned the corner into the waiting area by the hostess's podium. She nearly slammed into Jake's back because he'd come to a halt right in front of her. She peeked around Jake's broad back only to see Tyler Rhodes walking toward them from the bar side of the building.

He glowered at Jake as he got closer and saw them.

Brianna hadn't seen Tyler since Tiffany's funeral, but she'd heard he was still suffering and his life was off track. Grief could have long-lasting effects.

As he neared, the reek of fresh beer and the waft of stale cigarettes caught her by the nose. Since last setting eyes on Tyler, Brianna saw that he'd gone puffy around the eyes and his sandy-colored hair had lightened with silver. He was thirty but looked forty. Unkempt in scruffy work boots, old jeans, and a dirty denim jacket, he looked downtrodden. His eyes, though, were the worst. Pain seeped out of them and washed his face with loss.

Tyler's gaze widened when he saw her, but it quickly slid to Jake. "Who do we have here?" Tyler said with belligerent surprise in every syllable.

"Tyler," Brianna said on a puff of air. "I haven't seen you in years." She moved in to give him a hug, but he shrugged her off, glaring at Jake.

"Rhodes," Jake said bluntly. "This isn't the time to air your grievances."

"Why not? You killed my sister." It was as much a growl as a statement.

Brianna gasped and stilled between the two men. She looked from Tyler to Jake and back. Fifteen years and it still seemed fresh and raw for Tyler. Eyes turned their way and Brianna felt the heat of humiliation rise.

"I have to get out of here," she said to Jake. "Now."

Jake's gaze turned icy. "Yes," he said to Tyler. "I'll say yes if it will put an end to this right now." He clasped Brianna's elbow to usher her toward the door and the fresh air outside. She let him lead the way.

Once outside, she drew in a gulp of cool air. But her first words were for Tyler who crowded outside with them.

"No," Brianna said, with a shake of her head for Tyler. "Jake didn't kill her. Tiffany undid her seatbelt and—*Tyler*—you know she did." She pulled out of Jake's light grasp and reached for Tyler's forearms to give them a shake. He looked down at her earnest expression and gave her a crooked little smile.

"Brianna Bowler. I didn't expect to ever see you again." He tilted his head, curious. "But you're with him." He frowned as if trying to do math that was beyond him. Things weren't adding up for Tyler.

Jake put his arm around her, holding her by the shoulders protectively. She allowed it if only to keep Tyler from getting any closer. "We'll never really know what happened, will we?" Tyler said. "You made sure of that, Morrow."

"Believe what you want, Rhodes, but the investigation exonerated me."

Brianna remembered. The conclusion had been clear. Tiffany had unbuckled her seatbelt, opened the car door, and all hell had broken loose. She blinked against the memories, aching for Tyler.

"Come on, Brianna." Jake gently urged her away from the door because new diners were arriving.

Tyler followed them. Of course. This nightmare wasn't over. "That's not what your girlfriend says, Morrow. She told Denise Jones all about how you admitted you—"

Jake whirled and grabbed Tyler by the jacket collar. "Never happened, Tyler. None of it. I never said a word to Theda about that night."

"Denise Jones is a vicious woman," Brianna interjected. "Tyler, you know that." Of course, he did, but maybe he needed to be blind. Maybe that's where he was most comfortable.

Tyler looked chastened by Brianna's words. Then he covered Jake's hands with scarred fingers. "Let me go."

Jake released him. "Look. I've lived with the memories for all these years. I'm sorry your sister's gone, sorrier than you know. But I didn't shove her out the car door."

Ignoring him, Tyler turned and swayed while he looked around the parking lot. "Can't remember where I parked. You see my car?" He talked as if they weren't in the middle of a conversation about the worst thing that could ever happen. The thing that had messed them all up for years.

Again, Brianna stepped up and held Tyler by the forearms. "Give me your keys and I'll help you find your car, Tyler. I can drive you home and we can talk if you want."

"Umkay." He threw an arm across Brianna's shoulder and leaned on her just a little too much. She could see Jake's eyes gleaming in the fluorescent lights from the sign over the door. He looked furious.

Tyler dangled his keys over her outstretched hand and gave Jake a glittering look over her shoulder. "I think my car's around back."

Then he slipped his keys into her palm, making sure to stroke her fingers.

She drew in a breath for strength and kept her arms around Tyler's back to keep him from staggering. He snugged her close to his side as she guided him to the parking lot behind the building. The stink of cigarettes and old sweat made her want to gag.

Tyler had just admitted Theda was talking with Denise Jones. Maybe that was where Theda was staying.

"I'll drive you home," she offered. "But you need to know that Jake has broken things off with Theda. She's not his girlfriend. Not anymore."

"Oh? That's not what I heard."

"Is Theda staying with Denise?"

But instead of answering, Tyler began to whistle tunelessly and Brianna took the hint. He didn't want to talk about Denise or Theda, or their alliance. Brianna couldn't call it a friendship because she wasn't convinced Denise could have a friend.

BRIANNA CHECKED THE rearview mirror and Jake's pickup was still behind them. Jake was following as she drove Tyler Rhodes home in his fifteen-year-old beater. She hadn't asked Jake to follow them, but she was glad he was there. He could give her a ride home without her having to call her mom for a lift. Who knew where that man Duncan had taken her mother.

Tyler grunted beside her. "She used to laugh at you." He was mumbling so she couldn't be sure what she heard, but she assumed he meant Tiffany.

"We had fun together," she replied breezily as if her memories of Tiffany were easy. "I remember when you bought this car," she said, to keep him awake so he could get himself out the door and up to his house under his own steam.

He hadn't seemed this drunk when he'd been back at the Welcome Bar and Grill berating Jake. But he'd been angry and maybe that had sobered him in the moment. Now, though, Tyler looked heavy-headed and morose as he slumped against the passenger door. The fragrant scent of stale draft beer wafted through the car. His ashtray overflowed with old cigarette butts and the floor was littered with crushed empty packs.

Lovely. She cracked open her window so she wouldn't gag.

"Back then, I was happy," he said more clearly. "And I had a whole future ahead of me. I worked hard for two years to buy this car," he said, more to himself than to her. "Then everything went to shit."

"Losing Tiffany must have nearly killed your parents," she voiced her thoughts kindly.

"They're still walkin' around dead. Nothing I do can ever make up for her. My sister was golden."

"I know," she said softly. "You never married or had children?" She'd hoped by now Cassie and Phil Rhodes would have grandchildren to watch grow.

"Everything went to shit," he repeated. "I was planning on college, but I couldn't leave, not with them so messed up even two years later. Wouldn't be right to leave them like that." He rolled his head on the headrest.

She pulled to a stop in front of the neat bungalow where Tiffany had lived. Tyler still lived with his parents here. But the house wasn't the way she remembered it. The yard wasn't neat and tidy anymore. The lawn hadn't been mown and there was a tarp covering part of the roof. She hated the idea of sending Tyler into the place. "You take care, Tyler."

He looked at her again, as if surprised she was in his car. "She always laughed at you, dull, quiet Brianna. Tiffany was never your friend. That's why she laughed because you thought she was."

"What?" But another look at Tyler told her his words were the meandering of a drunk mind. Of course, Tiffany was her friend. A spike of old suspicion rose, but she cut it off before it could do any harm. But it was suddenly easier to send him into the house. Out of her sight. Tyler had turned into a mean drunk and she didn't need to hear anymore.

Not that he'd answered her blurted question anyway.

Brianna climbed out and went to the passenger side to help Tyler exit the car. Once he was on his feet, she locked the doors and slipped his keys into his jacket pocket. The denim felt greasy with dirt. Giving his breast pocket a pat, she set him on a course for his front door.

He swayed, but settled into a gentle, rolling stroll. He must have walked this walk in this condition countless times.

Jake parked across the road and she hurried over to him. "Thanks," she said as she climbed in and buckled up. "He's in rough shape."

"Yeah, I think something or someone set him off. We've crossed paths plenty of times and he's never approached me that way before."

"Theda?"

"Maybe." He drove away with a grimace. "Likely. When he mentioned Denise Jones I put it together. Denise runs into the bakery on her way to work every morning. Theda probably went to Denise today after I locked her out."

"Denise is the sort to encourage Theda's revenge." She remembered a conversation the other morning at the bakery. "I spoke with Denise a couple of days ago. Or rather, she talked and forced me to listen. She commented that Tiffany's family must really hate you." She'd tried to freeze the other woman out, but Denise had been determined to have her say.

Jake shook his head. "First I've heard of it. Her parents talked with me when the investigation was happening. They assured me they understood Tiffany better than anyone. At the time, what they said didn't make sense, but I was so torn up, nothing would have gotten through."

"Her parents believed the witnesses about what Tiffany did?" There had been a car behind Jake's pulling around to pass him and they gave statements about Tiffany's erratic actions. They'd seen everything clearly because their lights shone into Jake's car interior. It was a flash, but enough to corroborate Jake's account.

"I've run into Mr. and Mrs. Rhodes over the years and it's clear they're still grieving, but they've never *blamed* me. They're not the same people you remember, not by a long shot. And Tyler just sort of...stopped. He never went to college, barely works."

"He said he couldn't leave them at the time." She wouldn't ask Jake what Tyler had meant about Tiffany not being her friend. About Tiffany laughing at her for believing they were friends. "Before Tiffany and I became friendly, I wasn't very popular," she admitted. "I was too quiet and odd. My head was in the clouds. Leon used to tell me to talk to people more, but I needed a shove to do that. Tiffany gave me that shove. She was sweet to me when everyone else ignored me."

She turned to watch his expression, but he stayed looking straight ahead. Something about the set of his chin made her wonder.

"You were there the day she first approached me," Brianna said, her voice suffused with memory. Tiffany had been hanging on Jake's arm and smiling so widely it was impossible not to feel warmed. "It was kind of out of the blue. Like a princess noticing a pauper, deigning to include me in her wide circle of friends. I felt... embraced."

Jake made a sound in the back of his throat. It didn't sound positive and a quiet voice inside her head told her to stop talking.

"But I wasn't embraced, was I? She didn't think of me as a friend, did she?"

"It's so long ago," Jake responded on a husky note. "Leave it alone, Brianna."

"If we weren't friends, then what was I to her?"

Jake clenched his jaw. "She wasn't a kind person. I don't know where you got the idea she was."

"Through her actions, of course. She invited me over to her house. We talked and laughed together, shared secrets." Brianna even knew when Jake had lost his virginity with Tiffany. She'd giggled and explained that she'd told Jake it was her first time, too. But, she'd lied to him. Maybe Tiffany had lied about a lot of things. Jake had all but confirmed what Tyler had told her about their supposed friendship. "Oh," she said softly. "I get it now."

"Then why go over it?" Jake asked with exasperation. Was he feeling guilty about being in on the joke all those years ago?

She hoped maybe a little.

Finally, Brianna listened to that little voice in her head and quit talking because there was nothing else to say.

THE NEXT MORNING, BRIANNA received a group text from Elle. Shandy and Mercy were in the group, too.

Elle: "We've set the date. Meet us at the town hall at 4 on Saturday."

Elle: "Oh, Mercy, bring the kids. Mine will watch yours."

Elle: "Dinner at Welcome Bar & Grill."

And the ones that made her groan:

Elle: "Bring dates."

Elle: "Or not."

After that string of texts, Elle fell silent. Announcement over. Which didn't stop a series of whoops and cheers and smiley faces with hearts from making the rounds.

She was going to a wedding, she thought as she poured the first cup of coffee out of the freshly brewed pot. Brianna's smile stretched and her heart filled.

She could bring a date. Or not.

Brianna hadn't felt so included with a group of women before. That weird time with Tiffany didn't count. Not now that she knew it was all fake.

As an adult, she'd had women she could catch a movie with or have lunch with at work, but this was different. Since childhood, Elle had been the older friend she looked up to and now that she and Elle had returned to Welcome, Elle had enveloped her into her friendships with Mercy and Shandy.

"Mom," she called. "Elle and Logan are getting married at the town hall on Saturday." She took out a bowl for cereal, expecting to hear her mother's bedroom door open. "Do you want cereal with me or something more substantial?"

No response.

"Mom?" She set her coffee mug on the counter and walked down the hall that led to the bedrooms. She tapped on her mother's bedroom door. "Mom?" she asked again before turning the knob to peer into the darkened room.

Karen's bed hadn't been slept in. "Excuse me?" Brianna demanded of the empty room. She hustled back to her phone and called her mother, but before the call connected, she saw the kitchen door open slowly. Very slowly.

So slowly that the squeak was considerably quieter than it was during the busier part of the day.

"Are you trying to sneak in?" Brianna demanded when she saw her mother's hand, holding her shoes, precede the rest of her into the room.

Her mother faced her straight on, with a steady look. "Yes, I am. I didn't want to wake you."

Brianna's mouth moved. She knew it did because she could feel the muscles of her cheeks engage, but since her lips were numb from pinching them together, she couldn't get any words out.

"I'm glad you're up," her mother went on. "Duncan's taking a tour of the kennels before joining us for breakfast."

Brianna glanced down at her ratty, coffee- and toothpaste-stained terry robe, and squeaked. "No. No. You can't." And then she thought again. "You didn't?"

Her mother straightened her shoulders. "I certainly did." And then she smiled in a secretive, private way. "He'll be in here any minute. If you want to change, be quick about it."

Brianna pivoted, snatched up her mug of coffee and rushed to her bedroom. Maybe if she waited long enough, she wouldn't have to talk to that man. That man who—oh, no!—had seduced her mother. She felt ill and confused at the same time.

Her mother had been single for all of Brianna's life. Happily so, Brianna had thought. They'd always been a team, just the two of them. Sure, Brianna had left for college, but she'd settled in nearby Seattle. And she was back now when her mom needed her.

She pulled off her robe and pajamas, tossed them into her laundry hamper and quickly dressed for the day. A shower could wait until after she'd checked on the dogs and sorted out the volunteers. There were people coming to see dogs later this morning. They wanted a pair and a brother and sister set of boxer crosses needed a bath to put their best paws forward. Her mind raced between Duncan and her mother and all she needed to do for the dogs today.

Not to mention the wedding on Saturday.

There was no room in her head for thoughts of Jake, or Theda, or Tyler or Tiffany. She said a silent thank you.

As much as she wanted to hide in her room until Duncan had left, she wanted to know what was happening more. What was so special about this man that her mother would change completely at first sight of him? And how had he known exactly when to show up in her mom's life?

She drained her coffee and, feeling fortified, left her room and marched into the kitchen, empty mug in hand.

"Good morning," she said breezily as if it was an everyday thing to have her mother, dressed in last night's clothes, with a man she'd spent the night with sitting at the breakfast table.

Duncan stood as she entered and offered her his hand. She shook it.

"Nice to see you again, Brianna," he said with a happy glance at her mother who was busy at the stove.

He was tall, had a full head of long white hair and what looked to be his own teeth. But looks weren't character. Looks were window dressing and Brianna was more interested in the man's character. This man had to be the right kind of man to hang out with Karen. He had to be honest and kind. Good health and a happy outlook were important, too. She kept up the mental checklist as she took stock.

Her mother kept herself engaged at the stove. *Probably deliberate*, Brianna thought. The scent of bacon, blended with the smell of fresh coffee, made the kitchen seem homey.

When she still hadn't spoken, her mother turned and cocked an eyebrow expectantly at Brianna until she broke and smiled back at Duncan. "Nice to see you again, too."

"Your mother and I are very old friends," he explained. "We spent the night talking and laughing about old times and old friends. We share a lot of memories of growing up together."

"I see." And she did. Or at least she wanted to. "Are you staying in Welcome long?"

"I'm moving back. Now that I've reconnected with Karen, my decision to return to Welcome makes me happier than ever." He looked toward the stove with a fond smile for her mother.

"Duncan was widowed last year," her mother explained. "And we recently connected online."

Which meant he likely knew her mom was single. And the mystery of his sudden arrival was solved.

"I'm sorry," Brianna said about his wife and meant it. He did seem like a nice man and while her mother's reaction to him unnerved her a little, she didn't blame him for her mother turning into a simpering girly-girl. But she'd love to have ten minutes alone with her mother to get more details.

He took his seat again. "My wife and I were divorced and she'd remarried."

Her mother turned and looked him in the eye. Brianna could feel an intensity between them and she stilled with her hand on the handle of the coffee carafe, waiting. "His wife's second husband deserted her when she got sick. Duncan was there for her every step of the way." She turned her head toward Brianna, eyes burning with sympathy. "Right until the end."

Duncan went ruddy. "Nothing heroic, Karen. Anyone would have been there." He shrugged. "I'd recently sold my business and retired so it made sense and we actually became friends again." His voice had softened over the last words and Brianna lost a lot of her reservations about the man. He was kind, sympathetic, and generous. Not everyone would give up their lives to tend a dying ex-spouse.

"Are you going to the bakery this morning?" her mother asked.

The reminder of her usual routine brought a welcome change of mood, and Brianna shrugged. "I don't think that's a good idea. I may have to give up on writing there."

Karen nodded sagely. "Right. I forgot about the window for a moment. We can discuss it another time." She moved to the toaster and put a couple of bread slices down.

"Maybe I can find another place to go. The idea of leaving the house to go write somewhere else still works for me." The bakery had been nearly perfect.

"Karen told me about your book. I've never met a writer before." Duncan looked impressed. "You could try the library," he suggested. "It's quiet there."

"I'll think about it." Brianna took over turning the bacon and now she cracked eggs into the skillet and focused on cooking for a few minutes. Karen joined Duncan at the table. They seemed to find lots to talk about in spite of having *talked* all night.

She held back the wedding news because she found she enjoyed the sound of her mother talking happily with a man who clearly enjoyed hearing the same thing. Karen was happy and Brianna couldn't remember a time when she seemed so carefree.

Chapter Thirteen

"AND THEY'VE SPENT EVERY night together since," Brianna told Mercy and Shandy as they stood outside the Town Hall on Saturday afternoon. For the wedding, she'd invested in a dark purple dress with brilliant orange piping around the square neck and the hem. With the shoulder pads, she felt very 1940s. To complete the look, she carried a black clutch and wore orange peep-toe platform heels. She had a black fascinator on her head that veiled her face on her right side. One single black plume drooped by her left ear. If a breeze caught it, she felt a tickle. Disconcerting, but she'd managed so far not to rip the feather off her head.

She'd pulled the look together in an interesting little retro-Hollywood store called *TimeStop* in Bellingham. Mercy had been the one to suggest the store because of the Hollywood connection. The owner, Faye Grantham, was Mercy's friend and a wonderful source for unique clothes.

Shandy grinned. "I'd say your mother and her new man are rediscovering something they lost years ago. Nothing wrong with that. Rediscovering something you thought you lost can have the best, most lasting results."

"I suppose so," Brianna reluctantly agreed. But what had come between Karen and Duncan in the first place? "Whatever came between them before doesn't seem to have any bearing on their reunion."

Shandy nodded. "I'm sure they've cleared the air by now."

Mercy shifted baby Autumn to her other shoulder. "He's nice, though?"

"Very," Brianna admitted. "He's helping at the rescue and even taking over some of the things I do, like scheduling volunteers. He owned his own business so he's good at organizing."

Shandy leaned in. "Justin told me about you and Jake and Theda. What's happening there?" kept her tone soft for privacy.

Brianna shrugged. "Nothing. I'm not writing at the bakery anymore so I don't see Theda and I haven't seen Jake since the night she broke his window."

She didn't want to see Jake. Life was easier without all the emotions he aroused.

"Look who's here," Mercy cut in. "The bride and groom!"

Shandy nudged her shoulder against Mercy's affectionately. "Don't sound so surprised."

The three of them laughed. No couple was more committed than Logan and Elle. It had taken some hard work but once they'd booted their differences out of their personal equation, they'd become rock solid. There was no one for Elle but Logan and no one for Logan but Elle.

Clay pulled his SUV to a stop and hopped out to open the door for the bride and groom who descended to the ground. The bride wore a tea-length light blue gown trimmed in lace across the bodice and shoulders. Logan wore a tuxedo with a bow tie and pocket square in the same light blue shade.

The next car, driven by Logan's father, pulled in behind Clay's vehicle. The back door opened and Elle's children emerged. Daniel and the twins, Jorja and Liam, were dressed in matching tuxedos, except Jorja's was the same color as her mother's gown. And her shoes were bright pink. Her hair was a black cloud of curls and joy filled her face. She was normally a solemn girl, but today the sun shone out of her eyes.

Another vehicle pulled to a stop and a young woman exited from the passenger side looking nervous. From the back door, Elle's ex-mother-in-law and grandmother to Daniel climbed out onto the sidewalk. Susan Murdoch was one of the wealthiest people in town, and today, she looked quietly pleased. Her husband's dementia prevented him from attending, but Susan looked relaxed and happy.

The driver rounded the back of the vehicle with a baby in his arms. Elle's second ex and father of the twins had left Elle for the younger woman. That choice had driven Elle's desperation-fueled decision to return to Welcome.

Brianna watched as Logan and Elle embraced them all, one by one.

As the eclectic group of friends, ex-family, and new family ascended the wide concrete steps to the town hall's double entrance doors, Brianna pondered the love shared among the people in the small crowd. A lot of past grudges and hurt feelings had been sorted, discussed, and set aside for this happy day to happen.

Brianna hoped a time might come when Theda showed the maturity that all these people had. She wished with all her heart that Theda could move forward in her life. The young woman deserved to find whatever it was she was looking for. But Jake wasn't the man to give Theda what she needed.

Jake was not an easy man to get over or forget, but Brianna was doing her best to do both. She hoped Theda found her own way forward.

ON SATURDAY AFTERNOON Jake got off shift and joined his partner at the Welcome Bar and Grill. Doug had two pilsners from a favorite craft brewer on the scarred round table when Jake arrived. "Thanks," he said, lifting the bottle and taking the other chair at the table. "How is it?"

"Good flavor and ice cold." Doug raised his glass. "How are things with Theda? Any better?"

"Hard to say," he responded. "She's texting emojis all the time. I don't know what half of them mean." *Maybe less than half,* he thought. He sipped his beer, perplexed by how his life was going.

"No surprise considering the difference in your ages."

Jake snorted. "You got that right. What was I thinking?"

"Not with your brain, that's for sure." Doug's face turned serious. "Are you responding?"

"Not a chance. I told you she's staying with Denise Jones?"

"Yes. I don't know the woman, but you said she's mean. Probably not a good influence on a woman like Theda who thinks she has an axe to grind."

"When your boys go to school, you'll meet Denise in the school office to register them. Don't tell her you're single."

"No, I won't. My kids are in a different school district. But, thanks for the warning. If she shows up on a dating app, I'll swipe left." He blew out a frustrated breath. "I have no time for dating anyway. No one will want to take me on with my shifts and my two boys."

Shiftwork was hard on families. "Who's got the boys now?" It wasn't often Doug had this kind of time after work.

"My mom's here for the week. I'm taking advantage while I can." Being on shifts meant Doug's childcare was a patchwork to cover days and nights and daytime sleeping. He struggled like any other single parent. His mother visited one week a month to give him a break.

Over Doug's shoulder, Jake saw a large party of happy, lively people arrive, crowding into the entrance that served both sides of the building. From the whooping and the fancy dress, it looked like a wedding party. The restaurant host rushed to handle the crowd.

There were several people he recognized, of course, but he'd long since given up idly chatting with any of them.

Clay Foster stood out, not because of the classic suit he wore, but because he stood with an infant in his arms and a little girl clinging to his leg in the crush of people.

Jake had heard about Clay's first wife wrapping her car around a tree, but he'd never imagined Clay as a father. He looked at ease and happy with his life. Content, even. Jake felt a stab of something that he quickly set aside. No time for regrets for the life he might've had if things had gone differently.

The group of people began to disperse in small clusters as they were taken to their seats. The back half of the restaurant had been cordoned off and now he understood why.

Elle Foster must have married Logan Hughes. She beamed up at him, tucked into his side like a prize. But when they shuffled away toward the back of the seating area, the next person he saw stole his breath.

She wore a purple dress, orange shoes, and some kind of veil over one eye. Brianna looked as if she belonged in another century and outshone every other woman in the group, including the bride.

Beside him, Doug gave a low whistle. "Now, that's a stunning woman," he said under his breath.

Jake wanted to punch his teeth in. He'd have turned to glare at his partner, but just then, Brianna caught sight of them. Her lips parted in surprise, but she quickly— too quickly— glanced away. And then, she moved away toward the seating area.

He tried to see her date, but there didn't seem to be a man attached to her. Instead, Justin's ex-wife Shandy walked with Brianna. She gave Jake a brief wave and smile and moved on.

Maybe later he could pass a few minutes with her.

Doug sipped the last of his beer and set the bottle gently onto the tabletop. "Well, that's me done. I'll go home and tuck the boys in. Mom's cooking my favorite tonight. Where are you off to?"

"I think I'll stay and eat here."

"You're welcome to come home with me. Mom makes great lasagna." Doug was a mean wok cook, but when he made lasagna, it was pre-packaged and frozen, so homemade was a big deal.

Jake considered it but then thought again. He was too curious about the wedding party. No one in particular, of course, but he'd like to say hello to Shandy for courtesy's sake. "No can do. I don't want to hear you whining about not having any leftovers because I ate a second helping. And we both know I would. Plus, your mom would want to send some home with me."

"She does love to feed people," Doug said with a curious smile. "No more run-ins with Tyler here? Maybe you should eat somewhere else. If he comes in and causes you any trouble, just call. I can be back in no time."

"You live twenty minutes from here," Jake responded. "No way you'd make it in time. But I appreciate the sentiment. Besides, I haven't seen him since the last time." Maybe Tiffany's brother had come to his senses. Maybe he was dating Brianna now. They'd been friendly enough when Tiffany had hung out with Brianna, her *experiment*.

He'd hated Tiffany's silly games, even back then, but now he felt disgusted with himself for taking so long to see how nasty Tiffany was.

And here he'd fallen into the very same trap with Theda. He'd followed along with her because it was easier than setting boundaries. And look where that had got him? Stalked and threatened, his house insurance premium was higher and his high school girlfriend's brother had been belligerent and ugly.

"Okay, I'll get going," Doug said. When he stood, he added, "Don't get into trouble. If Tyler comes in, leave before he starts drinking."

"Will do. I'm having a burger and then going straight home."

Doug clapped him on the back as he left.

He should leave with Doug, but from the far side of the restaurant came the distinctive clinking of glasses and the low rumble of a man giving a speech. Bursts of laughter punctuated the speech and made Jake think of other weddings and happier times. He'd been Justin's best man and Shandy had been a glowing bride.

He waved the server over and gave her his dinner order.

"Sounds like a great wedding over there," he said with a tilt of his head toward the happy noise.

"Yes, it sounds like a good time," she said briskly. "Another beer?"

He shook his head. "I'll have a glass of water." He was driving. Too many accident scenes carried the stink of alcohol for him to take chances.

The laughter and clinking continued while Jake checked his phone. More texts filled with little pictures meant to represent words and emotions. All of them useless. He set the phone aside to give half an ear to the cheers and laughter.

He felt pathetic, sitting here missing happier times. Wanting them again. Wanting what he would never deserve.

Shandy and Justin had had a huge wedding. Her father had seen to it. He'd fancied himself a mover and shaker in Welcome and had insisted on going all out. Shandy had been steamrolled into agreeing with her parents, even though Justin had wanted a simple and fun get-together.

His friend would have been happy with what was happening for Logan and Elle but like always, her parents had had the final say.

His phone chimed that another text had come in. He watched as about fifteen texts appeared on the screen. The woman didn't know when to quit. She had stayed on at the bakery, so he'd avoided the place. As far as he knew Brianna had not returned to write there in the mornings.

He wondered idly if she'd found another solution or another place to hole up for peace and quiet in the morning.

Not his problem. And he needed to stop caring.

He smiled at the server when she set his burger and fries on the table. He unwrapped his cutlery and reached for the ketchup bottle. As he unscrewed the top, he saw the shadow of a body loom over his table.

The restrooms were on the bar side. No surprise given that at one time the whole building had been the local watering hole and a none-too-pretty one at that. Eventually, the wedding guests had begun to make their way past Jake.

One of them must have stopped for a chat. He kept his eyes down and pounded the bottom of the bottle to get that first glob out and onto his plate.

"Jake Morrow."

Jake looked up. "Clay Foster. I saw you earlier with a couple of kids. Hard to believe you'd turn into such an upstanding citizen." The jab was tired. He knew how much Clay had turned his life around; everyone in town knew.

"I've been the vet for a long time now." His eyes were happy but assessing. "Heard you're a paramedic."

"Yes." He leaned back in the battle-scarred captain's chair and watched. Any minute now he'd see the pity he'd avoided for years. The pity that had driven him into isolation.

"You should stop over at the wedding. People there would like to see you."

"I doubt that." All they wanted to see was the guy who'd killed his teenage girlfriend. None of them gave a shit about him. Except maybe Brianna. And Shandy. She'd always been sweet to him, even after her divorce from his best friend. He thought about walking over to the group.

Nah, safer here.

"No one at that table thinks harshly of you," Clay said as if he'd read Jake's thoughts. "We've had our own troubles and know better than to judge," he explained. "My sister Elle remembers you, too. And Brianna. You were friendly with her in school, right?"

"Tiffany. Tiffany and she were friendly."

"Well..." Clay hesitated. "Stop by when you've finished your burger. There's room for another friend over there."

He strolled toward the restroom but didn't stop again on his way back to the party. Soon enough, a steady stream of people trooped by. Most smiled warmly.

Jake ate, chewing and swallowing mechanically. He'd ignored so many people his own age for so long, he doubted any of them wanted to make room at the table for him. His only friends from his school days were Justin and Shandy, and that was only because they pushed.

And then Brianna walked in.

She stole the air from his lungs. She looked like a classic movie star from the top of her head to the soles of her feet. He wasn't sure what those shoes were called, but her sexy toes peeped out at him and he found himself pushing back his chair and rising to his feet. He couldn't help himself.

Then he stood there wearing a dopey expression because he couldn't think of a thing to say.

"Jake, Clay said you were still here." Her voice was soft. Much softer than he deserved. "I didn't think you'd spend much time in here after Tyler made an ass of himself."

The last time they'd seen each other he'd ended it badly. When they'd arrived at her home, he'd kept the engine running and she'd climbed out of his vehicle after a mostly silent ride.

That ride home hadn't been silent enough. No, he'd led her toward the truth about Tiffany and she'd rightly concluded that the girl she'd thought was her friend wasn't. He was such a shit.

He wiped his fingers on his napkin and dropped it to the plate. "I was just leaving."

"No," she said and set her fingertips to his forearm. "Stay and say hello. They're about to serve dessert and coffee and people are asking if you'll join us."

"No."

"Please."

He hesitated. Clay had seemed friendly enough and he knew Logan Hughes was a nice guy. And then, he saw Brianna's face cloud with doubt and his resistance melted away. He saw no harm in sharing dessert and coffee with people celebrating a wedding. And Shandy was there if he needed a friendly face.

It only took a nod from him and she slid her hand to his to lead him to the restaurant side. Her fingers felt warm and soft and caring and he remembered what a gentle soul Brianna had always been. When Clay saw them approach, he jumped up, grinned, and then grabbed a chair from near the wall and wedged it beside an empty seat.

Presumably, the empty chair was Brianna's.

Chapter Fourteen

THE REST OF THE EVENING felt like an out-of-body experience for Jake. Someone passed him a filled champagne flute, Brianna sat beside him, close and too far away at the same time. Conversation whirled, jokes ranged from corny to sly, to child-like for the little ones. A new baby, Clay's, he thought, got passed up and down the table and landed with Logan, who sat with his bride.

Apparently, handing the baby back was going to be a problem for the groom. He kept her swaddled body close to his chest, covered the small head with the palm of his hand and let her settle in.

Brianna leaned close so she could whisper. "Logan's so ready for a family. He and Elle will make great parents."

"And beautiful children," Jake said. If Elle's three children were anything to judge by, Logan would soon have a baby of his own to hold close. He felt the same stab he'd felt earlier. Kids. For the first time in his sorry life, he thought of children of his own.

Brianna went to settle back into her seat and, without thinking Jake set his hand on her thigh to stop her. Her eyes widened, but she stayed close. Pleased, he relaxed a little more into the role of old friend rediscovered.

An older woman sat on Jake's other side. She'd been introduced as Susan Murdoch, a grandmother of one of Elle's children, and she leaned forward to talk with Brianna. "How is your book coming?"

"It's slow going right now. I find I'm too busy with rescue work to get any quiet time."

"I would offer you my den if it would help, but with Graham, there's no way to know when he'll have a good day."

Graham Murdoch III, Jake thought. *He must be ill if she's mentioning good days.*

"Thank you for thinking of it, but I'll be fine," Brianna was saying. "I need to prioritize and put the writing first. It's the only way to get it finished. And then, I'll need to revise a lot."

"You could use my place, except for the shifts." He was pretty sure now that she'd given up on writing at the bakery. Good thing. Now wasn't the time to talk about Theda, but he wasn't convinced this thing was over for her. The texts were coming closer together and in clumps. The hours were erratic as well.

He couldn't talk about all that now, not when Elle's children were passing out dessert plates with slices of wedding cake on them. The bride and groom were cutting the slices in between kisses and catcalls for more kisses. He turned to Brianna. "This is a nice wedding. Relaxed and friendly." Look at me, he thought, sitting with a group that wasn't looking at him with judgment in their eyes.

"It's fun, right? Easygoing and lively."

"And warm," he added. For too many years he'd missed out on parties, stags, weddings, new babies. All the fun of life.

Tiffany's death had been a watershed moment. Jake's life before and after that night was totally different.

He'd become a loner; taciturn and well on his way to becoming a gruff old man. A lonely, gruff old man. When his parents had retired to a home in Arizona to finally escape the rainy winters, he'd become even more isolated.

Theda had changed things by shoehorning into his life. She'd invaded his home, insinuated herself into his bed and woken him up. Not in the way she'd hoped, but the tiny, pretty, narcissist had shown him what he wanted by being so very wrong for him.

He didn't want a woman like Theda. But at least now he knew he wanted *someone*. Before Theda, he'd denied himself every dream a man could dream.

"I don't want to be alone," he muttered under his breath as the truth hit him. He gently squeezed Brianna's thigh, causing her to look in his direction again.

"What did you say? I didn't catch it," she said.

"I'll tell you later." A serving of cake appeared in front of him. The cake looked fantastic; light and white with a ribbon of something gooey and red between each of the three layers. Clay grabbed a fork from an empty table and slid it across the table to him. "Thanks," Jake said with a grin. He tasted a mouthful of cake and the delicate flavor burst on his tongue. "This is fantastic." His compliment joined all the others.

Susan Murdoch flushed prettily, her cheeks glowing as the praise rolled toward her like a wave. "Thank you, everyone. Before I met Graham, I trained as a pastry chef. I don't often get to have this much fun in the kitchen." She leaned close to Jake. "This was my third attempt."

"Perseverance pays off," he said with a nod. "You're Tad Murdoch's mother?"

"Yes, he was Daniel's father," she said with a proud look at the teen.

"I was sorry to hear he passed."

"An accident at work," she said. "It was so sudden, it nearly broke us both. When Elle moved back to Welcome, my husband and I forced our way into Daniel's life." Her eyes filled. "I don't deserve to be here, but Elle"—she sighed—"well, Elle is just the kindest, most forgiving woman and I've been blessed because of it."

He remembered now. Tad had been trouble and the Murdochs had been difficult. But here she was, sitting at this table full of friends and extended family.

"This is an odd group of friends," he said for Brianna's ears only. Clay had said everyone at the table had had their own troubles and that no one here would judge him harshly.

He hadn't seen one pitying look, no morbid curiosity, and no judgment. He fit in and he'd been welcomed at this table of guests that included exes and former in-laws and children of different fathers. They were, each in their way, the misfits of Welcome.

And he did fit. He was one of them.

Even sweet Brianna belonged here. Her mom had been a single parent by choice. Brianna didn't know anything about her father and as far as he knew, she'd never asked or gone on a quest to find him. He wondered if being different from the other kids in that way had encouraged her to be so quiet.

"How's your mom doing with that Duncan guy?"

"You go from this is an odd group of friends to asking about my mom's love life?"

"Yeah. You have to admit the way they hooked up was unexpected."

"They seem quite happy." She frowned. "I'm still a bit in shock, but I'm coming around. It would have been easier if I'd seen her dating before, but I never have."

"Did Tyler ask you out?" he blurted because he had to know.

"No." She straightened in her seat and frowned at him.

"I shouldn't have asked." He'd come off as a jerk. Not a good look for him.

"That's right, you shouldn't have asked. Who I date is not your business."

HOW DID JAKE THINK it was okay to pry about Tyler? Brianna thought about explaining more about the conversation with Tyler the other night, but she'd covered plenty of that on the ride home in Jake's car. She didn't like to think about what she'd learned about Tiffany.

She didn't like to think about what she and Jake had done that night before the accident.

But maybe they should talk about it. About all of it.

Jake's hand still rested on her thigh. She hadn't had the heart to shift away.

"Your mother and Duncan aren't here," Jake commented. "Karen must have known the Fosters as children. You were neighbors." The change in conversation brought some relief.

"Yes, it turns out they were close when Elle and Clay were growing up. Unbeknownst to me, they used to come over and sleep on our sofa when they needed to. My mom never told me at the time. They had always gone home by the time I got up."

He frowned and his gaze flitted from Elle to Clay. He shook his head sadly. "Things were hard for the Fosters."

"They've changed all that now. They're happy and fulfilled. People say living well is the best revenge and I'd say Clay and Elle have got that down to an art form."

"So why aren't Karen and Duncan here?"

"They were at the ceremony, but had to take off to meet Duncan's family." She tamped down a feeling of dread at the idea. "I hope they like her. She's meeting his children, a sister, two brothers, and one elderly aunt."

"Whoa, that's a lot of people in one go." He knit his brows as he thought. Her mother wasn't known for a sweet personality. She could be abrasive and a gossip. Jake had seen her at her worst when she'd fallen down the steps. "But, don't worry. It's your mom," he said. "What's not to like?"

"Very funny." She noticed the younger children were tired and overwrought. Dilly couldn't sit in her chair anymore and ran from person to person, sticking out her tongue. By the time she got to her father she was blowing raspberries and only giggled harder when the spit flew. Clay put his hand on her shoulders, squared her face to his and told her to quit, but the stubborn set to her shoulders said it was time to go home.

Mercy stood and finally pried Autumn from the groom's arms. "It's time," she said with a gentle smile. "Dilly's about to blow and none of us needs to witness that."

Their departure signaled the other parents that it was time to leave the celebration to the adults. The nervous young woman now married to Elle's ex rounded up Daniel, Liam, and Jorja to take home with them. "Your mom and Logan want a long weekend away for a honeymoon so we have lots of fun plans for you," she said. Her husband, Ben, held their daughter, a pretty child who looked like her mother.

Daniel shook his head no. "I'm staying with my grandparents for the weekend." He refused to look at his former stepfather, Ben. *Clearly*, thought Brianna, *Daniel still harbored hard feelings over the breakup of Ben and Elle.* The teenage years could be hard when adults made decisions that disrupted lives.

Daniel looked to Elle and Logan for support. They both nodded and Susan rose to her feet with a smile. She set her hand to Daniel's shoulder affectionately.

"Thank you for the wonderful day," Susan said. "I enjoyed myself and now it's time to let you young people party," she said with a wide, beautiful smile. "It was lovely to meet you, Jake."

She and Daniel took their leave of everyone else with special attention to Elle and Logan.

"Susan seems like a nice grandmotherly type."

"She does now," Brianna drawled. "Things weren't always pleasant between the Murdochs and Elle. But with Tad dead and his father suffering dementia, the women came to terms and have joined forces to give Daniel all the chances he wouldn't have had otherwise."

"Sounds like quite a story."

"There isn't one person here who doesn't have one."

"Even us," he said softly.

She gave him a wan smile. "Even us."

Suddenly Elle rose to her feet, held up a glass of champagne and announced it was time to get the party started. As a group, the remaining people headed to the other side of the Bar and Grill, where they settled at various tables and ordered rounds of drinks.

Jake and Brianna naturally sat together at a small table for two next to the bride and groom. Logan's brother, Jamie, and their parents sat across from them at another table. Jamie had stayed with soft drinks all evening. Logan's parents seemed happy and relaxed. The affection they had for Elle was obvious. She'd lucked out having in-laws like Logan's parents. They were good people.

"I'm switching to coffee," Jake said. "I'll drive you home so you don't have to worry about drinking. Feel free."

Brianna waved her half-full champagne flute around in an exaggerated way. "Are you trying to get me drunk, Mister?"

"I'm not sure, am I?"

She laughed. "Maybe you should. This night might not be so awkward if you did."

"This is awkward? I had no idea."

Shandy exited the ladies' room and stood by the door looking uncertain. "Shandy," Jake called. "Come on over here and join us." He waved and she gave him a quick smile and made her way to the table.

"Thanks. I wasn't sure who'd still be here. Joshua's with a sitter so I'm free to dance the night away."

"Here?" Brianna teased. "Jake, ask her to dance," she demanded.

"You're next," he threatened as he rose to his feet and held out his hand for Shandy. They left her on her own while they danced on the small floor. The jukebox blared out a country-rock song and she found herself tapping her feet to the beat.

Jamie Hughes gave her a smile and raised his eyebrows in invitation.

"Sure," she said happily. And up they went, laughing and joining the other couple. Soon, the bride and groom were on the floor and, refusing to be outdone, the elder Mr. and Mrs. Hughes jumped in and did some dance from their youth. Brianna wasn't certain, but it might have been the Frug or the Swim, or some odd combination of both.

At a change in the song, Jamie smoothly moved in on Shandy. Eventually, the couples rearranged themselves and Brianna found herself dancing in tandem with Jake. When the song choice shifted to something slow and romantic, Jake stepped close and whispered. "Now, you're mine."

She welcomed the shiver that ran down her spine as she stepped into a slow and easy sway with him. He smelled of spicy aftershave and warm man. His scent enveloped her and she wanted to set her head on his shoulder and drift with him.

But of course, she couldn't. People would see and word would get out that they'd been dancing too close for people who were nothing but former classmates.

And if word got back to Theda, Jake could have more than broken windows to contend with.

"What is it with you and women?"

"I know what you're thinking, but I swear I haven't had any other women smash windows, or slash tires or send me two hundred texts a day."

Brianna tilted her head back to study his face. He had worry lines at the corners of his eyes and a frown line had etched itself deeply into his forehead since the last time she'd seen him. "Are you speaking to her?"

"No."

"Maybe you should. She may need to end things her way and not yours. What you did must have humiliated her."

"You want me to engage with a woman who's proven herself violent? I don't think so."

Chapter Fifteen

JAKE HELD BRIANNA CLOSE as they swayed to an old love song from their school days. The scent of her hair drew his nose and he nuzzled into the fruitiness of her shampoo. She pulled back with a stiff expression.

"We can't be seen like this, it'll get back to Theda," she said, bracing her forearms on his chest for added distance. "Please don't take me where you want to go. I can't follow you and it would be wrong."

Wrong. Yes, it would be.

"I'm tired of talking about her," he said, letting the ten-year-old that lived inside his head take charge. "I want to talk about other things." It was a small, petty thing to say, but he had Brianna Bowler in his arms. "Can't we just have this dance? Don't we deserve one dance?"

She settled then and he saw a softening around her mouth. "I'm tired of talking about her, too, but we don't have much else to talk about," she said, with no heat in the tone.

He feigned surprise. "You never bust chops." He loosened his hold and set her away from him so watchful eyes would see their sudden distance. "But, I think the harm's done now, anyway. We're dancing after you made a big display of coming to get me to join the wedding party."

She grinned as she was meant to. "I did not make a big display. This side was mostly empty when I found you in here all alone." Her teasing tone made him feel light.

"Maybe I wanted to be alone. Maybe that's how I liked it. Maybe I hated being around people who remember that night and look at me with pity or scorn in their eyes." He'd spoken in past tense and he wondered if something had changed and he hadn't seen it happen.

"Stop. That's not true," she said in a whisper. "People don't pity you. Look at all the good you've done since." Her eyes turned sad and wistful. Then she ruined the dance by walking out of his arms.

He stood there stunned. How did things go so wrong so fast?

Brianna hadn't been this decisive before.

Then she really shocked him by collecting her purse from the table. He blinked and realized she was leaving him behind.

It was what he deserved. It was what should happen.

But he wasn't going to let it.

He followed her outside, not caring who saw them leave together. Shandy watched him chase after Brianna from the dance floor. She'd probably call Brianna right away. Women were like that. They cared about their friends, asked questions and were there when they were needed. The only guy who'd been there for Jake during his darkest days was Justin.

At the time, Jake had wanted to bust Justin in the face for hanging around. But now he felt grateful for every time Justin had forced himself into Jake's life.

Brianna halted outside the door of the Bar and Grill as if uncertain which way she could storm off. She glanced back at him. "What? Do you believe people blame you? That they only see that night and nothing else you've done since?"

"I haven't done *anything* since Tiffany died. I'm frozen," he said fiercely. "Stuck in this place with these nightmares. Nothing I do takes them away because I don't *do* anything." But he wanted a life. He wanted to break through his carefully constructed barriers. He grabbed his head before it exploded with the breathtaking realization. *He wanted a life!*

"You're not making sense." She clutched her purse to her chest as if he might grab it and run.

Frustrated, he ran his fingers through his hair. "I know. There's no sense to anything anymore." There used to be sense before Theda showed up. "I used to get up, go to work, save lives, bandage knees, and even deliver a baby some days. I did my best and kept to myself. What the hell has happened to that guy?" That life was gone, replaced by this unbelievable *wanting*.

She shrugged. "I don't know. I came home and you had a live-in girlfriend and I was happy for you. You'd found something I haven't."

What she said barely registered. His mind was on the recent past, trying to track all the changes. A month ago if someone had told him he'd be at a wedding dinner with people he knew from school he'd have laughed his ass off. And dancing with Brianna? Holding her close in *public*? Not a chance.

All the parts of his life, the ones he depended on, the ones he let the world see shattered like a blown-out windshield. Tiny shards of glittery tempered glass littered his thoughts.

But one thing came clear. He needed to sort this mess out with Theda before he moved forward and reshaped his life. "I have to talk with Theda. She's part of this and I need to thank her."

"Thank her," Brianna repeated in a flat tone. "Now I'm really confused."

"Hang tight, I'll be right back." He left her to wait and rushed inside the restaurant. Shandy was sitting with Jamie Hughes and when he stepped toward them, she caught Jake's eye. She rose immediately and came over.

"Hi, what's up? I thought I saw you leave." She tossed a glance back toward Jamie. "This is nothing, by the way. He's the only single man my age here so we're catching up on—"

"I know," he said, cutting her off. "I've known you for years and can tell when you're interested in something or not," he reassured her. "But I need you to do me a favor and take Brianna home. She doesn't have a ride."

"I thought—"

He shook his head. "I have somewhere else I need to be." He wanted to clear the air with Theda as soon as he could. He pulled out his phone to see five more texts from her. "I need to go right away." Strings of emojis ran across his screen. Half of them were hearts or flowers. Some crying faces and a few eggplants. Nothing made sense or followed a logical pattern.

"Okay, I've got my car. No problem." Shandy turned back to where Jamie sat and picked up her purse. After a brief goodbye to Logan's younger brother, she followed Jake outside.

"Now you've been seen leaving with two women," Brianna quipped when they met her outside.

"Perfect," he responded. "Nothing like confusing people to keep the rumor mill fed." For years he'd gone about his business unnoticed, but now he felt like he was living in a display window. Even Brianna's mom had known about Theda breaking his window.

Shandy snorted. "What will the gossips make of this?"

Brianna grinned. "Not sure. A threesome, maybe?"

Shandy laughed through Jake brushing a light kiss to her cheek. "Thanks for getting her home safely."

"Thanks for giving me a graceful exit," she replied, with a significant look at Brianna.

BRIANNA CLIMBED INTO Shandy's Mustang and buckled up. "Jamie Hughes?" she asked because she didn't want to talk about Jake.

Shandy shrugged. "He's single and seems okay. A bit shy, actually. We didn't get much of a chance to talk. We were too busy dancing." She pulled out of the parking lot and headed south to take Brianna home. "And before you say anything more, I'm aware of his struggle with drugs. But, for now, he's doing okay. I hope he keeps it up, but it's a hard road."

When Brianna said nothing more, Shandy cleared her throat. "And you and Jake?"

She thought quickly. "When I realized he was sitting in the bar alone eating a burger I thought he might like to join us. Clay suggested it, actually. I didn't know Jake was there until Clay said he saw him." Which was mostly true. She'd seen Jake when she'd first stepped inside the building and was waiting to be seated.

He'd been with his partner, Doug Marton. She and Jake had locked gazes and she'd felt the punch of deep recognition, the recognition between a man and woman, and had wanted to run back out the door. But, she hadn't. She'd walked on unsteady legs behind the restaurant host and taken her seat just like everybody else in the wedding party.

If Clay hadn't mentioned Jake, she thought, she'd have left it at that.

Now, she was lying to herself. *Pathetic.*

She had to change the subject. "Did you tell me that your husband wants to spend Christmas here?"

Shandy shrugged. "I haven't decided if I want that. Justin's parents don't live here anymore and I think he'd expect to stay with us."

"He could stay at the hotel he usually stays at."

"I guess. Last weekend he stayed with Jake." She hesitated and Brianna wondered if she had anything more personal to say about her ex. "Josh would like him to stay with us for Christmas, but I wish he'd go see his parents and be done with it." The last was said briskly as if Shandy were mentally washing her hands of her ex.

"You'd prefer it if Josh didn't see his own father at Christmas?" Brianna blurted in surprise. This wasn't like Shandy. She'd never indicated there were leftover emotions around Justin before.

Shandy stiffened. "No, of course not. Justin's a good father and they should be together. Of course, they should."

Brianna saw her lip quiver. "Are you okay?" she asked as Shandy bit her lip.

They stopped at a red light and Shandy turned her face toward Brianna's. Tears sparkled in the blue light from the dashboard. "Sometimes I wonder if our divorce was a mistake," she said in a soft whisper.

"Oh, Shandy," she whispered back. "I'm sorry."

The light changed to green and her friend smoothed her fingertips under her eyes. "I'm fine. I shouldn't have said anything. *We're fine just as we are.*"

Brianna wondered if *fine* was enough. "But, surely you could talk to Justin."

"No. This will pass. I've just been lonely and—now I feel like a terrible friend—but seeing Elle get married, and Mercy having Autumn, and now you talking to Jake after all these years..." she trailed off. "It would only confuse things if I brought my doubts up with Justin. And Josh has accepted the divorce. He really has, in spite of this Christmas wish of his."

"So, there's no going back?"

"There can't be. Justin's moved on and so have I. Honest." She smiled a little shakily. "It's just loneliness and that's no reason to be with a man who doesn't suit."

"I've heard that before and I agree."

They drove on in silence for another mile until Brianna broke the silence. "There's nothing going on with Jake and me, either." She patted Shandy's arm. "He left me outside the Bar and Grill to go see Theda." And he'd just delivered her into Shandy's care like a child. "I could have called a cab, but he went inside and got you."

"I'm glad he got me but going to see Theda? She's lost her mind. I've been hearing all sorts of stuff about her. How she basically moved into Jake's place without an invitation. How she's living with Denise Jones and hanging out with Tyler Rhodes. She's surrounding herself with some of the nastiest people in town."

What kind of woman moved into a man's home, into his *life*, without being invited? "Where'd you hear all this?"

"From Justin, of course. Justin never liked Theda and told me she's been possessive ever since she moved in. She's kept tabs on Jake and has tried to come between the Jays more than once. Nasty woman."

Brianna sat, shocked into silence. What was Jake walking into tonight? At the very least, a scene. But at the worst? She had no idea what Theda was capable of. She'd already shattered his front window. "Do you know where Denise Jones lives?"

"No, I don't," her friend replied. "Do an internet search. I assume you want to drive by?"

"I do. Jake's gone to see Theda and if Denise took her in I assume that's where he's headed. He said he wanted to thank Theda for something."

"Thank her?"

"Yes. Weird."

"She smashed his window. Justin said Jake's had all the locks changed and installed a top-of-the-line security system because of her." All of which Brianna knew, but still, hearing it again disturbed her. Brianna's stomach rolled with dread. She did a quick search on her phone, found Denise's address and told Shandy.

"Great. I know that street." She pulled a U-turn and headed north, toward the older subdivisions in town.

Fifteen minutes later, Shandy pulled to a stop across the road from a small, square bungalow. Jake's vehicle was not in sight.

"Do you think he took her somewhere to talk?" Brianna asked.

"He could have. He'd want privacy because I doubt he'd want Denise listening to their conversation."

"We should wait a while," Brianna suggested. "In case he comes back with her and there's trouble."

Shandy nodded and turned off the ignition. "We'll stay for an hour. That seems long enough."

"He'll either bring her back or take her home to live with him again."

"No way. He doesn't want her in his life."

Brianna wedged herself against the passenger door to stare at her friend. "How can you be so sure?"

"Justin. Jake's wanted her gone ever since you returned to Welcome."

"What?!"

"I swore I wouldn't say anything, but that was before you two started talking." Shandy mimicked Brianna's posture so they faced each other squarely. "Jake saw you one night when you and I and Elle went out for dinner. It was just after you came back to town. Probably our first girls' night out."

Brianna felt off-kilter and stared off into nothing as she sorted her bafflement. Jake saw her and wanted out of his relationship with Theda right away? She didn't know what to make of that. When she didn't speak, Shandy went on.

"Jake didn't say it this way, but Justin realized that as soon as Jake saw you, he started talking about how things weren't working out with Theda. Her possessive behavior began to chafe. Jake started avoiding going home by hanging out at his partner's house more often. He'd go to Doug's instead of going home."

"I had no idea. Things between Jake and I are complicated." She'd never imagined that he'd been as aware of her as she'd been of him.

"I've never figured out why."

Brianna ignored the leading comment, forcing Shandy to continue.

"But I know he basically insisted you leave for college when you wanted to stay home and grieve. Losing Tiffany that way derailed your plans for college until Jake said otherwise."

"You've been talking to Elle," Brianna guessed. She was the only one who knew about those conversations with Jake in the weeks after the accident. She and Jake had been an ugly mess back then. Both of them feeling guilty, responsible, confused.

Unworthy of happiness.

She closed her eyes and sank into silence, letting the memories wash through her.

Jake with tears in his eyes, pushing, pushing, pushing her away. Telling her to leave.

To never come back.

So she'd gone and kept her visits home short. Her mother knew something was wrong, but she'd put it all down to grief over losing her friend Tiffany. But Brianna had lost so much more.

Jake had hated her. She'd been so convinced. Absolutely certain. But now, they'd laughed together, held each other.

But things still weren't right and she feared they never would be.

Chapter Sixteen

THREE HOURS AFTER LEAVING Brianna with Shandy at the Bar and Grill Jake arrived home with nothing to show for his time. He walked around the outside of his house, checking for broken windows and jimmied locks. When he found everything in order he cautiously walked in. After a quick check of all the rooms, he laughed at himself for his over-the-top reaction. Theda had him spooked.

He'd gone to Denise Jones's place and knocked on the door, only to find he'd roused the owner of the house and Denise lived in a basement apartment. He'd apologized and headed down the side of the bungalow to find Denise's door.

He tried there, too, but she was unhelpful; downright hostile if he wanted to be truthful. She'd refused to even admit she'd taken Theda in, and denied knowing her whereabouts. But then, he *had* woken her from a sound sleep. Anyone would be out of sorts.

He explained patiently that he was looking for Theda to talk with her, not to argue or cause her any harm. Denise had relented and asked, "Are you here to beg her forgiveness? Because you should."

He didn't let on that she'd just admitted that Theda was staying with her. He'd balked at answering Denise's question directly but decided to keep her talking. Maybe she'd let slip something he wanted to know. "Is she out with someone else?" He'd put on a worried expression.

"I already said I don't know where she went. But she wasn't alone when she left and that's all I'm saying about that." She sniffed as if she was looking at something distasteful. In other words, Denise wore her usual expression.

"Anyone I know?" he prodded, because she was awake now and interested, not any smarter, but interested.

Denise pulled her robe across her chest and crossed her arms. "You might want to look at your past for that answer. Who do you think would want to steal your girl from you? Huh?" With that last dig at his ego, she'd slammed her door shut and bolted it with a solid thud. Even if Theda came back tonight, she'd have to wake Denise to get in.

After that conversation, he'd driven around town uselessly looking for Tyler Rhodes' car. He checked the Rhodes family's driveway three times until he saw the car parked out front. He had no way to know if Tyler had brought Theda home with him or had left her at Denise's.

He hadn't knocked because he hadn't had the heart to disturb Phil and Cassie Rhodes at two a.m. He'd do anything not to involve the still-grieving couple. They'd suffered enough without hearing about this new mess.

He tossed his keys and wallet on his nightstand. He'd have to be a fool not to get the broad hint Denise had offered. Tyler must be the person Theda had gone out with.

But Theda had kept texting him, despite being with Tyler. The last three texts, spaced five minutes apart, had chilled him through. He read them again.

Theda: "You'll see."

Theda: "See what you made me do?"

And finally, the last one which made his blood run cold.

Theda: "She'll be sorry."

"Who will be sorry, you insane bitch?" he asked his silent phone. The texts had stopped half an hour ago.

At least Brianna was home safe and sound. Shandy had sent him two thumbs up ninety minutes ago so he knew Brianna had been delivered to her place. By now he figured Denise had told Theda he'd stopped by, which made him wonder why Theda's texts still seemed threatening. Denise should have explained Jake had gone over to talk, not argue.

If Theda was out enjoying Tyler's company, as Denise had hinted then why was she texting Jake?

Women were different from men, no doubt, but Theda was different from everybody.

He wondered at her logic, but with Theda logic didn't factor in. If she wanted to use Tyler to prick at Jake's male pride, then she'd use him until she'd got through to Jake and to hell with Tyler's feelings.

He was too exhausted to think anymore. He'd had a long shift, and had enjoyed some time at the wedding dinner, danced with Brianna and searched all of Welcome for Tyler and Theda.

Tomorrow he'd deal with Theda. They'd talk, clear the air, and she'd understand it was time to move on.

As he undressed, he ignored the fact that he'd told himself this very same thing too many times to count in the last couple of months. All he wanted was for Theda to move on so he wouldn't feel so damned guilty when he thought about Brianna.

BRIANNA ROLLED OUT of bed to a strange stink of bitter or rancid coffee. Last night she'd come home late and distracted after playing amateur sleuth with Shandy and hadn't bothered to set the timer on the coffee machine. Maybe the automatic timer to shut off the warming plate had died, leaving yesterday's coffee to burn in the carafe. Yuck. She wrinkled her nose at the stench.

She slipped into her terry cloth robe and an old pair of her mom's slippers and scuffed her way into the kitchen. A glance at the coffeepot told her this was a fresh pot. In fact, the last of it was dripping into the full carafe. Whatever this new flavor was, it was a capital M mistake. Hard to believe her mom would make this smelly stuff. She opened the window over the sink to help freshen the air.

And then she remembered. Her mother was away with Duncan so she could meet his family.

With a grimace, she lifted the carafe and sniffed it, her nose protesting. Recoiling from the smell, she dumped the foul brew into the sink. *Who the hell had made coffee with vinegar?*

A chill rose up her back and along her arms.

Horrified, she ran through the house to her mom's room. Her bed hadn't been slept in. Brianna had been alone all night.

Strangers had been here. In her home. *While she was sleeping.* Her hands shook as she pressed them to her temples. She jumped and turned in a circle, searching for something, anything to tell her why someone had crept around inside her home.

And what else had they done? That question pushed her to go from room to room looking for whatever was out of place or weird.

"My laptop's gone," she said aloud when she looked at the dining room table. She'd taken to writing there in fits and starts, but with Elle's wedding in the final planning stages, Brianna hadn't touched her laptop in a couple of days. But she knew it was there the last time she saw it. The power cord draped the back of the dining room chair.

So whoever took it didn't plan to *use* the laptop. But why steal a laptop if not to use or sell it? *Hard to pawn a laptop without a power cord.*

She fumbled her phone out of the pocket in her robe and called 9-1-1. Since there was no imminent danger, the operator told her to wait until they could get an officer out to take her report. She could be waiting for a while.

She hung up and let indignation build. Her fright was over and now she felt furious at the nameless losers who would do this creepy, weird stuff. Had they watched her while she slept? Every creak and sound in the house amplified until she felt skittish with anger.

She called her mom, ignoring the tremor in her hands.

"First of all, I'm fine," she said as soon as her mom answered. "But the house has been broken into. It happened when I was at the wedding." At least, that was what she hoped. She walked through to the kitchen. "Oh, and the coffee was made with vinegar."

"But you're okay?" Her mom's shock rolled from the phone into Brianna's heart.

"Yes. I'm fine." Nerves notwithstanding. She'd had time to think now and was counting her blessings. "They didn't break a window to get in and the locks on the doors look okay to me, but I'm no expert. As far as I can see they only took my laptop."

"Have you checked my jewelry box? There's not much of value in there except my mother's pearls and an antique brooch."

Brianna hurried to her mom's room and checked. "All fine. And no other damage either." She walked back into the kitchen.

"And the dogs? They're okay?"

"I'm standing at the back door and everything looks normal from here. Sandra O'Neal is feeding them right now. If anything were amiss out there, she'd have told me right away." An old friend of her mom's, Sandra had been volunteering with them for at least five years. No way would she ignore a problem.

Brianna watched as Beau patrolled with Sandra, looking every bit the interested, happy pit bull. "Should we leave Beau outside his kennel at night?"

"No. He'll be blamed for any defensive action on his part. We don't want that."

"Then we need a security system." She shivered inwardly. She hated to think they needed one, but even a sleepy town like Welcome had its less-than-upright citizens. "Jake just had one installed."

Silence while her mother let that sink in. "Theda," her mom said after a moment. "Could it have been her? She did smash Jake's window and she might think you and he are more than old friends."

In the background, Brianna heard a man's voice. Duncan's low murmur sounded concerned.

"I prefer to think this was a random thing," Brianna said to soothe her mother's fears. "Maybe it was kids playing a prank with the coffee machine and one of them snatched my laptop on impulse."

Her mom relayed Brianna's thoughts to Duncan. More murmurs while the couple mulled things over.

"I don't want to believe it was Theda," Brianna broke in. "Or that she's making an assumption about Jake and me. Besides, Jake went to talk to Theda last night and I think they cleared things up between them." But she didn't know for sure. She and Shandy had waited the full hour and like disappointed detectives on a stake-out, had to give up when nothing happened. Her mind skipped to the way Jake had held her close for the slow dance at the Bar & Grill. How he'd nuzzled her hair, and how he'd walked her outside last night.

"We're coming home." The question ended Brianna's whirlwind of thoughts. "We'll cut our visit short. Duncan's family will understand. And if they don't, too bad."

"Absolutely not. Duncan's family is your priority. Everything here is fine. I'm okay. The dogs are good," Brianna said. "Whatever this is will be over when we get a security system. I'll call for one right now."

"Ask Jake for a recommendation. And I think you should stay somewhere else. I don't like you being home alone tonight."

"I'll call Jake for the name of his security guy and I'll consider going to a friend's place for the night." They said goodbye after Brianna reassured her mother again that her coming home early wouldn't help anything. Besides, Brianna didn't want to worry about her mother being hurt if the person came back to do anything else.

The more she thought about this, the more she believed Theda was behind it. Her talk about kids playing pranks was just to calm her mother. Maybe Theda had come over before Jake talked with her last night. If so, she'd be calmer now and less likely to cause any more trouble.

She called him and quickly filled him in on the break-in.

"What about your laptop? Want to borrow mine?" he asked after the news sunk in.

"No thanks. I'll buy a new one and check with my mom about her house insurance. It could be covered under her policy. Once the police get here and they file a report, I should be good."

"What about your book?"

"It's backed up online. I'll buy a new laptop with my word processing program installed. This won't hold me up for any longer than this morning." After this episode, she had more ideas for the book and a better understanding of emotions that could drive bad decisions.

If Theda had meant to frighten her off, she'd be disappointed. That was one of the fun things about being a writer; creating characters based on real people and giving them the fate they deserved. "I thought you talked to Theda last night. It didn't go well?" Her heart picked up its already too-quick pace.

"She wasn't home. I drove around trying to find her, but she wasn't at Tyler Rhodes's house either. I couldn't wake his parents looking for him because they've been through enough. But Tyler's truck was gone for a couple of hours." He sighed. "I have no idea where he was."

If Shandy had brought Brianna straight home, instead of to their fruitless stakeout, Brianna may have walked in on Theda and maybe even an angry, drunken Tyler. She gave an inward sigh of relief that nothing more serious had happened.

"My mom wants me to stay at a friend's place."

"Stay here with me," Jake said brusquely. "I'm just starting my days off this week."

Staying with Jake would throw salt in Theda's wounds and put Brianna's heart in jeopardy. She wasn't over her high school crush on Jake Morrow and it was time she faced it. The man was all kinds of trouble. Their shared guilt and shame were too much to overcome.

"I'll stay at Elle's place," she replied decisively. "Elle is our closest neighbor and they're away honeymooning for a few more days." Brianna had responsibilities with the rescue. Sandra was great with the dogs, but Brianna couldn't abandon her best volunteer and make her responsible for the whole operation. Her mom was depending on her to keep everything running smoothly. "Elle will be happy to have me stay in her empty place."

Something else crossed her mind. "We don't have proof it was Theda. Maybe it was Tyler?" she suggested. "Forget I said that; it's too far-fetched. It's you Tyler has the grudge against, not me."

"Up until recently, Tyler never said anything to make me think he'd want revenge. And he wouldn't have any reason to take his anger out on you. He always liked you." Jake blew a loud breath into the phone. "We might have something to implicate Theda. I got some very strange texts last night. I'm coming over to show them to the police. When will they be there?"

She wanted to say no, that she could handle all this on her own, but what Jake said made sense. If he had something the police could go on he should show them. "They'll be here sometime this morning." The police might want to see the whole picture surrounding Theda and Jake and those texts could be incriminating. At least they'd be interesting enough to have Theda questioned. "When can you be here?"

"ETA thirty minutes."

"Bring me coffee, will you? I have to deal with this coffee machine and I shouldn't have to do that without being caffeinated."

JAKE ARRIVED ONLY A minute after Officer Branson, a woman in her early forties. She inspired confidence immediately that she'd find out who'd been inside the house. She might even learn why Brianna and her mom had been targeted. Jake presented three takeout coffees, one for each of them.

"Thank you, Jake," Officer Branson said with a raised eyebrow and accepted the paper cup. "It's been a busy shift already and I missed my first cup." But Brianna noticed she didn't take a sip but put the cup on the kitchen table. "You two are friends?" She directed her question to Jake.

"High school," he responded.

"Are you involved in this matter?"

"Briana called me because this may have something to do with me." He slid his phone across the table to the officer. "These texts came in last night from my ex-girlfriend."

"She the new one at the bakery?"

And Brianna was reminded again of how small Welcome was. Everyone knew everyone and a new face was noticed. She wondered how much she'd been gossiped about since coming home.

"She's been there a couple of months."

"When did you break up?" This time the woman's gaze encompassed Brianna too and made her squirm inside. She hadn't been the cause of the breakup, but she could see how the officer could think so.

"That's the problem," Jake said. "I've been trying to get her out of my life and my house for over a month. Theda won't accept it's over and I think she may have come out here to mess with me."

"Which brings me to the reason I'm here. Ms. Bowler's break-in. We'll start there." The officer gave Brianna a level look. Jake nodded and leaned back, apparently content that his concerns would be heard.

Brianna started from the beginning and explained how she'd come home, neglected to set the coffee machine timer and woke to the rancid stink of coffee made with vinegar. The officer glanced down at her take-out coffee when Brianna got to that part. "I ran through the house looking for anything else that had been tampered with or was out of place. Saw that my laptop was missing and that's when I called you."

Officer Branson jotted notes as Brianna spoke. She asked a few more questions about people who might hold a grudge against the rescue, but there was nothing to report there. "We get the odd complaint in the local paper about dogs barking, but that's nothing new. Before we set up the rescue my grandparents raised prize poodles here. There have been dogs on this property for over fifty years. The neighbors behind us have been here for two. They can hear the dogs sometimes."

"They ever come over here to speak directly with you?"

Brianna shook her head. "Not with me. But with my mother when they first moved in. She told me she paid for some saplings for the back of their property. They planted those and more at the edge of the property line. They make a good sound barrier."

Officer Branson jotted down their names, but Brianna couldn't believe the Johnsons would be petty enough to break in and steal her laptop. Still, the officer was being thorough.

"And now we'll discuss these texts." The statement was bald, flat and revealed nothing of Officer Branson's thoughts. The officer turned to a fresh page in her notebook and looked steadily at Jake.

"And the fact that Theda broke my living room window," Jake added.

The officer leaned forward at that and her eyes sparked with curiosity. "Start at the beginning," she ordered Jake. She gave Brianna a steady look. "And you wait until he's finished before adding anything."

"Fine," Jake said. "But this is not a formal complaint. If I decide to make it one, I'll call you directly."

It was Jake's turn to tell the officer about the broken window and his breakup with Theda.

The officer's eyebrows rose when he explained that he'd changed the locks and left Theda's belongings on his front porch. "I couldn't come up with another solution. I fully expected her to go to Pastor Reeve. If she had, he'd have helped her."

"He does good work," Officer Branson conceded.

At the end of the interview, Brianna was even more confident that Officer Branson would find Theda and get the answers about the meaning behind her late-night text messages. Really, there was no one else to consider as a suspect especially since Brianna's laptop had been taken and the power cord left behind.

"I feel like a fool for not having a password on my computer, but I really only use it for my writing and research. All my banking is done on my phone and I don't have them networked so the person who took it can't cause any financial damage." She had enough saved to live for a couple of months and without rent to pay, she could last longer without needing to work. Still, she hoped to pick up some work as a virtual assistant. She'd already put out some feelers with previous colleagues in her field.

"I'm sure Officer Branson will get to the bottom of this," Jake offered as they stood on the front stoop and watched her drive away.

"Do you think Theda went into work?"

"If she didn't she'll look guilty. But she could have left town. Maybe this was her last kick."

"You think?"

He shrugged. "I don't know what to think. I never would've imagined her doing any of this stuff. Not my window, not your house. You must feel creeped out."

She rubbed her chilled arms. "I do. Especially if I was asleep and Theda was wandering around my house." She shuddered. "Will you still talk to her?"

Jake tucked his chin. "Yes. What I have to say may help her move on. But I can't say it in a text. This has to be in person. We can hash things out."

"So, you didn't go looking for her last night to get her to come back to you?"

His eyes widened. "Of course not. What gave you that idea? I want her gone now more than ever. And not just out of my life, but out of Welcome."

His firm tone made her want to believe him. "But, you said you wanted to thank her. To me that sounded friendly rather than confirming a breakup."

Jake turned to face her, his expression earnest. "If I get Theda to understand the shift in my life, how she changed me and woke me up, maybe she'll calm down and see reality." He moved closer and brought his hands to Brianna's elbows. His touch made her soften, his eyes made her believe. He tugged lightly and she stepped into his arms. He set his mouth near her ear and a thrill coursed through her. "Brianna, I want to live again. And I have Theda to thank for that. She needs to know."

Brianna nodded stiffly, even though she didn't understand.

"I want to kiss you," he whispered clearly. "But I can't. Not yet. Not until I finish this with Theda."

And then, blindingly, she understood. She closed her eyes. "I want that, too. And you're right, it's best if one thing ends, before..."

His head reared back so he could look into her eyes again. "Before *we* begin. And this is a beginning, Brianna. This will be the beginning we didn't have last time."

"We were wrong when we were kids. It was awkward and unkind. We'll do things differently this time."

"I'm trying."

She set her fingertips to his bristly cheek. "You haven't shaved yet."

"Couldn't spare the time. I needed to get here, to see that you were okay."

"You're caring and kind and I see why Theda's in a mess because she doesn't want to lose you."

"It's her own mess, but I have to help her with it."

"Will you go to the bakery?"

"That's my next stop. I hope she's there. But I'll give Officer Branson time to ask her questions first. I want Theda to have the full picture before I talk to her."

JAKE WALKED BRIANNA around the house and out to the kennels to explain to everyone why the police were here. The volunteers were kind and supportive and he left Brianna in good hands with Sandra. Sandra mothered and fussed and when he left, Brianna looked more at ease than she had since he'd arrived. He left to head to the bakery and his chat with Theda.

They both had errands to run, thanks to Theda. He'd ordered a new window for his living room and Brianna needed to buy a new laptop. She also needed to get the key to Elle's place from Clay. Her new laptop should be safe enough away from the Bowler house. She should be free from any more hassle if she stayed at Elle's. And her safety was paramount.

Jake hated that Brianna had been driven out of her own home to write. He hated that she had to suffer because of his soured relationship. But maybe forcing Brianna out of her home was what Theda wanted. Maybe her ultimate goal was to drive Brianna out of

Welcome altogether. All the more reason to make Theda come to her senses.

As he pulled into a parking spot across the street from the Welcome Bakery, a police cruiser pulled away from the curb up ahead. Office Branson hadn't wasted any time. He thought about not going inside, but he couldn't wait to clear the air. If he'd got to Theda last night maybe she wouldn't have gone to Brianna's at all.

He walked into the welcoming scent of yeast and dough and sugar, with an overlay of rich, dark coffee. A couple of booths were taken, but it was still too early for the lunch crowd and he'd missed the early morning rush by an hour.

"Jake, what are you doing here?" Theda asked in a hoarse whisper. She had a smudge of something white on the tip of her nose and he realized that when they'd first met he'd have thought she looked adorable. Now, he wondered if she'd put it there so he'd notice it and respond. Damn, now he questioned everything about her.

Alyce Markham, the owner, stepped out from the back and Jake realized the poor woman must be exasperated with the interruptions to her morning. It wasn't every day an employee was questioned by the police and now Jake was here, too.

Alyce was a thin woman with the full-bodied rolling accent of her home country of Jamaica. She'd been in Welcome for over ten years; baking and sharing her common sense with anyone who'd listen. She liked Jake and had taken Theda on for his sake. But as time had moved along, Alyce had made it plain Theda had a knack with customers and with baking and was a legit asset to the business.

But today, her eyes were quite naturally troubled. "The police were here, Jake. What is this nonsense?"

He cocked his eyebrow at Theda, but she wore her perfected forlorn expression and kept her gaze on the floor. Poor Theda, sorry

Theda, sweet Theda. She bit her lip and widened her eyes, the picture of innocence.

"That's what I'm here to talk to Theda about, Alyce."

"Good." Alyce waved in a shooing motion. "Take her and go. Sort out your differences away from here." She leaned into Theda's ear. "You don't need everyone knowing your business."

Theda nodded and stepped into the back. A moment later she returned minus her apron and hairnet and wearing a jacket. She had her purse with her. Theda lifted the counter lid and headed for the door while Jake followed her out.

She walked stiffly beside him, up the block toward Clay's vet clinic and away from his car that he'd parked in front of the credit union. "You sent a police officer to my work," she said accusingly.

"Someone stole Brianna's laptop last night right off her dining room table. After the texts you sent me is it any wonder Officer Branson wanted to talk to you?" Maybe he should have reported her for breaking his window, but he saw it as an impulse, not a planned, deliberate act. "I should have called it in when you broke my window, but I thought that would be the end of your petty temper tantrums." If he had made a police report, this would be Theda's second time under police scrutiny. "I don't want to mess you up about the window. But this thing at Brianna's is too much."

"Officer Branson asked me about your window. I told her you'd forgiven me. And since you didn't report it, I thought you *had* forgiven me. That you understood."

"Forgiving you is not the point." And understanding her? No way. Forgetting her was the point, but she was in no mood to hear the stark truth. He had to tread lightly or there was no telling what she'd do.

The park was up ahead. "Let's take a picnic bench beside the river. We can talk there."

"Fine." She marched straight ahead, head held high, refusing to look at him or say anything more.

This would be one helluva conversation.

Chapter Seventeen

JAKE WAITED FOR THEDA to settle atop a picnic table, facing the river. She took the right side as if she expected him to sit beside her. Instead, he stood in front of her, well back and wary in case she lashed out. "I went to Denise's last night to talk to you, but you weren't home," he began, although Denise must've told her about his late-night visit.

Her back straightened even more and she looked to the ground. "You mean after you danced with Brianna at the bar? After you cozied up to her and made a fool of yourself all over her. I know you left with her, too." She kept her voice soft and hurt. She raised her face and unshed tears filled her sad blue eyes. Her face paled as he looked at her.

"Yes. That's when I knew I had to clear things up between you and me."

She tilted her head and her eyes brightened. "You mean you want me back? Oh, Jake. That's wonderful." She climbed down and stood inches from him and clasped his forearms. "I knew you'd come to your senses. You just needed the right motivation." She raised herself to kiss him, but he reared back.

She frowned, her eyes going dark. But she released him and stood silently.

"Breaking into my friend's home and stealing her laptop is not motivation for me to take you back. There is no going back, but hear me out before you jump to any conclusions." He settled on top of the table, giving her ample room to sit beside him. She nimbly took the space. He stared at the river, the water level higher than levels in the summer. Rains in the mountains had fed the rivers and streams now, in late September the water rushed more than babbled.

He cleared his throat. "I am grateful to you, Theda."

She made a surprised sound but kept still.

"Before we met, I was locked into a life I thought I wanted. I was alone. I avoided old classmates who still live here. Fifteen years ago I stopped acknowledging waves from friends and neighbors. I became churlish and rude and liked it that all the people who used to know me gave up trying to talk to me. I wasn't invited anywhere but to my parents' place and, to be honest, I rarely went over."

"Really? I'd give anything to have people who recognize me, who wave at me like friends, who want me around."

He turned his head to study her and for the first time, he saw raw honesty. Until now, he hadn't realized how alone in this world Theda was. "You were hitchhiking when we met. Where were you going?"

She shrugged. "I don't know. I didn't have a destination. I was just on the move, the way I usually am."

On the move. In her way, Theda had been as alone as he'd been. "Is that how you liked your life?"

She shook her head. "I wanted to settle. I wanted to find what we found, Jake. I still do."

"Theda, I don't know what to say." At last, a real conversation with the real Theda. The young woman she'd kept hidden. He had a plan for the way this would go. All he had to do was stick to it.

"Don't say anything, just hold me." She moved toward him, fully expecting him to take her into his arms.

He kept his hands clasped between his knees. "That won't happen, Theda. I came here to talk and that's what we're doing. Nothing more."

Her lips turned down at the corners and she got a petulant look in her eyes. "What good is talk? We do better when we don't talk. When you fuck me it's good, right?"

He hung his head. He hadn't wanted her for so long, he couldn't remember a time when it was good. Expedient, yes. Easy, yes. Never good. But he wouldn't hurt her with that truth. "We're past that now. And if you think about it, you'll see that's true." But the conversation was veering from the direction he aimed for. "I came here to tell you what you did for me."

Her eyebrows rose. "What do you mean?" She sounded suspicious.

"You gave me back my life. You walked into my house and took over and forced me to see what I could have; a partner, a mate, someone to come home to. The thing I liked the most in the early days was coming home to you. You'd kiss me and have a meal ready. Then later, we'd watch a movie and eat popcorn."

Her lips wobbled as she remembered those times, too.

"But that didn't last long, did it?" he said gently. "After a couple of weeks, you had to know why I was later than usual. You never understood that the last call could run past quitting time. You hated when my parents called. After a while, I found out you wouldn't even pass along a message from them."

She raised one shoulder and cringed away from him. A truth she couldn't deny was hitting her hard and he knew he had to press on to get through to the end. He had to make her come to her own conclusion.

"Nothing to say?" he prodded. When she shook her head slowly, he took that as permission to continue. "I found it easy to stop coming home right after work. Doug's on his own with his boys and he's a good cook." He spread his hands wide. "I shouldn't have imposed on him, but, hell, Theda, you made my place a war zone."

She sniffed. "Because you weren't there. You didn't want me to be there, either. Everything I wanted was slipping away."

"Not slipping away, being pushed away. The more you clung, the more I felt choked." He stared at the river rather than look at her.

This was the bare truth, the ugliest part. But, he had to keep going so she'd see that there was no going back to what they had early on. "I think you've been here before. I believe other men have been choked, too."

She snorted and an odd, small chuckle escaped into the air around them. "So what if they have? What you and I had was more real. It was everything I've ever wanted."

"The funny thing is you made me want more out of life. You gave me a fresh perspective and without you showing up at my door, I'd still be stuck inside the walls I put up between myself and other people." She'd driven him to visit Doug. And being there with his kids made Jake see what he was missing. What he'd denied himself.

"You know what happened when I was in high school. My girlfriend died while I was driving her home. After that, I couldn't take the pitying looks and the outright scorn and blame I saw in some people's eyes."

She craned her neck so she could look at his face during his confession. He raised his gaze to hers. "I became a paramedic because Tiffany died in my arms and there was nothing I could do about it. I didn't know how to help her. I was panicked and screaming and holding her in my arms. The next day I knew I never wanted to feel that helpless again."

She blinked back tears. "I understand," she said softly and patted his knee. "I saved you from your own prison and I'm so glad. But, don't you see? We can go back to the beginning. We can start again, from fresh. We'll save each other this time."

He shifted his knee out from under her hand. "No, that's not what I want."

"What else is there? We'll have each other and we won't need anyone else." She jumped off the tabletop and bounced excitedly in her sneakers like a four-year-old. "I'll cook dinner every night and take care of you. We'll binge-watch your favorite shows. And I'll even watch football with you."

She cupped his cheek in her palm while he wondered desperately how this conversation had gone so far off the rails.

"No, Theda. That's not what will happen." He paused and removed her hand from his cheek. The hurt in her eyes magnified, but he had to move forward. "You asked what else is there? There's you leaving town. You've got the police asking questions about Brianna's laptop, and I could report you for the smashed window at my place. If you leave, all that will go away. I won't make a formal complaint about the broken glass."

"Your neighbor saw me. She thought I didn't know she was watching, but I didn't care. I wanted you to know it was me."

He shouldn't ask, but the workings of her mind were bizarrely intriguing. "How would breaking my windows make me want you back?"

She blinked and stopped her excited bouncing. She narrowed her gaze. "Don't think she can get away with this."

The mysterious "she" again. "Who? Get away with what?" His heart sank as he realized she was fixated on Brianna. But he refused to bring her name into this.

She opened her mouth, then closed it again, her expression crafty. Clearly, she was planning more trouble.

"Theda, you need to calm down and think about everything I've said. You helped me get my life back and I'm grateful, but you'll never be happy with me. I can't be the man you need." He didn't think any man could live with her possessiveness. "I'll always work shifts, be home late, be sleeping when you're up and want company. That's my life and I won't change it."

"She's confused you," she muttered more to herself than to him. "She made you think of the past when you shouldn't." Theda's eyes scanned the ground from right to left, and back again, her voice getting higher and faster. "You shouldn't relive the past, there's nothing back there for you or anyone. You need to be more like me, always looking ahead, never looking back. *Never.*"

Without looking at him again, Theda broke into a run and dashed across the park.

Jake stood and watched her go. He considered following her, but there were families with young children near the play area. If Theda caused a scene things could get ugly. He pulled out his phone to call Officer Branson and make a formal complaint about his broken window.

CLAY UNLOCKED ELLE'S door for Brianna and she walked into her friend's double-wide, carrying her new laptop box. "This place can't be seen from the road, so I doubt anyone outside close friends and family know it's here."

She set everything on top of the kitchen's sandwich bar and turned to him. "Thanks, Clay. I'll be fine here."

"I'll get a key cut for you and drop it back later. I'll leave you to it," he said and left her on her own.

Clay had provided the home for his sister when he learned Elle was returning to Welcome with four children. She'd needed more rooms to house her three children and a foster baby who'd since been returned to her family. With Elle's marriage to Logan, Brianna wasn't sure where the new Hughes family would live. They had a choice between this spacious three-bedroom that shared the lot with Clay and Mercy or Logan's snug three-bedroom bungalow in town.

But for now, Brianna had free run of the place and a brand new laptop to set up. She told herself to focus on dealing with getting her new machine up and running, but it was hard to concentrate on anything but Jake's conversation with Theda.

Whatever Jake said, she hoped he'd put an end to Theda's vandalism. Brianna didn't want to get the young woman in trouble, but she'd been scared out of her wits and she'd been forced to call the police in order to make an insurance claim for her stolen laptop.

She should have used a password to secure the laptop, but since she was the only one to use it, she'd never bothered. Whatever was on there was wide open to prying eyes. Officer Branson had shaken her head when she'd heard. Brianna felt foolish, of course, but what was done was done. She had no intimate images or videos on her devices. The most intimate thing was her writing.

There was nothing in her writing that would upset Theda. Almost certain, she nibbled her lip, rethinking some key plot points. Theda couldn't possibly believe she was the model for the stalker, because the book was about a victim standing up for herself.

Shrugging off the useless merry-go-round of thoughts Brianna unpacked her new, sleek laptop. She unwrapped the power adapter and then plugged it in, a small thrill of anticipation running through her. She'd be back into her story in no time.

From outside came the crunch of tires on gravel. A visitor. Brianna moved quickly to the window beside the door to peer through the side of the drawn shade. Breathing a sigh of relief, she opened the door so Jake could come in.

"I feel like I'm in hiding. Give me some good news," she said as she stood back to let him enter.

"This place looks like a bomb went off. What happened in here?"

"Oh, I hardly noticed," she said, as heat rose to her cheeks. Elle had at least three bras tossed over the kitchen stools. Make-up and hairpins covered the kitchen counter. Discarded clothes and shoes littered the living room. Elle kept a clean house, but Brianna could see why Jake looked bemused and mildly appalled at the same time. Clay's glance had taken it all in, but he'd said nothing when she'd swept aside the makeup bits and pieces to set her laptop on the counter.

"This is what happens when a bride prepares for her wedding. There hasn't been anyone in here since Elle, Shandy, and I left together. Mercy would have been here too, but that would have meant bringing Autumn and, well, we needed every moment to get ready. The baby would've been a distraction."

Jake had his hands up, palms out. "Your secrets are safe with me," he promised.

"I'll just tidy up a bit," she said as she gathered the clothes and folded them over one arm. "I think you'll find the makings for coffee in the cabinet next to the fridge if you'd care to make a pot." She left him there as she took everything back to the bedroom for Elle to sort when she got home from her honeymoon.

Next, she collected the remnants of the makeup and hair products and returned them to the bathroom. The scent of coffee made with fresh water wafted through the living area. The brew burbled into the carafe while she gathered dirty dishes the women had used for snacks. She loaded everything into the dishwasher.

Those chores done, Brianna had nothing to occupy her mind except Jake. He'd already poured two mugs of coffee for them. When he passed a mug to her their fingers brushed and she felt the heat to her toes.

Jake wore a deep blue and gray plaid shirt that looked warm and cozy to the touch. She wanted to run her hands over his shoulders and down his chest to see if Theda had wounded him, physically or emotionally. Instead, she settled on a stool beside him and cupped her mug between both hands, enjoying the warmth between her palms. This was the kind of warmth she should want from him, not the man/woman kind.

Jake watched her with a gaze so keen she wondered if she had something distracting in her hair or on her cheek. She lightly swiped her palms across her face and took a quick glance at her reflection in the door of the microwave. Nothing out of place.

She shrugged and took note that his hair had grown since she'd come back to town. His lush, thick curls now touched his collar but his eyes were trained on her as she took inventory. She self-consciously smoothed her hair and then sipped her coffee.

"Well?" she prodded, to keep her mind off kissing him. "How did things go with Theda?" She wanted desperately to know what it was he was grateful for with that woman, but she daren't ask.

"Not the way I expected them to. I'd hoped she'd see for herself that we can't go back to the way it was. Not after all this. I wanted to lead *her* to conclude we were split for good, but somewhere, somehow, she took a sharp left and winged off into her usual rant."

"Which is?"

"All about what she wants. How no one loves her, and I should be the one who does, basically. She pretended to hear me, but then dismissed everything I said. Everything I confessed."

"Confessed?" That was an odd word.

He looked at the floor. "I told her about...about holding Tiffany as she died in my arms." His voice roughened over the words.

"Oh, Jake. I never knew..." she trailed off because the depth of his despair washed through her.

"No one did but the first responders. They took her out of my arms but there was nothing they could do. She was gone." He blinked, hard.

"But they tried?" Tears threatened, but he didn't need her pity.

"Yes, they did what they could, but her head wound was too severe. In the dark and the confusion, I hadn't even seen it. I didn't know the other side of her head was bashed in."

"She must have hit the road."

He shook his head. "Actually, it was the car door on the way out. They found—"

"No," she pleaded, interrupting him. "Don't say it. Please."

He dragged in a long, shuddering breath and let it out slowly. "Anyway, I told Theda how helpless I felt and how I decided to become a paramedic so I could save lives instead of standing by and watching more people die."

"She listened?" How could she not? Any normal person would be deeply affected by his nightmarish story.

"Yes, she was sympathetic, so I told her that when she showed up at my door and I let her in, she changed my life. I explained that I'd been hiding behind walls for years, not letting anyone in but Justin, and that was only because he forced me."

Brianna nodded slowly in remembrance. "You drove me away." He'd been adamant she leave town and him behind.

"Pushing you out of my life was only the beginning." He looked at her then, sorrow etched into his handsome features. She never wanted to see that kind of grief again. Raw, savage, he'd been torn apart and the scars from that night still lingered.

She was sorry she'd left him to suffer alone. "I should have been braver and stayed for you."

He jerked at her statement. "No, you needed to move on the way you'd planned. College was the right place for you. I slid into dark times and I didn't want anyone I cared for seeing me like that."

He'd shuttered himself away, that bright, funny boy who'd had a plan for his life. He wanted to study business and move to a big city. Any big city. Instead, he stayed in Welcome to be the hero he hadn't been able to be for Tiffany. Brianna clasped his hand where it rested on the counter. "It's all behind us. You've come through to the other side."

He pulled his hand away to rest it on his lap. "Except Theda latched onto the part where I thanked her for waking me up, for making me see what it was I wanted. She brought me to awareness of my life passing by. For that, I told her I'm grateful."

"But she took that to mean you wanted her back?"

"I thought I'd said it all so carefully. I told her no. I told her how it was nice at first, but she soon got possessive and strange. Explaining her odd behavior didn't make a dent in her understanding. Theda ignored everything she didn't want to hear."

Brianna took a sip of her cooling coffee. "I believe you. Some people are like that, especially emotionally unbalanced people. She's so alone in the world that maybe she can't see that clinging is the wrong way to love someone."

"She ran off across the park after making another vague threat."

Brianna felt a chill at the words. "What was it?"

"That 'she wouldn't get away with this.' I asked who she was talking about, but she bolted like a deer and raced away." He shook his head. "I wanted to follow her, catch her and make her explain herself, but people saw her running off and I thought better of chasing down a young woman in public."

Brianna was shocked into silence.

"In the end, I didn't call Officer Branson to make a formal complaint about my smashed window," he concluded. "I was going to; I had my phone in my hand, but I'm still holding out hope that Theda will leave town. I hope she finds whatever she's looking for and doesn't mess it up again."

"So do I."

Jake ran his fingers through his hair, looking apologetic. "I'm sorry I disturbed you here. I know you came for solitude to write."

"Pfft. It's not like I can focus on a fictional story when so much is going on in real life." She'd prefer to escape into her writing, but let the story thoughts drift away. She'd have to be content to set up her laptop and meet with the security company when they arrived.

"About real life," Jake said doubtfully. "I want to move forward. I want a life." He turned his head and looked right into Brianna's eyes.

Everything stilled inside her. Her breath. Her heart. Her pulse. All still. Her mind blanked as she stared back into Jake's seriously sexy blue eyes until she couldn't look anymore and she let her eyelids droop closed.

He must have leaned in because the next thing she knew, his lips brushed against hers in a tentative touch. She shuddered and everything—*everything*—inside her woke up at once. The feeling was so powerful she shuddered against his lips and moaned.

OhGod. OhGod. OhGod. It felt good. Right. Wrong. Delicious. *Alive.*

One brush of Jake Morrow's lips and she was seventeen again and in love with all her girlish heart.

Chapter Eighteen

THE BRUSH OF JAKE'S lips ended as quickly as it had begun. Brianna popped her eyes open to find Jake smiling two inches from her. "That was nice," he said in a coaxing tone that curled her belly. "Can we do it again?"

The curl in her belly rolled into excitement and trepidation at once. "Are you sure?" she asked. "This is a path we tried before." *And look at what happened that same night.*

"We're different now. My responsibility to Theda is over. Even if she doesn't grasp it now, she will when she has time to think it through." He looked certain, confident, that he'd done everything he could to convince Theda it was over between them.

She licked her bottom lip and thought she tasted Jake. Wanted to taste Jake. In every way. "Then let's do it again." She got to her feet because if she was going to kiss him, she wanted the feel of his whole body pressed to hers.

He rose as well and put his arms around her, bringing her in close. Brianna cozied up exactly where she wanted to be, against his broad chest covered in warm, soft flannel. He smelled of soap and clean man and she drank in his scent. This time his kiss was certain and sweet and tasted of coffee and desire.

He didn't press, didn't demand, but his fingertips found her cheek and stroked lightly. She melted inside and gave a little shiver of acquiescence as she moved closer still. "Kiss me like you mean it," she said against his lips. "The way you did before." It had been so long ago maybe she'd magnified the power of Jake's kiss, made it seem superhuman. A teenage girl couldn't possibly feel all the things she remembered feeling.

A footstep thudded on the stoop outside. She stilled and Jake raised his head, bright flags of red on his cheeks, a sure sign he'd wanted to show her how much he wanted the kiss to mean.

One brisk knock broke them apart. Brianna moved to the window for a peek outside. Two more knocks and, after a quick glance back at Jake, who stood frozen, she opened the door to let Clay in.

He looked discerningly from Brianna to Jake. "Am I interrupting something?"

"No," they both blurted and shook their heads.

Clay rolled his eyes. "Right." He clapped his hands lightly. "I'm here to see if you need anything, Brianna."

She glanced around the now-tidy living area. "I'm fine," she said and gestured toward her brand new notebook. "I'm setting up this puppy and will be writing within the hour."

"I'm sure you will," Clay said with a look at Jake. "I'm also here to give you the key I had cut for you." He handed it to Brianna. "Elle said to use the place for as long as you need. They'll be moving in to Logan's house because it's closer to school." He glanced around the living area in assessment. "I guess we can sell this back to the place I bought it from. I hope. Elle's only been here a few months."

"Logan moved a lot faster than I expected him to," Brianna commented with a chuckle. "It's the nice guys you have to watch." She warmed at the thought of the wedding and how the love between Elle and Logan had grown. She cast Jake a sidelong glance.

"In the meantime, being here to write is perfect," she added. "I'll be close to home in case anyone at the rescue needs me, but away from distractions at the same time." So many people supported her dream to write this novel, she couldn't set it aside.

"I'll tell Mercy hello," Clay responded. "She said you should stop in this afternoon when you get a minute. She'd appreciate some grown-up company."

"Of course." To be polite, Brianna offered Clay coffee, but he declined saying Mercy needed him to run errands.

"I'm taking Dilly with me. When you're five, a trip to the store is still an adventure and she loves buying baby supplies for Autumn."

Jake stirred. "I'd better be going. Theda must have borrowed a vehicle last night to come out here, so I'm curious who lent it to her. We've got a good idea, but I'd like confirmation. When we find out who's helping her I want to make them see sense. I'll ask them to help put a stop to this."

"It wasn't Denise. Her car was parked on the street last night," Brianna mused aloud as she rolled the problem over in her mind. A sudden stillness alerted her that the men had been shocked to silence and Jake glared at her.

"What were you doing at Denise's house?" he demanded. "And why didn't you mention it before?" Jake had thunderclouds in his eyes. Rather intimidating.

"Don't play detective, Brianna," Clay warned, looking concerned. "Denise Jones is nasty. She tried to bully Elle about getting her kids enrolled in school."

In the bright light of day, and after her house had been broken into, the stakeout last night seemed foolish and reckless. Brianna shifted, uncomfortable with two men's complete focus trained on her. "There was no need to tell you that Shandy and I wasted an hour doing nothing and seeing nothing. If something had happened or we'd gleaned any useful information then I'd have mentioned it to Officer Branson."

"Why did you go to Denise's house in the first place?" Clay asked.

She flashed a look at Jake who'd left the Bar & Grill to go see Theda. "I learned from Shandy how Theda's been possessive and a little scary and I grew concerned about Jake seeing her alone.

I—*we*—thought we could help if she got violent." At the least, she and Shandy could bear witness.

"I went to *talk* to her about how things went down between us. It was personal," Jake said, exasperation dripping from every word.

Clay frowned. "You think she's violent?"

"It wasn't directed at a person. Theda smashed my living room window. A moment of frustration. An impulse," Jake explained as if it was nothing.

Brianna shook her head at the sheer male arrogance. "Look at you two men; strong, virile, and in the prime of life. You seem invincible. What you don't realize is how dangerous a woman can be. Theda's small, but that doesn't mean she's not treacherous. She probably uses her tiny, perfect body to lull you into a false sense of security, like how tiny spiders can have the most toxic venom." Both men looked disbelieving, which made her point. At least to her.

Brianna went on. "Look at the facts, Jake. She wanted to control your every waking moment."

He shook his head in disbelief while Clay studied him with interest.

"Did she isolate you from anyone?" Brianna wanted to know. "I mean, more than you did yourself? I heard the nasty comment she made about you and Justin. That was said to drive a wedge between you two and humiliate you." Brianna had been surprised at the insinuation, but then, now that she had more knowledge of Theda the surprise trickled away.

"My parents," he said, with a note of wonder. "Theda stopped giving me their messages."

Brianna didn't enjoy being right. Not in this case. She lifted her hands in emphasis. "These are things abusers do." She looked from Jake to Clay and back again. They wore identical expressions of doubt.

"Don't think men aren't abused by women," she went on in a softer tone. "They just take longer to see it because they see themselves as strong, invincible, and in their prime."

"You're saying Theda was heading toward abusing me? *Me?*" After shaking his head a moment, Jake stared at the floor, his chest heaving. "I guess she was. On the job, we're trained to see it, but if a man wanted to hide it, I'd believe a lie, for all the reasons you said."

Clay huffed out a long breath. "No way. Really?" He frowned, but his gaze turned inward. "Women can be tough. My mother gave as good as she got with my old man. No one seemed to have the upper hand, though." He stared off into the middle distance as if sorting through memories.

"But Theda hasn't done anything physical to me," Jake added uneasily. "I doubt the cops would consider it abuse. The window was vandalism and done out of spite and in a moment of rage."

"Jake, you wanted out before she had complete control. Things might have escalated if you'd waited."

"When I was packing her stuff I found a stack of pictures of other guys she's been with. I'd love to talk to them to see how things ended there. I'd like to know if she went ballistic or acted out the way she has with me."

"I'll look her up on social media to see if she's shared any names. It shouldn't be too hard to find one or two of these men." She made a mental list of places to look.

Clay came back to the conversation. "I've got a security camera on the side of my house that faces your place. I'll aim it at your property, Brianna. I don't like where this is heading and the camera should be able to catch your driveway." He shook his head. "You should stay with us."

She considered his offer for all of a second. "No. You have a brand new baby and I need my sleep. Also, my house shouldn't be empty and I need to be available for the dogs and volunteers." She smiled to reassure both men.

"I'll be fine with a security system in place. They're coming over in an hour." She checked the time. "I'd best finish setting up my new toy and get back home."

Jake shook his head. "They have to check your place out before they can install. The soonest they'll be able to come out to get the system in place is tomorrow. You have tonight to get through."

Brianna stared him down. "That gives you today to find Theda again or get help from whomever it is who's helping her."

"I'll check with Tyler Rhodes," Jake said after a moment to think. "He could be more connected to this than I thought. Since our female detective friend saw Denise's car last night, Tyler may have lent Theda a vehicle or he could have driven her out here himself. She can flash those big blue eyes and make a man regret he ever met her."

"Wish I could do more," Clay said. "Autumn is keeping us up half the night and Dilly wakes up bright and early wanting to climb into bed with us. We don't know which way is up half the time." He frowned. "Plus we're swamped at the clinic and Mercy needs me as well." He yawned and scrubbed his face. "Keep us posted, Brianna. If anything seems suspicious tonight you come straight to us, hear?"

"I promise," she said with a smile and with one last curious look between them, Clay took his leave.

When they were alone, Jake looked sheepish. "I never dreamed things could go this far, Brianna. All I wanted was to break it off with her."

"Jake, I think we should back off with each other," she said with her heart in her throat. She wasn't sure what had changed in the last few minutes, but pushing forward into whatever this was between them seemed like tempting fate. And the more she thought about what she'd said about abusive women, the firmer her conviction. "We need to be very cautious with Theda."

He frowned and held himself straight and stiff. "And?"

She shifted and geared herself up for what she had to say next. "We've been caught up in reunion fever. Just because we kissed back in school, doesn't make us right for each other today." No matter how good it had felt to kiss him, to be in his arms, she had to keep her distance.

He nodded. "I see." He blew out a breath.

"We need to slow down and think objectively," she went on. As a teenager, she'd had a secret crush, but that was no reason to act on it now. Especially with a scorned woman on the loose who'd proven herself violent and willing to break and enter.

Jake stared hard at the counter, a muscle in his jaw jumping. With one brisk nod, he tore open the door and fled as if he couldn't bear the sight of her.

He moved so quickly he didn't see how she held out her hand to him.

JAKE LEFT BRIANNA AND called the Welcome Bakery, but Alyce hadn't seen Theda since she'd left with Jake to talk. "I thought you two were busy making up," Alyce said with a sly chuckle.

"No, she left me in the park. I assumed she'd go back to work."

"No, my dear, she did not." She sighed. "You tell her she still has a place here if she wants it."

"Will do," he said, distracted by the news. Theda was in the wind again and he didn't have a lot of hope he'd find her if she didn't want to be found. Next stop, the elementary school.

A few minutes later he waited until Denise was alone at the front desk before approaching her. "Do you know where Theda is?" he asked quietly.

Denise shook her head. "I have no idea. She told me you scared her in the park and she had to leave my place." She folded her arms across her chest and glared at him.

"Scared her? She wasn't scared, not by me. She was angry when she stormed off."

"Did you hurt that girl? Put your hands on her?" Denise demanded.

Appalled but not surprised by any lies Theda told, he responded. "Of course not. Is she claiming I did?"

Denise bit her lip and shrugged. "I don't know. She just sounded scared."

"She sounded scared. Well, Theda can sound all sorts of ways," he muttered. "And you should know there were witnesses at the park that saw her run off away from me and me walking in the opposite direction." He'd headed along the riverfront walk for a while to clear his head and to try to figure out where this drama might end.

He glared at her until she pursed her lips looking only slightly mollified.

"You don't know where she went after the park?" he pressed her.

"Back to my place to get her things I imagine."

"Do you know of anyone else she's made friends with? Anyone else she might go to?"

"No," she insisted, but Jake knew she was lying. She'd given him broad hints last night that Theda was seeing a man. Someone from his past who might want to steal his girl. In other words, Tyler Rhodes.

Denise made a show of pulling her keyboard forward and resting her hands on the keys. "If that's all, I have work to do."

"Right," he said. "I'm finished, but don't be surprised if you get a visit from the police." The scared shock in her face gave him a righteous thrill.

He pivoted and left the office. He needed to share all this with Brianna. But the thought of her and her last words to him gave him pause. She didn't want to continue exploring what they'd started with that kiss. Her taste filled his mouth, his mind and he may never taste her again. Her integrity unmanned him. Instead of breezily moving into a thing with him, she was putting Theda's feelings ahead of theirs.

Guilt was an interesting motivator. Theda wasn't Tiffany, and the situation was different. He'd made it plain he didn't want Theda, probably never really had wanted her, but still, Brianna would stick to her decision

Sometimes having integrity stunk. He felt his shoulders slump as he accepted that Brianna was likely right. It would be best for everyone if Theda accepted the end before Jake and Brianna shared a beginning.

He thought of calling her, but he didn't want to hear her voice. Didn't want to hear it catch on the words. Didn't want to hear a sigh or an indrawn breath. Didn't want to think about what she'd say next. He texted her instead.

Jake: You were right about us.

It was cryptic, but she'd know what he meant. Storming out the door of Elle's place the way he had made him look like a jerk, but he'd been surprised and disappointed. They'd been making headway and she'd slammed the door on them and what they could have.

Some days it wasn't worth getting out of bed. His mind filled with sour thoughts of sacrificing Brianna because of Theda. Dammit! He'd avoided complications with women for years and now this.

He rubbed his chest because he felt a hole opening up in there. Brianna was right, of course. Until Theda was out of town, Jake couldn't let anything grow with Brianna. From here on out, he'd keep his distance because that was the only way he could focus on finding Theda and convincing her to leave.

What was it with him and drama queens? Tiffany had been a handful, but he'd been so driven by rampaging hormones that he'd been willing to tolerate anything she handed out.

But then she'd started her experiment with Brianna and he'd seen what Tiffany was really like. The blinders had come off and when he'd looked around, it was Brianna he'd seen.

The agony of seeing her with Tiffany all the time had eaten away at him. It had been clear Brianna had been smitten with the idea that Tiffany had finally noticed her. Had befriended her. The shy girl transformed into a confident, friendly person who understood him.

He hadn't meant to kiss her and she hadn't done anything to make him think she wanted him to.

But he had. The kiss had been almost accidental. They were waiting together behind the bleachers for Tiffany. Brianna had slipped on some wet leaves. He grabbed her upper arms to steady her and when he'd looked into her wide, startled eyes he knew he had to taste her.

And she tasted just the same today as she had all those years ago. Sweet, tart, giving.

He squeezed his eyes shut and remembered the sweetness that was Brianna. He'd had lots of experience with Tiffany and if he thought hard about it now, he'd admit she'd been experienced when they'd begun seeing each other.

He and Tiffany had been a star couple, thanks to her. She had a shine about her, an appeal that put other, quieter, less-beautiful girls to shame.

But she had a dark heart. Tiffany Rhodes could be cruel, demanding, spiteful and nasty. He knew it deep down, so when he'd kissed Brianna, he saw trouble.

He knew Brianna was too sweet and kind not to be awkward around Tiffany after they kissed. They hadn't stopped at one, maybe if they had things would've been different. But once he'd tasted her, he'd asked for more and she'd freely given it.

She'd kissed him back with all her inexperience showing. Her lips had sought his, her mouth had opened, her tongue had explored and he knew, *he knew,* he was the first boy to kiss her this way.

But, he took what she offered. He was a horny teenager and when she kissed him back it was their undoing. He'd nuzzled her neck, her ear until she groaned. That sound brought him back to reality.

They'd broken apart, both flustered and red-faced. Brianna had stuttered an apology as if it was all on her. As if the kiss was her doing and he'd hated the shame he read in her gaze.

He'd reached for her, cuddled her close and talked. About how much he liked her, how much he appreciated her sweet nature, her kindness.

He never said a word about what Tiffany truly thought of her. To tell Brianna about Tiffany's plan to embarrass her at the prom by putting her in the spotlight, drunk, would've been cruel; like hitting an adoring puppy.

His stomach had turned at the thought and he decided then that he had to tell Tiffany they were through. He couldn't let this prank happen. Not to Brianna.

Tiffany had called out looking for them and Brianna had run out from under the bleachers. She ran past Tiffany, upset and near tears. But Tiffany, like a cat with prey, had pounced on Jake, demanding to know what had happened.

The prom was a long, hellish evening spent defending himself and warding off a thwarted Tiffany. By the time he'd started driving Tiffany home, she'd wound herself up to a crescendo of screaming, crying, and when that failed, bullying.

Finally, Jake confessed. He'd kissed Brianna and he *liked* her. In that way.

Tiffany tried to grab the steering wheel, but when he blocked her hands, she'd screamed that she'd jump out of the car. She unbuckled her seatbelt and hit him on the temple with her purse.

Her door flew open as he tried to correct his steering after being hit and suddenly, Tiffany was gone. He slammed on his brakes, skidded to a stop and ran back to find her in the gravel beside the road. Another car screeched to a halt ahead of his and those people appeared next to him as he'd cradled Tiffany in his arms.

They were the ones to call 9-1-1. They were the ones who told the investigators that they'd seen Tiffany swing her purse at his head. They'd seen the interior light come on in the car as she bailed out onto the shoulder.

He'd blanked so much of those minutes out that even now the memory blurred and seemed to have happened to someone else. Someone he'd watched from above.

Chapter Nineteen

LATER THAT EVENING, Brianna shut down her new laptop and shook her head. After the security company promised they would be back in the morning to install their top-of-the-line system, she'd settled in at Elle's place to do a quick Internet search for Theda Levi. Old pictures of the actress, Theda Bara, appeared onscreen, including footage from nineteen seventeen. Lots of people shared the surname Levi, but nothing for Theda Levi surfaced. Maybe Theda was her middle name or maybe it was a short form of some other name. She checked Theodora and came up empty, too.

She called a colleague from her fact-checking days to see if her friend could learn anything about the now-mysterious young woman. Grant Thomas was a great researcher and if there was anything anywhere on the Internet about Theda, he'd find it.

Brianna had carefully set aside thinking about Jake ever since her decision to cool things between them. She'd told herself it was for the best five hundred and ninety-six times. Call it superstition or misplaced nostalgia, or some other emotional trick, she refused to allow her longing for a relationship to cloud her judgment with a man she barely knew. And really, the new Jake was not the same as the Jake she remembered.

She really didn't know him. The old Jake would never lock a woman out of his home and would never leave a note telling her to move out. Sure, Brianna wasn't aware of how many times he'd tried to get Theda to leave, but still, it left a bad taste in Brianna's mouth that the new Jake would resort to what was clearly abandonment.

All this was no excuse for broken windows and creeping through Brianna's house, but still, Theda was a young woman alone in the world. She was clearly high strung and sensitive and her heart may well have been broken.

Yes, Brianna had told her friends and her mother she wanted to meet someone to have a family with. There was nothing abnormal about being sure of what she wanted. At thirty-two it was time to think about the rest of her life. Past time.

But Jake was probably the worst man in the world for her.

Returning Jake's kiss had been a terrible mistake all those years ago. Enjoying his kisses was quickly followed by guilt for kissing her best friend's boyfriend. And then, to hear Tiffany calling for them just out of sight had nearly done Brianna in. What if Tiffany had seen them? Her friend would have been devastated. Brianna had felt a choking sob rise up and she'd run past Tiffany with her hand over her mouth in case she embarrassed herself.

The three of them had planned to drink a bottle of wine and anything else Tiffany could steal from her mother's stash, even though Brianna hadn't wanted to. She remembered seeing Tiffany with a bag of bottles dangling from her hand as comfortable as could be.

The sight had made Brianna's stomach clench harder and she'd run as fast as she could away from her greatest shame. She wasn't sure how she'd ever face her friend again.

Turns out, she hadn't had to. Tiffany died only hours later.

How convenient. The shame and guilt threatened to swallow her again and she was glad, *glad*, she'd set Jake aside. Then and now.

She wasn't built for subterfuge and sneaking around. She'd known it at seventeen and she knew it now. As long as Theda felt there was a bond between her and Jake, Brianna wanted no part of him.

There, settled, she thought.

She shrugged into a rain jacket and went to check on the dogs before settling in for the night. Really, she didn't need to check all the latches, but often, the new arrivals needed one last pat and cuddle. Beau came out of his kennel, happy and confident. He enjoyed this routine every night and delighted in his job.

The white and black pit bull, with his black saddle and half-black face, was a handsome dog who owned the ground he walked on. He was never intimidated, nervous, or out of control. Clay called him their Judas because he calmed the other dogs with his steady presence.

"Beau," she said softly, "you understand why I had to give Jake up, right? Why aggravate a situation I stumbled into? I didn't bring on Jake's dissatisfaction with Theda, but she seems to believe I'm the cause."

Beau snuffled her hand in reassurance. She patted his head in thanks. "I agree. It's best to let Jake sort things while I get my head on straight." A couple of dogs had knocked over their water bowls so she filled a jug and went through the kennels refilling their bowls where needed. She took solace in the mundane task. The company of the dogs with their easy affection and soulful eyes eased her heartache.

One last pat for Beau. "Thanks, sweetie, I can always depend on you to make me feel better."

She closed the latch on his kennel gate and walked into the house. Tomorrow night, she'd be setting an alarm code for the house and the kennels. Cameras would be everywhere recording every movement.

The idea saddened her that life had come to this. But then, she was sad about a lot of things tonight, Jake among them.

It bothered her that she couldn't find anything on Theda Levi on the Internet. She wasn't sure how a person her age could avoid any mention anywhere. But she had Grant working on the case now and he loved nothing more than a challenge. Between them, they'd find a trail and follow it. She just hoped it would be soon.

Darkness had fallen while she'd checked on the dogs. As she crossed the yard toward the back door of the house, she had a moment of hesitation. While she'd been out last night, or even maybe while she'd *slept* some nameless person had entered her home and looked around at her and her mom's personal space. She shuddered as she climbed the back stoop to the door. It creeped her out to think about someone turning on her laptop to see whatever they wanted and then taking it away with them to see more.

To what purpose? Not to sell. To inconvenience her? But what would be on her laptop that would cause someone to steal it? She'd likely never know. The whole episode belonged in the unsolved mysteries of life category.

She bolted the kitchen door securely and called Mercy next door to let her know she was settling in for the night. "Hi, all set. It's quiet and the dogs are settled."

"Are you sure you don't want to come over here to sleep?" Mercy asked.

"Absolutely. I'm fine. I want to be here. Sometimes, people leave dogs tied up by our mailbox by the road in the middle of the night."

"We've heard the odd dog crying out there, but we never knew what it was. We assumed the sound came from a kennel in the back."

"People can be ashamed that they can't afford their pets anymore and leave them secured so we'll be sure to find them. It's a terrible choice to have to make when they love their dogs." She hoped nothing woke her tonight. It had been an emotionally exhausting day and she was weary to the bone.

After assuring Mercy again that she'd be fine on her own, they hung up and Brianna checked all the doors and windows one more time before taking her new laptop to bed to re-read what she'd written so far. She was afraid anything she'd written today was an ugly mess. With all the upset and upheaval she felt disconnected from the story and needed to reassure herself that the plot still worked and the characters were still true to themselves.

Her heroine was finally taking charge of her life. But first, a name. She'd used XYZ as a placeholder but it was time to come up with a real name that fit the character and the woman she would become. Brianna could do that much right now.

She had a vague notion of how the heroine looked and now that she was a bit stronger and more in control, she couldn't be XYZ any longer. The romance-heroine-like names she'd considered before popped into her head, but they still weren't right for a woman facing real peril. This character had to be confident, capable, and even a little kick-butt. That eliminated names that sounded soft. She jotted some names down on a piece of paper she kept on her bedside table. *Joan. No, too old.* She thought again, rolling more names through her mind. *Kailey.* That one had possibilities. She considered it for another full minute but then wrote *Jaye,* a name that came to her like a stone skipping over her head.

Jaye. Jaye. She wrote it down three times. It was right. The woman in this story had to be Jaye. It was short, punchy and couldn't be shortened into something cutesy. Jaye was Jaye and there was no messing with her or her name.

She returned to the first page of the story and replaced all the XYZs with Jaye. A couple of clicks and the heroine became Jaye and Brianna felt even better. At least something had turned out all right today. When a surname came to her she'd put that in where appropriate.

Her mind settled and she finished reading the rest of what she'd written and, pleased with what she'd read, smiled. This was rough writing, first draft writing, but it had form and rhythm and she could work to make it better once the story foundation was laid. She sighed with contentment. Writing did that for her. Made her happy.

She saved her work and shut down. Sliding the laptop onto the floor, she took the added precaution of shoving it under her bed. If a thief came back for this, they'd have to go through her to find it.

She let her mind drift until sleep came. After the stressful day she'd had, dreams turned to nightmares as the sounds of dogs barking intruded into her sleep. She woke groggily and looked at her phone. Three ten.

In the morning.

She'd dreamed the dogs were barking. Hadn't she? Rolling out of bed, Brianna grabbed her robe and made her way to the kitchen. Rubbing sleep out of her eyes, she peered outside to the kennels. Beau circled the yard, nose down. When she turned on the outside lights, he came to the door barking and bouncing with excitement. Dread filled her. "You shouldn't be out," she said as if Beau could answer.

She scuffed her bare feet into an old pair of sneakers they kept by the back door and stepped outside. As the screen door slammed at her back, Beau turned and raced to the kennels whining and yipping. She turned on the lights for the kennels and gasped.

Every door swung open.

The dogs were gone.

Beau ranged back and forth in front of the gates as if to point out that they were open. Then he cocked his head and tore out of the kennel area, turning a corner toward the back of the deep lot. A large stand of trees provided a good windbreak and a walking path wove in and out of the spruce, poplar, and maple trees. When she and Elle had been children they'd wander around back there pretending they were explorers. Elle, being older, would lead the way, telling Brianna stories and pointing out nature's beauty. But tonight, all Brianna could think was that half a mile behind those woods was a trail that led to the highway. And all the dogs were roaming.

"Beau! Come back!" But he'd peeled away so quickly, she knew he was determined to go where he needed to go. The pit bull wouldn't be back until he was ready to return.

Brianna dashed back into the house and called the police. "There's been another act of vandalism at Bowler's Rescue. This time, it's the dogs." Oh God, she could hardly catch her breath.

The 9-1-1 dispatcher was calm and collected. The questions she asked kept Brianna grounded. "No, they're not dead, they're gone," she explained. "I was dreaming—no, that's not right—I heard them barking, but I was asleep. The only one who hung around was Beau, our pit bull. But he just tore out of the kennel area."

"Is he dangerous? Has he bitten anyone before?"

"Aren't you listening? This is the second night in a row my property has been vandalized. Last night, they stole my laptop from *inside* my house!"

"Ma'am, is the dog dangerous? Our officers need to know."

"No, he's not dangerous. And if you tell your officers to be ready to shoot him, you can just forget I called." She slammed the old kitchen phone down and wanted to scream.

She called Clay next. "Clay, sorry to wake you."

"Brianna? We're awake with Autumn. No problem. What's wrong?"

She told him about the dogs and about Beau being on the loose. "I'm afraid the police might come prepared to shoot him."

"We'll explain about Beau. He's got distinctive markings so they'll recognize him. I'll be right over." He hung up and she went back outside, armed with a flashlight and her cell phone.

Clay joined her by hopping the fence between their properties. He checked out all the empty kennels and starting calling for Beau.

Two minutes later, Beau rounded the corner into the yard, leading a pack of five dogs Brianna recognized. "He went and brought them back. Good boy! What a hero," she said and rubbed his ears affectionately. Beau wiggled and groaned.

The other dogs milled about, happily back where they belonged. These were the older dogs, harder to adopt, who'd been here the longest.

She and Clay grabbed their collars and put the dogs back into their kennels. They all went happily. "I thought I heard dogs barking, but Autumn was crying and Mercy's exhausted so I got up to bring her to our bed. I ignored the sound of the dogs. I'm sorry, Brianna, I should have investigated."

She waved away his apology. "I thought I was dreaming about the dogs barking, so I took too long to get out here."

Brianna's phone rang and she read the display. "It's Mercy," she said to Clay. "Hi,' she answered. "We're out by the kennels. I'll put you on speaker."

"I'm looking at the security footage from the camera that's pointed at your driveway," Mercy said, sounding loud and determined in the chill night air. The sound of baby Autumn came through, as well. She sounded happy and very much awake. "Just out of clear view there looks to be a recreational vehicle or camper van near your mailbox."

"Really? That's odd. Can you see anything else?"

"A dark figure runs along your driveway to the back, then a stream of dogs races toward the road and then the figure returns and drives off."

Clay stood transfixed. "Dammit," he growled. "Bastard." And then he added a few other choice words. Beau began circling the yard again, nose down. When he headed off toward the driveway, Clay grabbed his collar. "No," he commanded. Beau rolled his eyes and groaned a protest.

"Mercy, thanks," Brianna said. "We'll lock Beau up and be right over."

Clay shook his head. "You stay here for the police and I'll email you the footage. I'll also grab a jacket and boots and be right back." She realized then that he'd run over barefoot wearing jeans and a T-shirt. And she was in her sleeping T and pajama bottoms.

"Okay, I'll call the volunteers to let them know what's happened. Maybe some of them can come out tonight to get a jump on rounding up the dogs. If the dogs are gone much longer, they could keep on running." She'd dress while she talked to Sandra. "Clay, the highway's not far," she said, struck by a quick paralyzing fear.

"Don't think about it, just stay on task," he said as he loped back toward the fence. He hopped it in one smooth jump.

Stay on task.

Right.

Chapter Twenty

STAY ON TASK BRIANNA reminded herself. She kept thoughts of the highway under control. Too much thinking could stall her and she couldn't afford to stall. Not now. Not with the dogs roaming toward who-knew-what disaster.

She threw on clothes and decided to call Jake about the dogs being released. Even though she'd hoped to avoid him, he needed to know that Bowler's Rescue was now a target, too. This was way more serious than creeping through the house. What kind of person would put innocent dogs in jeopardy?

She called Sandra O'Neal to ask her to call half the list of volunteers and Sandra's calm efficiency reassured Brianna. "I'll get everyone over there to help. Don't worry. We've got this. You do what you have to do."

Grateful for Sandra's steady calm, Brianna called Jake to let him know about this new act of vandalism. "It's more like terrorism," she said to wind down her explanation. "These dogs have been terrorized and sent out into an area they don't know. Most of them won't be able to find their way back on their own." The task ahead was monumental, but with Sandra's help, she had faith they could get all the dogs back where they belonged. "There's footage of a camper van at the road by the driveway. Clay had his camera aimed there."

"Good. That'll help. I'll be there as soon as I can."

BY THE TIME JAKE ARRIVED at the dog rescue, Brianna looked to be in full command of a small group of people who'd arrived before him. Some looked only half-dressed with jackets tossed on over pajamas and shoes without socks. But they all wore concern and determination on their faces.

The girl of his dreams smiled and waved when he made his way past the cars in the driveway. Clay stood beside Brianna and nodded at him brusquely. "Glad you're here, Clay," Jake said. "What was this about some footage from your camera?"

"Here," he said, and passed Jake his cellphone. The image was small, but it was clear what was happening. The vehicle was almost out of range of the camera, but it was obviously some kind of camping vehicle.

"The vehicle looks old, and the person's short." Theda. "I'm pretty sure who it is," he said for Clay's ears only.

Brianna turned and stood with them in a tight triangle. She looked agitated and bone-weary. "We think it's Theda," she said softly. "She's so short she had to hop down from the passenger side."

"No way to know who drove?"

"Actually, when she runs back, she gets in on the driver's side," Clay said as the video played for Jake. "She could have slid over to exit on the passenger side when she arrived."

"So, she could have been alone or had company."

"Right."

"But why would someone help her do this? It's way beyond petty vandalism." Brianna asked. "She must have been alone."

Jake nodded. "At least now we know what kind of vehicle she's been borrowing to come out here."

Clay agreed. "This is unlikely to be a younger person's camper. And from what Brianna has told me about Theda's circumstances it must be borrowed. She wouldn't have the money to buy this."

"Absolutely not. And it's way too old to be a rental," Jake said as he studied the image again.

"Who does she know who's older?" Clay said as he held up a hand to forestall any response. "Sybil, what are you doing out here?" he asked as his receptionist rushed up to them.

"We heard about the dogs getting out and came to help." It stood to reason she'd be a dog person. Brianna smiled her thanks at the older woman. "I saw a post about it first thing," Sybil explained. "So we came right out. Isn't that so, Bud?"

"That's so," Bud said with a nod. "It'll be lighter soon, make it easier to find 'em."

"Thank you both for coming," Brianna said. "I'm sending people out to the back by those trees if you've got walking shoes on. It can get muddy back there."

"Let's go, Bud, time's wasting," Sybil said and stalked off.

"Bud, there are some leashes over by the kennels if you need them," Brianna called to them.

"Brought our own," he tossed back as he followed his wife.

"I wonder who posted the call for help?" Jake asked. "It's still too early for most people to be up."

"It was Sandra, one of our volunteers. She's very efficient. I was too rattled to even think about posting anything. Apparently, she has a group site for concerned citizens."

"Which means your mother will know as soon as she wakes up," Jake said. "This must be how she knows all the gossip. An online group."

Brianna's mouth ticked up in a faded imitation of her usual smile. "I don't want my mother to feel like she needs to come home. I can handle this."

Jake patted her shoulder when all he wanted was to take her into his arms for a hug. "Where was Beau during all this? Didn't he cause a ruckus?"

She explained about thinking she was dreaming about dogs barking. "By the time I got out here all the dogs but Beau were gone. He actually took off and led five of them back. I kenneled him again in case the police got antsy about a pit bull running loose."

"He's a hero," Jake said. "I'll take one of those leashes for him and see if he can find some more dogs."

"Good idea," Clay said, "but I'll take him. He's my dog and will take my commands better than a stranger's."

Jake nodded. "Good," he said to Clay. He turned to Brianna. "I'll go wherever you need me, Brianna."

For a moment she looked stunned, overwhelmed, and ready to cry. But she controlled her features and drew a deep breath. She looked around as if uncertain where to put him. Then she gave a brisk nod. "Coffee, I need you to make coffee."

"I'm on it," he said and gave her hand a quick squeeze in reassurance. "Whatever you need, I'm here."

The group of searchers parted to allow two uniformed police officers to approach. Brianna moved quickly toward them. "Call me if you need me," he called after her. She responded with a wave.

Most men would balk at doing kitchen duty in the midst of a search, but Jake could see what looked like half the townspeople milling around in the pre-dawn darkness. Coffee was likely the most helpful thing he could do.

He called the fire station for supplies and grinned at the response. The guys razzed him about doing dog rescues again because they'd heard about the pup he'd brought out here.

There were times he loved his job.

In twenty minutes, he'd received paper cups, an industrial-sized coffeemaker, and all the sugar packets and creamer containers they'd need.

He played Clay's security video on the television in the living room. Every volunteer who'd come in had taken a look to see if anyone recognized the vehicle. No one had.

Sybil and Bud came in after rounding up two of the younger, more skittish dogs. "Good job," he said as they joined the short lineup for coffee.

"Cops are outside. And it looks like more have arrived," Bud said. "It's a woman. She's looking at the cages and stuff."

"That's Officer Branson. I'm sure she'll get to the bottom of this."

"Take a look in the living room and see if you know who owns the vehicle on the TV video footage," Jake said. "We think the vandal borrowed it from someone."

Sybil cocked a curious eyebrow, her gossip radar obviously tingling. She filled her paper cup with coffee and wandered into the living room to see. "I know this camper," she said clearly at first sight. "It belongs to Cassie and Phil Rhodes. They have a son, Tyler."

She turned and gave Jake a knowing look. "They were Tiffany's parents. But you already know that."

He walked closer to the television to get a better look and to avoid Sybil's curiosity. "Yes, I already know that," he muttered. *Damn!* Did her parents hate his guts, too? Enough to mess with Brianna and a rescue full of innocent dogs? *No, not them, but Tyler. Maybe.*

Brianna drifted to a stop beside him, silently staring at the screen. "Officer Branson is outside and she needs to know this. All of it." She turned stark eyes toward him and Jake nodded. Brianna wanted to tell their secret, their long-ago shame, and he had to let her.

Damn. The whole sorry mess would have to be aired.

AN HOUR LATER AND IT was still early morning. Most people were just rising and dawn had brought pretty blue skies for a change. The air was crisp and clean and as Brianna stood with Jake at the end of the driveway, Clay walked toward them with a trail of missing dogs behind Beau. "No leashes required for this group," he called. "Once they got wind of Beau they came out of hiding. Most were in the underbrush, cowering from all the strangers wandering around."

"We need to take a count," Brianna said with a tight smile, "but we may have found most of them."

A quick headcount proved Brianna right, most of the dogs had been found. Those that hadn't been brought back yet were reported to animal control and she had promises from everyone who'd come out to search that they would continue watching for the dogs all over the area.

One of the volunteers was already working on signs to go up beside the highway to watch for wandering dogs and report them. Everyone hoped none of them had run that far, but just in case, drivers could report in if they spotted any.

While she kenneled, Clay fed the latest batch of returnees. Most seemed relieved to be home, especially the ones who'd been there awhile.

Clay went home. By the time she returned to the kitchen, Jake had collected all the coffee fixings to return them to the fire station. In silence, she helped carry a box of cups and supplies to Jake's car.

He stowed everything and then closed the hatch on his SUV. Brianna lifted her hand in a half-hearted wave. She dreaded reliving their past with the police officer, but Officer Branson needed the full picture of how that night fifteen years ago may be affecting current events. Jake agreed, but she hadn't been able to look at him since Sybil had narrowed her eyes at Jake in the living room. "I guess that's it, then. The regular volunteers will continue the search. There are what? Three dogs left to be found?"

"Yes. I'll take Beau out again, too." She chewed her lip. "Officer Branson had another call and left. But she'll be back soon. She wants an in-depth interview, she said and with all the activity here, she thought it best to wait. She inspected the cages and downloaded the video to study. I'm glad Clay thought to aim his camera over this way."

Jake studied her with heavy-lidded eyes. His total focus unnerved her.

"Don't," she said. "Don't look at me like that."

He blinked and shifted his head to look into the distance. A muscle flexed in his jaw. With a tight nod, he took the three steps to his car door. Opened it.

"Wait, I wanted to tell you something odd and now that we have a moment alone..." she trailed off.

"What is it?" he kept his tone detached.

"I couldn't find anything anywhere on the Internet about Theda. She's a ghost."

His brows furrowed. "Surely, there's something. There's got to be. An old school grad photo or mention of her playing sports? She told me once she was on a softball team that won the state championship. Her name and photo would be online for that." His expression fell into puzzlement.

She shook her head. "No, I didn't see anything like that and I've been a fact-checker for years. I know how to dig deep." But, he'd given her a clue so she'd go look again. "What state?"

He frowned. "Iowa? Or was it Ohio?"

"No matter. I'll find her now that I've got something to go on."

"Still, it's odd that she's avoided being mentioned more recently. Don't people that young live online?"

"Was she on her phone much? Posting?"

He shook his head, rubbed his lower face as he tried to recall. "No, not really. She loves to text me, but other than that, no."

"Did you say you'd seen photos of her with past boyfriends?"

He nodded. "A lot. She had a collection. Maybe ten or twelve. And those are just the ones she kept. There could be more she didn't want reminders of."

"I'll keep looking. I'll search for images online from a few years ago." That could take days, but if the police went searching too, it could go faster. Her phone rang. "It's Officer Branson, I'll tell her about this and they'll likely help with the image search."

Jake climbed into his car. "I'll let you talk. Meanwhile, I'm going back to the bakery to talk with Alyce again."

A second ring sounded. "I'd hoped you'd tell her about what happened to Tiffany with me." She didn't want to have to deal with this long, sad story alone. "About that night and what we did."

"I will. I promise." His eyes looked haunted. "You shouldn't have to talk about that alone. I'll be back soon. What I need to ask Alyce needs to be asked in person."

JAKE WAITED FOR NATE Talbot, Mercy's father, to pull out of a parking spot in front of the bakery, and then slipped into the vacated parking spot. He was relieved to see a new counterperson inside with Alyce. Good to know all this business with Theda wouldn't hurt the bakery owner. Alyce was a wonderful woman and didn't deserve to have her business disrupted. This was the morning rush and it seemed almost as chaotic as it had been out at Bowler's Rescue at four a.m.

He stepped inside and a few heads swiveled in his direction. "Jake," someone called. "Did you get all the dogs?"

"Most of them, yes. The last three will likely be found today. Brianna's got her regular volunteers still searching." He recognized more than one person who'd pitched in for the roundup. He held up both hands and addressed the crowd. "You folks were awesome out there and you saved lives today. No telling what would've happened if the dogs had gotten as far away as the highway."

A quiet cheer went up and Jake saw a few backs slapped. Most of these people had run to lend a hand long before they were usually awake. So many of these folks had been the ones Jake had cut out of his life. His high school coach sat on a stool at the window counter and held up a cup in salute. The girl he shared his first kiss with gave him a friendly smile. A Sunday school teacher clapped at his grateful announcement.

So many welcoming smiles from so many people gave him pause.

Alyce slanted him a shrewd look and tilted her head toward the counter where it lifted. He took the invitation to join her. Once behind the counter, she led him into a cramped office where it seemed she did her paperwork. She slid the pocket door closed so their conversation would remain private. She leaned against her tiny desk while he positioned himself against the lone file cabinet on the opposite wall.

"Theda's left me in the lurch," Alyce began. "I had to bring in inexperienced help this morning and handle the till myself. I've got pies to finish, too." She shook her head sadly. "That girl's way more trouble than she's worth. Is she the one who set those dogs free?"

"Likely. We think she borrowed a vehicle and drove out there about three this morning."

Alyce clucked her tongue and set her hands on her hips. "What else can I tell you?"

"We can't find anything on the Internet for Theda Levi. Can you tell me why?"

"I thought you knew," Alyce said with her eyes rounded by surprise. "That's not her real name."

Chapter Twenty-one

JAKE WASN'T SURPRISED when Alyce told him Theda was using a phony name. But he wondered why Theda would trust the bakery owner with her secret.

"I suspected Theda had changed her name when Brianna's search came up empty." There was more he wanted to know and he had to hurry. Officer Branson would be at Bowler's Rescue any time now and he wanted to be there for the conversation. He dreaded talking about his past with Officer Branson, but it had to be done and he had to be there to support Brianna through the whole messy story.

"How have you been paying her?" he asked Alyce. "There are employment records you need to fill out. How have you dodged that?"

"I paid her in cash, as she requested," Alyce responded softly so the sound of their voices wouldn't carry outside her minuscule office. "She told me Theda Levi wasn't her real name because she was hiding from an ex-boyfriend with a mean temper. It's not the first time I've helped out a woman who was outrunning her past." She frowned. "I do what I can when women need a helping hand," she said with a shrug. "She's not the only young woman in her predicament."

Except Jake didn't believe Theda was in the fix Alyce believed she was in. No. The more he thought about it, the more convinced he was that she was the abuser in her past relationships. Brianna was right. Men were abused, too and stayed silent.

Alyce looked concerned and her brows knitted. "Are you going to report me?"

"No. You thought you were helping a victim keep a low profile. I can't fault you for that." And he knew how convincing Theda could be. He had no doubt Alyce had believed Theda's story.

"I have to get back to the rescue. The police will be there. I won't say that you've confirmed my suspicions, just that I suspect Theda is using a false name." And now that he suspected Theda could be hiding from her own violent past rather than a violent man, he'd tell the police that, too.

"You're a good man," Alyce said with a sigh and a gentle pat on his shoulder. "Go and deal with this."

Fifteen minutes later, Jake parked beside the police cruiser in the Bowler Rescue driveway. He yawned and realized that in the rush of the morning, he hadn't had time for coffee, even though he'd been providing it for everyone else.

He didn't have long to wait for one. Officer Branson and Brianna sat at the kitchen table and the fresh scent of brewing coffee filled his nose. "Good morning," he greeted them and hooked a thumb over his shoulder. "Any news on the three remaining escapees?"

"We got them all," Brianna responded with a pleased smile. "Sandra rallied half the town to help in less than an hour. And with you manning the coffee station and showing everyone the security footage, we managed the whole crisis quickly and efficiently. "

"I just stopped at the bakery after returning the coffee supplies to the station and a lot of the breakfast rush customers had been out here. I told them how well everything went."

Officer Branson assessed him critically as he focused on helping himself to the delicious- smelling brew. He pulled up a chair and settled in for this private and painful discussion. "We have something we need to explain that happened a long time ago," he said in a rush. He rubbed his hands in preparation.

"Does this also have something to do with the broken windows at your house?" Branson asked with a raised brow. She picked up her pen, ready to take notes. "Start at the beginning." Her hazel eyes held a determined gleam, but something about the officer reassured Jake.

Brianna's hand reached for his under the table and he squeezed her fingers lightly. "Back in Welcome High I had a best friend," Brianna began.

"My girlfriend, Tiffany Rhodes," Jake added. He looked at Brianna's shame-filled eyes and knew he had to ease her mind with the truth. "She wasn't a nice girl," he said. "She had plans for Brianna that would embarrass and humiliate her. It was prom night and Tiffany was about to put her plan into action."

Brianna stiffened and pulled her hand out of his. "What?" Her eyes rounded in shock. "Explain," she demanded, sounding nothing at all like the quiet, unassuming girl she once was. This woman could handle the truth. This Brianna could hear it all and move forward.

"Tiffany knew how shy Brianna was," Jake explained. "Everyone did. She hated being the center of attention. Hated everyone staring. She got tongue-tied if she had to read aloud in class." He smiled at her. "But she was sweet and kind and once I got to know her, I hated what Tiffany planned to do."

Brianna frowned and looked a little sick at the revelations. "You kissed me," she said. "You wanted to humiliate me, too? That was what the kiss was about?" She looked more enraged by the second. "Because you have. Right here, right now. I thought you liked me. I thought we could be friends and maybe even more." She rose to her feet, red-faced and angry. So angry.

Jake wasn't sure if she was talking about the kiss behind the bleachers or the more recent, mind-blowing ones they'd shared. He wasn't sure it mattered which ones she meant.

Office Branson watched carefully, apparently accustomed to emotional outbursts.

"No. Nothing like that, I swear. Let me explain." He looked at the other woman and waited for her nod. Brianna went and stood by the back door, staring out toward the kennels, but he knew she wasn't seeing them. She was seeing what happened between them behind the bleachers.

"I kissed Brianna because I realized she was the girl I liked," he said to the officer. "I'd been allowing my teenage hormones full rein with Tiffany and I finally saw the truth. Brianna was the girl I wanted so I kissed her."

"I take it she kissed you back?" Branson prodded. "Can we move on to how this affects what's happening today?"

"Sure." He drew in a breath and gathered his memories. "Tiffany's plan was to get Brianna drunk before we went into the prom and put her in the spotlight. She planned to egg her on. To make a fool of her. I knew Brianna would never recover from something like that. She was so sweet." He'd wanted that sweetness for himself. He'd been a selfish bastard. Still was if he was being honest, because he still wanted her sweetness. Wanted her kind thoughts and her smiles and for her eyes to light on his.

Brianna's shoulders stiffened. He imagined every word he uttered was a blow. She'd been so certain of her friendship with Tiffany.

"Brianna never made it into the dance. After the kiss, she ran off when Tiffany arrived. Tiffany was furious with me. The rest of the night went pretty much as you'd expect. By the time I was driving her home, Tiffany was enraged. To shut her up, I told her I wanted to end things because I'd kissed Brianna and knew she was the girl I wanted."

He'd been blunt and deliberately goaded Tiffany. He'd felt a weight lift off as he'd shouted back at her. Tiffany had gone quiet as she'd finally stopped spewing hateful things about Brianna. "And then she said it."

"Said what?" the officer asked, pen poised over her notebook.

"I'm so done with you and that bitch. You'll be sorry for this. No one treats me this way. If you don't take it back I'll jump out. After that, she swung her tiny purse at my head."

"I read the report. The metal clasp on her clutch left a mark over your eyebrow."

He stared at her because he'd almost forgotten the small gash. "It cut me, yes. He still had a small scar. He touched it lightly.

"I also saw you were cleared of any wrongdoing in the accident," Branson said clearly.

"Huh," Jake muttered. "You must be a good investigator if you checked me out, too."

"I'm thorough," Branson admitted, without a trace of pride. "And I like to get the full picture. So, how does all this old news pertain to today? Theda Levi is not Tiffany, and in fact, I don't think she's anybody."

Brianna turned back to face them, her shoulders held stiffly, her face wet from tears. "I can't find anything on Theda. She's a ghost."

When Branson raised an eyebrow at Brianna's comment, she explained that she had been a fact-checker and knew how to dig for information.

The officer nodded. "She's clearly using a false name. The question is why and what's she hiding from?" She put her hazel eyes to work on Jake again. "Any ideas?"

He told her about the photos of men Theda kept among her few possessions. "They must mean something to her if she's carrying them around. Everything she owns is in a hiker's backpack."

"Do you have a photo of her?"

He pulled out his phone. "Here," he said. "We took it and she had it printed to put on our fridge. It's just like the others in her pack." He emailed her the photo. "You should know we've learned that Tyler Rhodes is hanging out with Theda, or whatever her name is. He may have lent her the vehicle she drove out here."

"Rhodes. Tiffany's brother?" At Jake's nod, Branson went on. "And Theda broke your window when you told her to move out of your place?"

"Yes."

"And then she came out here and stole your laptop?" she asked Brianna. When Brianna affirmed with a nod, the officer continued. "Any idea what's so interesting on your laptop?"

"No idea, but as you saw, she didn't take the power cord, so she's not planning to sell it."

"In her texts, Theda keeps saying that 'she'll be sorry,' but Theda never says what she'll be sorry for," Jake added. "I'm not even sure that Theda is talking about Brianna, but it's a good bet, right?"

Officer Branson's expression was noncommittal. More note-taking while the officer sipped her coffee. Jake did the same as he mulled over everything else he thought might be of interest to the police.

The sound of car doors slamming in the driveway alerted them to visitors. A moment later, the sound of the front doorbell sounded.

"No one ever uses the front door," Brianna said with a concerned note in her voice. The officer looked out the living room window and then followed Brianna to the door. Jake stood back to give the women room.

Tyler Rhodes stood framed in the open doorway, flanked by his parents. "May we come in, Brianna?" Mrs. Rhodes asked.

Chapter Twenty-two

BRIANNA HAD HAD ENOUGH surprises for one day. First, the dogs were released, and then her high school best friend turned out to be a liar and a user. The woman who was targeting Brianna with these pranks wasn't who she said she was and no one knew where she'd gone or what Theda would do next. And now Tiffany's family stood waiting to enter her home. Phil and Cassie Rhodes, older and sadder, wore identical contrite expressions, while Tyler looked aggravated.

Not to mention Jake had held back the news for fifteen years that Tiffany had planned to humiliate Brianna at the prom. Hard as she tried, she couldn't understand why Tiffany would concoct such a cruel plan.

For all this time Brianna had felt guilt and shame whenever she thought of that night and those young, inexperienced kisses with a boy who belonged to her friend. When all along Tiffany wasn't her friend at all, was, in fact, an enemy.

And now, just to remind her again what a fool she'd been, Tiffany's mulish looking brother Tyler and her grieving parents stood at Brianna's front door hoping to slice out the rest of her heart with even more revelations.

Brianna drew up her shoulders, heaved a heavy sigh and motioned them inside to join this bizarre party. After all, half the townspeople had been here rounding up dogs in the half-light of early morning.

"You've missed the excitement," Brianna said flatly. "All of the dogs are back now." She saw Tyler flinch ever so slightly. Officer

Branson caught his reaction as well. "Everyone's gone home. But there's fresh coffee in the kitchen. You can join us there."

Without glancing at Jake, who stood beside her, she introduced the family to Officer Branson and led the group through the house into the kitchen.

As she recalled, Mrs. Rhodes had always been kind. She had seemed to genuinely like Brianna. Cassie Rhodes had welcomed her into their home, provided snacks, and had asked friendly questions. Mr. Rhodes had been the kind of father who would drive Tiffany anywhere she wanted to go at any time of the night. He never censured Tiffany for being out too late, or running around with the wrong crowd or getting into teenage scrapes. All was forgiven all the time.

Brianna had been a little jealous of Tiffany for having a family who took such loving care of her.

Not to slight her mother, but Karen had been focused on keeping a roof over their heads and providing for Brianna. There was little time for dealing with teenage angst and trouble. Brianna had been expected not to rock the boat and to get good grades. For the most part, she toed the line. Growing up, she'd never wanted undue attention and being a troublemaker would have brought all sorts of attention; all of it stressful.

The only time she'd felt daring was that night before the prom. Tiffany was bringing wine and some stronger liquor to the bleachers so Brianna could loosen up a bit before facing the crowd in the gym. But Tiffany wanted to do way more than see a loosened-up Brianna. Her so-called friend had wanted to sabotage her.

Something about what Jake said about the plan to humiliate her rang a bell of truth inside her and she believed him. Not that understanding Tiffany's twisted intentions changed what Brianna had done. She'd still kissed her friend's boyfriend. Still felt the guilt of that betrayal.

At the time, Brianna had believed in Tiffany's friendship, more than anything and she'd let Jake kiss her anyway. In fact, she'd kissed him back.

There may even have been a moan or two.

No matter now. She had other problems to deal with, namely another girlfriend of Jake Morrow's to contend with. Seriously, she thought, how could one man find himself hooked up with two nasty women in one relatively short lifetime?

Inexplicably, the Rhodes family, who had been through enough, had been caught up in this current drama too. After leading the group to the kitchen, Brianna spoke. "Please, Mrs. Rhodes, take a seat. Jake, please bring in a chair from the dining room for Mr. Rhodes."

"I'll stand," the older man responded and covered his wife's shoulder with his palm. It was a kind and loving gesture and, as she recalled, typical of the man. Brianna smiled at him and he crooked up a corner of his mouth in response.

"It's Cassie and Phil, Brianna," Tiffany's mother said with a soft smile. "Please."

Brianna nodded and offered them coffee, which they refused with nervous looks at each other.

Tyler gave her a brusque negative shake of his head. He'd ignored the offer of a seat and stood in the corner of the room, away from his parents.

"Let's get this over with," Tyler said with a chastened look at Jake.

"What brings you out here?" Officer Branson asked with more authority in her voice than Brianna thought warranted as the officer settled into a seat across the table from Tiffany's mom. She kept her pen at the ready for notes.

Cassie Rhodes reached across the table and took Brianna's fingers in hers. "We're here to apologize for Tyler's contribution to this whole mess. He lent our camper van to a new girlfriend and we didn't know what she planned to do."

Cassie glanced at Jake apologetically. "She came out here and let all the dogs free. We're sorry."

Tyler cleared his throat. "Yeah. I had no clue what she was up to."

"That's not all she's done," Brianna interjected. "She stole my laptop the night before last."

"I know," Tyler admitted, shamefaced.

The officer raised her eyebrows and put pen to notebook. She scribbled furiously and Brianna noted absently that it was in old-fashioned shorthand, the kind secretaries used decades ago.

"Why?" Brianna demanded of Tyler. "She didn't even take the power cord."

Tyler shrugged. "She wanted to read your book."

The answer surprised the entire table. "What? Why?"

"I dunno." Another shrug. "She just did. She never said what she read in there, but it made her real mad."

"But you wanted to get back at me for your sister's death and you knew Theda wanted to get at me as well," Jake threw in with a hard stare at Tyler. "I wasn't to blame for Tiffany doing what she did. I wasn't." The tone of his voice made Brianna think that this was the first time Jake believed that he wasn't completely to blame for what Tiffany had done that night. He flashed Brianna a look stunning in its ferocity.

Phil Rhodes straightened and looked Jake in the eye.

"We know," he said quietly. "It wasn't the first time Tiff threatened to harm herself when she wasn't getting her own way. She unbuckled her seat belt with me at least three times before that night. Twice, I held off giving in to her for so long, she had her hand on the door handle before I let her have her way."

"Tiffany had ways to get what she wanted and she wasn't above threats," Cassie added with tears filling her eyes. "She was a spirited girl," she said with all the love a mother could put into her voice. "My girl," she ended.

Officer Branson let the family talk as they filled in some blanks about why this vandalism was happening. Obviously, Theda had manipulated Tyler's grief to her own ends.

"Tyler had a hard time facing the truth," Phil continued brokenly. "She was his big sister and he thought the sun shone out of her. We encouraged their closeness. He never saw her at her worst, not really."

The officer stared at Cassie Rhodes, calculatingly. "You're saying your camper van was used without your knowledge in these two incidents here at Bowler's Rescue. Now, Theda Levi has use of your camper and that means she's able to stay anywhere out of sight in this van? It has a water tank and propane?"

Phil nodded. "She could last three or four days, maybe even a week if she's careful."

"Or she could leave the area altogether," Branson declared. "We'll put out an alert for the van. If you hear anything from Theda Levi, Tyler, you call the police. If you don't, I'll consider charges." The threat hung in the air as the family looked at each other with trepidation.

"I'll call. I promise."

Phil Rhodes cleared his throat. "Damned right he will." His wife nodded in full agreement.

"We'll see to it," she promised as well.

Brianna felt a pull of sympathy for Tiffany's parents. First, they'd lost their daughter and now this.

"I'll alert the State police," the officer said. "Meanwhile, I have to find out who Theda Levi really is."

"My friend, Grant Thomas, a former colleague is digging for information, too. I'll let you know if he unearths anything," Brianna promised.

Jake mentioned the state softball championship that Theda claimed to have won. "That's another place to look," he offered.

The officer leveled a steady look at Tyler. "Unless she told you her real name?"

"No, ma'am," he said. "She only ever called herself Theda."

BY NOON THE RHODES family and Officer Branson had cleared out. Brianna made certain to walk them out to their cars when they left. She hadn't wanted to be alone in the house with Jake.

In the driveway, she crouched in front of Beau, caressing his silky ears and staring into his soft brown eyes. Cowardly, yes, but she didn't have the strength not to reach for the comfort of Jake's arms. She needed a hug and Jake would give that to her and more, but she couldn't allow it. At near-collapse with all that had happened in the hours since she'd been woken by barking and baying, she was afraid if she accepted Jake's comfort, she'd never give it up.

"I'll go take down the signs by the highway," Jake offered from behind her shoulder. She startled at the sound of his voice.

How had he snuck up on her?

"I'm relieved everything worked out and we got all the dogs back," he added.

Brianna sniffed, surprised that she was near tears. "Me, too."

She should rise and thank him, but that would be temptation itself and she couldn't bear to give in. She stayed where she was, well out of harm's way and Jake's arms. "I hope the police find Theda before she does anything else."

Beau settled on his haunches, prepared to sit all day and have his ears stroked. He was such a baby.

"You should stay somewhere else for a few days." Jake's voice sounded tired and stressed. "I'm sorry I brought all this down on you."

"Don't," Brianna snapped, still aiming her words at the dog because she couldn't look at Jake. "None of this is your fault. You couldn't know how Theda would react."

"There were signs she was possessive."

Brianna blew out a huff of breath. "She's a stranger here. No one knows her or her background. Don't forget she's using a false name, so she wants no one to really know her, even you. The question is what is she hiding from?"

"The police will find out and then we'll all know," he said. "You've rubbed that dog's ears raw, but I take it I should leave now."

"Yes." She blinked. Hard.

"Just take my advice and stay with someone," he said as he turned to stalk off to his car.

"Maybe after my mom and Duncan come back," she said in a conversational tone to Beau. "They'll be home in a few days."

Beau rolled his eyes and moaned in pleasure.

"I'd be welcome to stay with Clay and Mercy, but they have their hands full with Dilly and Autumn."

Shandy would take her in, but she didn't want to involve her and her son in all this.

Wherever she went to stay, she should be alone. Elle's place would be perfect and Brianna already had a key. As soon as her mom got home, Brianna would move to the mobile. Duncan would be easy to convince to stay at the house. He seemed happy and content with how things were going with her mother. Brianna just had to get through the next few nights until they found Theda and figured out who she really was.

THREE NIGHTS LATER, right at the end of Jake's shift, one more call came in. "This better not be another false alarm," Doug muttered. "Pain in the ass all night long," he groused. Jake had to agree.

The station rallied and the trucks rolled, everyone tired and pissed off. Four false alarms in one night were malicious disruption of service. If a member of the public suffered because first responders were chasing their tails, then it was more than mischief, it was criminal.

"Hey, Jake," Doug said. "This is your address. Apparently, someone's choking and there's the smell of smoke in the air. You got anyone staying with you?"

"No. Dammit! This must be Theda," he said and grabbed his phone. When his call went to voicemail, he left a message for Officer Branson. Doug wound his way into Jake's subdivision. The neighbors were stepping outside in nightwear or work clothes to see what the commotion was about. Great, he'd be the talk of Welcome for weeks.

Branson returned Jake's call as they pulled to a stop. "I couldn't get to the phone," she said, and he realized she'd be getting ready for her day shift. "What do you need?"

"Theda's been giving us false alarms all night sending us on wild goose chases. This time it's at my house and I'm sure it's another false alarm. But at least we know it's her."

"How?" Her voice sounded distant like she was moving around the room and he was on speaker. "How can you be sure?"

"Because I'm looking at my house and it's plastered with eight by ten photos." He and Doug stood staring while the fire crew did their check. The crew sent him dark looks and he knew they'd demand answers when they got back to the station. After a while, a few weeks maybe, the jokes would start.

But Jake saw nothing funny in the photos or in Theda's behavior tonight.

Nothing funny at all.

"I'll meet you there in twenty," Officer Branson said, pulling him back to the conversation as she ended their call.

"Choking," he muttered. "There's no one choking. She knew damned well I'd be here for that. And the mention of smoke would bring out the fire crew." The only one in danger of choking today was Theda when he got his hands on her, he thought darkly fifteen minutes later. The front door and living room windows were covered in images of him looking at Brianna and Brianna looking back. The clapboard was spray-painted with foul language.

The pictures had been taken over the past week at various locations and sometimes he and Brianna were nowhere near each other. They weren't all images that showed affection, but sometimes Theda caught a mooning expression on his face. Those pictures had caused the most comments from the crew.

Some of the milder language went: "Get your personal life together, Morrow." His supervisor called with: "Deal with this or you'll be looking at disciplinary action." And from the fire captain: "Good thing you've already got the cops on this because I'd call them myself if you didn't."

The uniformed police officers that had responded to the 9-1-1 call stood with him as he waited for Officer Branson. "Theda must have been stalking both Brianna and me to get these photos."

"This security system will allow you to view your footage from your phone," the younger officer said.

"It's a brand new system. I forgot that feature." He'd been too angry to think of checking it out.

Officer Branson arrived a few minutes later and he showed her what he'd found on his phone. "There, see? Theda's disguised herself as a boy in a hoodie. Just at the edge of the frame, you can see her drop a bike to the ground and run up to the house with a sheaf of papers." She'd taped the pictures onto every glass surface but had used a spray can of red paint for all her other "artwork."

When Theda had finished, she pulled a phone out to make a call and then she sprayed the camera lens for good measure. "The call she made was to 9-1-1. I'd bet my life on it."

"You could be betting your life," Branson said sternly. "A woman fitting her description is wanted in Arizona, Iowa, and Nevada for assault and attempted murder. You need to get out of town for a few days. Somewhere she doesn't know about."

His world tilted on the words assault and attempted murder. "What? That can't be right."

The officer kept her face impassive and inside Jake thanked her for her calm and confident presence. He blinked and pulled his thoughts together. He knew people went off the rails. He just never expected it would happen with someone he knew. Not like this. He'd cared about Theda. Had let her into his life. He scrubbed his hands through his hair.

"I'd suggest a protection detail," Branson said. "But the budget's tight and it would take more time than I think you have to set it up." She frowned. "Frankly, I believe Theda is escalating and things may come to a head sooner than we think. Get yourself out of harm's way right now. But stay in touch."

"Can I go inside to get some gear?"

"Has the fire crew cleared the property so you can enter?"

He nodded.

"Then get in, get out and then let me know where you land. I'll keep you informed."

"YOU'RE COMING WITH me." Jake's voice had taken on a strained tone as his explanation about last night's and this morning's events wound down. It was barely seven fifteen and already Brianna could feel her heart pounding with distress over Jake's safety. He'd called only minutes before, waking her from a sound sleep. Sleep she'd badly needed. Here she stood, groggy and dressed in her rattiest robe again, vowing inwardly to toss it out as soon as Jake ended the call. What if he'd come over instead of calling?

"Wait," she said, as the rest of Jake's hasty explanation replayed in her foggy brain. She squared her shoulders, fully awake now, her pounding heart making caffeine unnecessary. "Did you say assault and attempted murder charges?"

"I did. Who knows what else she's done that no one's reported."

"You're sure it's Theda that has done all these things in other states?"

"Branson was certain enough that she told me to get out of town right now. She believes Theda is way past coming to her senses and will escalate faster than we think. There's no way to be one hundred percent sure, but we've got to believe the worst at this point. No foolish chances."

A chill ran through her chest at his words and she took no satisfaction in being right about men being abused and denying it. "Regardless, I'm staying at Elle's. The place is empty. I can stay until this business with Theda is cleared up. They'll find her soon and life will go back to normal."

"I don't want my life to go back to the way it was." His tone had gone husky and thick and she knew his heart was talking. She closed her eyes and held her breath for a few beats. It wouldn't do to listen to Jake's heart.

"Officer Branson wants you to leave town, but I can't go." And certainly not with Jake. Plus she didn't believe she was Theda's main target. No, Theda wanted to get back at Jake for breaking up with her. Brianna had had no part in that.

"You can't or won't go with me?" he sighed against her ear and she could almost feel his moist, heated breath against her skin. *Jake was in danger and she was giving him a hard time.*

"I doubt Theda knows the double-wide is at the back of Clay's property." Hidden by a huge hedge of cedars, Elle's place couldn't be seen from the road and it was situated on the back half of Clay's large lot. "I'll tell my mom she and Duncan should stay at a hotel."

"Branson let me pack a bag and gather my stuff, but I'm not leaving town, not if you won't come with me. Besides, we're short-staffed and I need to be here for work."

"How can you think of going to work when you're being stalked by a woman who's been violent in at least three other states? Your supervisor will give you time off." She spoke firmly, but it was a lost cause. Jake would never abandon his job when Welcome's citizens needed him.

"I didn't ask for leave or vacation. He's pushing me out the door, in fact, he used the same words you just did, but — listen—I can't keep talking about this on the phone. I'm coming out there." And he hung up.

Chapter Twenty-three

JUST AS JAKE HUNG UP, Brianna heard a sound that made her half-jump out of her skin. The back door had opened. Then she heard voices, one male and one female.

Her mother was home with Duncan.

She slipped her phone into her pocket and braced herself for filling her mom in on everything. But before she could change into a nicer robe to join the new arrivals, her mom burst into her room and threw her arms around her.

Brianna hadn't been squeezed like this since she was seven and had taken a header off her bike. Still, she squeezed back and clung for a moment. Relief was spelled M O M.

Her heart twisted and Brianna leaned back and basked in the comfort and the love and the very sturdiness of her mother's devotion.

"It's okay, Mom. I'm okay, really."

Duncan cleared his throat from the hallway. "She didn't sleep a wink last night fretting about everything going on here. We got up at three and started driving." He gave them a hesitant smile and all her reservations about Duncan Starling fell away. This man was good for her mother.

"You're home a day early, I didn't expect you, but I'm glad you're here." Now when she left to stay at Elle's the house here wouldn't be empty.

"My daughter's in danger and you expect me to stay away?" Karen said with a sigh. "Fat chance."

"Let me get dressed," Brianna said, "and you get the coffee on." Her mom needed something other than fear to focus on and Brianna needed time to gather her thoughts. She didn't want to scare her mother, but Karen would insist on the whole story. "Jake's on his way out here."

After they met in the kitchen and settled into their seats with steaming mugs of coffee in their hands, Brianna couched the whole story in gentle terms. She didn't use the phrases "crazed bitch," or "maniac," or "attempted murder charges."

"Theda is hiding in the bush somewhere in the Rhodes's family camper van, riding some kid's bike all over town and taping pictures of you and Jake Morrow and, just for good measure, spray painting filth on the walls of his house?" her mother summed up.

"And she came here to cause you grief," Duncan added. "That's what I hate about this. You're more vulnerable than Jake and the dogs might never have been found." He looked like he wanted to growl.

"That woman is a dangerous you-know-what," her mom said with a decisive nod. "What is Jake doing now? He's on his way over, right?"

If Brianna protested that she wasn't privy to Jake's decisions and that they were no more than old acquaintances, her mom would know for certain that Brianna's high school crush was back in full force.

It was ridiculous to go backward in life. It was time to set the past aside and move ahead. Move on. Go forward. Think of her future. The thoughts hummed in the back of her brain while Duncan and her mother discussed if Duncan should stay in the house with her mother or not.

It was a very short discussion.

Duncan won, but Karen looked content with the outcome.

One strong knock on the kitchen door announced Jake's arrival. He opened the door and walked in without an invitation. Brianna shook her head at his presumption. Duncan cocked an eyebrow, but Karen pointed to a cupboard. "Mugs are in there, help yourself."

He waved his hand in dismissal. "Need sleep more than coffee." He still wore his uniform.

"Have you just gotten off work?" Karen asked. His eyes were rid-rimmed with exhaustion.

"Theda called in four false alarms. The last one was my place. She must have ridden all over town on the bike to make herself a nuisance. We thought we were done with the wild goose chases by five a.m. but no, she took about an hour taping the photos up and spray-painting my place. Her last call was just before the end of our shift."

"Sit down, man, before you fall down," Duncan said, in male sympathy. "So, every call meant a full complement? Fire, police, and ambulance?"

"Yes, she said exactly the right things to get us all out every time. Everyone's pissed. She made her point on the last call though. It was all about me." He shook his head in disgust and sat heavily. "Branson's convinced I need to leave town. But we're short-staffed for the time being and I'm not going."

"Where will you stay?" Duncan asked. He shot Brianna a look.

"With me at Elle's," Brianna blurted without thinking it through. "It's perfect. Theda probably doesn't even know the house is back there. I'll be close to home, but out of the way and Jake can come and go quietly."

"Are there alternate routes to get here?" Duncan asked.

Jake nodded without looking at Brianna. "I could take a different route every time. There are several cross streets."

Her mom nodded and made a sound of assent. "Good choice. With Duncan here, I won't be alone and I'd feel better knowing my daughter wasn't by herself either."

"You both should stay at a hotel," Brianna said to Karen and Duncan.

Her mother shook her head. "Theda will know for certain everyone's gone into hiding. With Brianna out of the house, she won't bother with us here." She gave Duncan a look that said not to argue, but there was no need. Duncan was nodding in agreement. "I'll also put it on the grapevine that you've left town for job interviews," her mom continued. "I'll say you're staying with friends in Tacoma and Seattle. Word'll get around."

Brianna glanced at Jake. His lips firmed as the plan came together. "I'm in," he said in a brisk tone. "Now, show me where I'm sleeping."

And there it was, decided. No matter how they might have tried to stay apart, no matter how much Theda wanted them apart, Brianna would be sharing quarters with Jake Morrow.

Fate had an ironic sense of humor.

"I'll give you the key," Brianna said and went to get it out of her purse under the bed in her room. She'd been paranoid since the break-in and kept important things hidden.

As she moved through the house she realized the sleeping arrangements at Elle's place could be interesting. When she returned to the kitchen she decided to use a no-nonsense tone.

Afraid to brush Jake's fingers if he reached for the key, she set Elle's house key on the table carefully.

"You take the boys' room and I'll take Jorja's," she said. "She sleeps in the master suite and has an ensuite bathroom. That way we have our own rooms and each have a bathroom." Elle slept in the third and smallest bedroom because she believed growing children needed more room than she did. And for a short time, Jorja had shared the larger room with a baby foster sister.

Jake picked up the key from the table as a yawn overtook him.

He'd just had a long, hard shift with his personal life splashed all over the fire station and his neighborhood. He and Theda would be the talk of Welcome for months unless the police caught her soon, Brianna thought with some sympathy. Jake needed a break and some peace and a good day's sleep. Brianna's heart squeezed with everything he'd been through.

If she knew Jake at all, she understood he'd feel terrific guilt over Theda's actions.

"I'll be quiet when I come over with my things," she vowed. "I'll write in the living room and then unpack after you get up for work." She wasn't sure she could order her thoughts for writing, but she had to try. Time was running out and soon she'd have to get serious about making an income. "This will only be for a day or two. The police will find Theda and that will be the end of all this vandalism and petty revenge."

With a grateful nod, Jake left as quickly as he'd arrived.

Karen and Duncan exchanged a look that made Brianna slam the coffee carafe back onto the burner. "What?"

"Nothing. It's just that Jake seemed like he had more to say," her mother commented in a leading tone.

"Maybe so, but whatever he wants to talk about is for my ears, not yours." But she wondered, too, how much more Jake had to say about this insane situation. "What are you hearing on your gossip highway?"

"Theda has Tyler Rhodes wrapped around her finger and if he's not careful he'll be the next one she ensnares."

Brianna dismissed the idea. Tyler lived at home with his parents. Theda wouldn't want that. But she'd certainly used him for the use of his parents' van. Thankfully, that source of help had already dried up. "She's running out of options in Welcome and I think she'll leave soon. She could already be gone. She must know how serious it is to call in false emergencies. And four in one night is excessive."

"Everyone in town knows about her letting the dogs out. That escapade has cost her, as well," Karen said with a brisk nod.

Brianna stilled inside, a little shocked at the inference. "Are you saying some people were okay with her breaking Jake's windows? Wasn't that enough to turn people against her?" Maybe they thought it was nothing more than a lovers' spat. Some people may have thought the whole thing amusing and not in the least serious.

"Jake has been surly for years and thinks he's above everybody else in town," Karen explained. "He's always been that way. He has no friends and rarely speaks to anyone he went to school with."

"He has his reasons," she responded, appalled that his self-imposed emotional exile would be taken as some twisted form of snobbery.

Karen sniffed. "It's strange," her mom continued, "because he was so popular in school. Everyone liked him then." Her mother's cocked eyebrow meant she wanted more details, but the effect on Jake after Tiffany's death was not her story to tell.

The need to defend Jake welled, but she refrained. He was a grown man and didn't need her defending his friendliness or lack of it.

"Not my place to say," Duncan interjected, "but Jake seems like the kind of man to carry things inside. I've seen it before. Men shut down and think they can handle their burdens by shoving them deep. Not always the best course."

Karen reared her head back and stared at him. "And where did you pick up this gem?"

"I served and saw it myself. The quiet guys suffered the most." Then he rose and helped himself to a second mug of coffee, effectively ending his contribution to the conversation.

"Thanks, Duncan. You guessed right." Brianna left the kitchen to get her essentials for a couple of nights at Elle's. With Jake.

Chapter Twenty-four

"MERCY OFFERED ME A security service," Brianna said as she poured Jake a mug of coffee. "In Hollywood, she knows people who have been under siege by stalkers and paparazzi, so she knows where to get help." Morning for Jake today was two p.m. She'd been at Elle's for hours, writing and plotting her book while he slept.

"I bet Mercy knows lots of people in that position," Jake replied with a brisk scrub of his hand across his face. He'd just risen from a deep sleep and stood, bare-chested and with his jeans yanked up but unzipped. He'd stumbled out into the kitchen looking adorably confused. For a moment Brianna had wondered if he'd remembered coming to Elle's place to sleep. But he'd caught sight of her and grinned; full-on with all defenses down.

Adorable.

"But I said we didn't need a security detail. That would feel weird, wouldn't it? We'd look outside only to see a black SUV with a burly bald man doing a crossword puzzle while keeping half an eye on the trees for Theda." She'd added a whole new chapter in rough draft and surprised herself with a few twists in the plot. One of which was a character exactly like the one she just described. She smiled at Jake, pleased with herself.

Jaye, the heroine, had turned into a kick-ass woman who learned what she needed to learn as she went. She took self-defense classes for hand to hand fighting. Jaye had learned how to hide in plain sight, how to read body language, and how to lure her stalker into a trap. Brianna felt good about the story and even happy with the romantic hero. Not that Jaye actually *needed* a hero, but the romance added a certain zing to the plot.

223

Jake's eyes widened as she ended her wild little speech. "You are a writer. Quite an imagination you have there." He brushed her fingers as he accepted the mug of coffee, making her wish she'd set the mug down on the counter so he could pick it up without shooting sparks of sexual energy through her.

She wasn't going to make it through this time with Jake unscathed. Worse, she wasn't sure she wanted to. Maybe she needed a good scathing. Maybe she should be scathed from head to toe. Or, she could do the scathing. As she thought about it, her tongue itched and her insides melted.

He blew air across his coffee twice then tested it with his lips. Reassured he wouldn't be scalded, he took a tentative sip.

"This is great. Thanks." His mouth stretched wide and his shoulders sank into a comfortable stance as he leaned against the counter. She mimicked his posture beside him.

Shoulder to shoulder with Jake, Brianna felt at peace for the first time in days. For now, here, they could be themselves and the rough edges inside her smoothed out. She'd been uncomfortable for so long, it felt strange to stand in perfect harmony with Jake Morrow. "This is nice, Jake. We don't need to wear our masks around other people."

"I know it's been hard for you since we started talking again," he said companionably. "People in Welcome speculate and have long memories. They like to believe the worst." He took a long drink and then set his mug on the counter and crossed his arms over his bare chest. "I've kept myself apart from old friends and classmates and I can't blame them for thinking I'm an ass."

"The people you've helped don't think that. I've seen lots of people wave to you and you wave back."

"Really? When?" He cocked his head toward her, one eyebrow raised.

When? For all the time she'd been in Welcome. Every time she'd seen him from across the street or through a window or driving by. But admitting she watched for him seemed creepy now, given their circumstances with Theda. "Oh, just around town." She gave him a vague wave.

"You watched me?"

She shifted her shoulders. "I noticed whenever you were around. It's not the same thing as *watching*."

It really creeped her out to think of all the photos Theda had taken of her while she was oblivious. She gave herself a mental shake. "I'm glad I haven't seen all the photos she took of me and you. And us. It's disturbing that I didn't even know it was happening."

"Me, neither. If I'd known I'd have reported it."

"She hid her true nature from everyone." She stared at the wall. "It's her fault, not ours." *This time.*

"I watched you, too," he confessed. "Every time you loaded up with dog food or ran into the credit union, or walked into the bakery. Just seeing you go about your day, here in Welcome, made me smile."

She straightened. "In front of Theda?"

"I guess..." He looked inwards, trying to recall.

"So she knew before we did that we..." she trailed off because she couldn't come up with the right words.

"Still have feelings for each other?" Jake supplied exactly the right words. "She must have," he said.

Brianna took two steps away and turned to him. He took a step, too. When their chests bumped she put her arms around him and he drew her in close and tight. "Brianna. Don't ask me to let you go. Not now."

She shook her head no and then set it to rest against his shoulder. He rocked her in his arms and held her tight.

"I feel safe here with you," she whispered. Warmth and want eased through her body as Jake held her. "What a mess we've made of things."

"You *are* safe with me. You always have been." He tilted his head and put a fingertip to her chin. "Look at me."

She raised her lashes to see him staring hard into her eyes. "We were kids kissing under the bleachers. It happens every day. I didn't plan it and neither did you. After she hassled me all night about me ruining her plans for you, I told Tiffany the truth. I liked you. I don't know why she wanted to humiliate you, but she did. I couldn't stomach the idea. When I told her how I felt about you after prom, Tiffany flipped out. End of story." He firmed his lips, looking hard. "No one could have predicted what happened."

"And now?"

"One look at you when you returned to Welcome made me see I'd been dragging my heels about Theda. We never suited each other." He shrugged. "She needed a place to crash and regroup and I wanted to help her out. That doesn't make for a real relationship. She's confused and alone and messed up for reasons we'll never fully know."

Brianna nodded. "I feel bad for her." But being held in Jake's arms was Heaven on earth. No wonder Theda couldn't let go.

"Don't feel sorry for her. She's been violent. Assault and attempted murder charges are serious." He held Brianna close and set his chin next to her ear. "If you see her or even feel someone's eyes on you get somewhere safe. Better yet, don't be alone today. I can't bear the thought of you being scared or feeling threatened."

"Maybe we should take Mercy up on her offer of a security team." She'd do it if it made Jake feel better about leaving her. He needed the distraction of work and if Theda was still lurking, she'd know where he was. She'd focus on him and would likely be caught sooner. "Maybe the police can cruise by the fire station more often."

"I'm sure they will when I let Branson know I'm not going anywhere but to work. She's confident they'll find Theda quickly," he responded with certainty. "She's the object of a statewide manhunt. Now that they know who they're after, they understand her tricks. We just have to hang tight."

He pulled back and searched her eyes. "Call Mercy right away. You should have extra protection."

Brianna nodded. "Okay. I wish you wouldn't go to work, but I think you want to somehow draw Theda out."

A surprised look flashed across his handsome features. But just as quickly he covered it. "We're shorthanded," he said. "That's all." He gave her a nod. "Doug will be with me. And if it's a quiet shift I won't have to leave the station much. And if I do and Theda shows up, we'll have her."

"The police will be watching you and will show up at every call?"

"Yes. Every first responder in town knows what's happening and what she looks like." His stomach growled and he patted it. "Do we have anything but coffee in this place?"

"Elle said to help ourselves. The fridge is stocked and the cupboards are full." She opened a cupboard to have a look. "Here's some chocolatey cereal. But you need something more substantial if you're going to work." She wished he wouldn't go. She'd like to spend the rest of the afternoon with him. Alone.

He opened the fridge. "Bacon and eggs," he said, happily. "I'll make." He rummaged around and pulled out a block of cheese. "Scrambled."

Instead of spending time doing what she'd like to be doing, Brianna settled for watching Jake work in Elle's kitchen, which involved a lot of cupboard searching and delighted discovery as he found everything he needed.

"Settle in, sweetheart, and you'll soon be eating my world-famous scrambled eggs deluxe."

"World famous? Have you been written up in some fancy cooking magazine?"

"Absolutely. But I will carry this recipe to the grave." The whole effect turned hilarious when he lifted his wooden spoon over his head and a glop of half-cooked egg landed on his shoulder.

Brianna burst into laughter and as Jake's gaze found hers, the laughter died away, replaced by sudden awareness. Silence descended until the egg slid farther down his shoulder, pulling Jake's attention away. He grabbed a dishtowel and, with a sheepish grin, gave his shoulder a wipe.

Brianna mentally shook herself and searched for plates and cutlery. "Scrambled eggs wait for no man," she said.

As it turned out, his secret ingredient was a quick shake of dried parsley. "For color," he said with a grin. She passed him the cheese she'd grated and watched as he stirred it into the eggs.

"I wrote a whole new chapter this morning and then had lunch with Mom and Duncan." She caught his intake of breath. "Don't worry, I was careful not to go where Theda might see me. I hopped the fence. It can't be seen from the road. Besides, Theda's not watching for me. Mom has let people know that I've left town for job interviews."

Jake dished up and they ate and talked of mundane things, just like normal people. Except breakfast was at three in the afternoon and they were in hiding from a violent stalker.

"I also kept the blinds closed all day."

"Good."

But half of her said keeping the blinds closed meant they were literally blind in the house and wouldn't see Theda coming if she found them. She kept that thought to herself. Why rattle the man when he was heading off to work, leaving her alone?

"Promise you'll go to dinner with Karen and Duncan."

"Yes." She glanced at the kitchen. "After I clean up your mess," she said with a grin. The warmth in Jake's gaze brought hope to life.

"I wish things were normal for us. Just once," he said. "I want to be with you when we don't have a dark cloud overhead. Any minute now we could be picked up and blown apart by a tornado."

"A tornado named Theda."

Chapter Twenty-five

JAKE WATCHED BRIANNA pop the last bite of bacon into her mouth as she razzed him about the mess he'd left in the kitchen. "Some people don't appreciate the cook," he quipped just to see her eyes lift and her smile fill them. They hadn't had many moments like this; light, fun, and flirtatious.

He wanted to flirt with Brianna. He wanted to make her laugh and wanted to kiss her senseless. Just wanted her.

But none of that would happen again if Theda got to either of them. He bit back another request for her to leave Welcome with him. She'd never agree.

In too short a time, duty called and Jake left Brianna with her mother and Duncan. Jake liked the man. He'd promised not to leave the women on their own and his steady gaze had reassured Jake.

Brianna had taken a call from Mercy who reported that a security team was on the way. Jake agreed with Brianna that Theda likely believed Brianna had left town, but it was better to be safe than stupid. It went against the grain to ask for help, especially since he'd done everything he could in this town to be left alone, but he'd set aside his pride for Brianna. Hell, he would set his whole life aside for her.

He loved her.

The feeling washed over him as he pulled into a parking spot behind the fire station. He shut off the ignition but kept his hands squeezed on the wheel.

Parking; such a mundane thing to be doing when your whole life changed. He stared at his hands on the steering wheel and then turned his gaze to the rearview mirror.

That guy. The guy reflected in the glass loved Brianna Bowler with every beat of his heart.

He loved Brianna and he'd do whatever it took to keep her safe, from Theda, and from any other threat to her happiness.

He should have stayed with her, but even as he thought it, he heard the sound. A call on the speaker inside. He jumped out of his car and ran into the station, keeping close to the wall to avoid the fire rig already pulling out. Doug was tossing a mug of coffee into the sink. "It's their call," he said, "so far."

But they jumped to get ready in case they were needed. Moments later they knew the call was a brush fire out by the highway. Easily handled and no more support needed. Jake and Doug relaxed into their routine duties.

All the while they worked quietly, he thought about Brianna and what to do about his feelings. He was pretty sure she wanted something with him. She'd kissed him goodbye after he'd made breakfast and she'd let him hold her as they'd talked today. There hadn't been time for more and he doubted she'd have given him more anyway.

He understood her reluctance to become physical. Brianna wanted him to be totally free of Theda before they took their feelings to bed.

He got it, he did. But that didn't make the want go away.

Still, he had a teenage boy inside him who'd seen Brianna run off in tears that time under the bleachers. That terrible awful time he'd messed up all their lives: Brianna's, Tiffany's, her parents, and Tyler's. And his own.

BRIANNA SENT OUT A group text to Mercy, Elle, and Shandy.
Brianna: We need to talk in person.

Shandy: Man trouble? Or that lunatic?

Brianna: Man...

Mercy: Jake? What's he done other than P.O.ing the lunatic?

Elle: What part of in person don't you 2 get? I'll be back in an hour. That soon enough Brianna?

Mercy: LOL Yes, I get it – Meet here – you do recall I have a newborn, right?

Shandy: Man trouble, the best kind, unless it's your ex. LOL

Brianna: I love you all! See you in an hour...

The idea that Elle would take time from her brand new marriage and Mercy would host this girls' chat time spoke volumes about their friendship. Brianna was touched and so, so happy that she'd connected with these women.

If she stayed in Welcome she'd have these friends close by for every major milestone in her future. Couldn't get much better than that.

An hour later, Brianna walked into Mercy's living room to find a radiant Elle holding a sleeping Autumn while Shandy and Mercy looked on. She leaned in for a peek. Sweet Autumn had already changed a bit. "She's so perfect," Brianna whispered, feeling a rush of something maternal. Yearning? Maybe.

For a minute or two, four women stood gazing and cooing at the little bundle of love.

"How was your honeymoon?" Brianna asked Elle.

Elle looked to where Dilly was busy with a couple of baby dolls by the fireplace. "Hot. Sexy. Wonderful." Elle kept her voice low while she beamed with happiness.

Brianna sighed. "You and Logan deserve every joy." She hugged her friend. "I'm so happy for you."

Mercy chuckled. "Right, we're all thrilled, but Elle and Logan are old news now. What's Jake done?"

Brianna chewed her lower lip, and then all resistance to sharing fled. She needed to talk this out. "He's making me think we may have a future, but I'm not so sure. We've been thrown together in this mess with Theda and what we're feeling could be the anxiety around the situation."

Elle frowned as she accepted a mug of tea from Mercy. "And residual feelings from your time before. You liked him in high school. Has he changed so much that your feelings have changed?"

"I don't trust that our feelings are real and strong enough to go beyond this threat. I guess." She frowned, confused. But *her* feelings were strong even before Theda acted out. And Jake had admitted earlier that as soon as he'd seen Brianna, he'd felt ready to finally end things with Theda. All of those feelings were still inside them both. "Theda seemed to catch on that Jake and I still cared about each other, even before we did."

Shandy looked up from Autumn's sleeping face. "Then why doubt yourselves? Jake's wild about you and has been for years. This Theda girl never stood a chance with him. Not really." She carried the sleeping baby to a cradle in the living room and set her in it. "Justin's told me many times that Jake wondered aloud about you over the years. He'd check you out on social media once in a while and tell Justin what was new with you."

"Really? He never made contact." She'd have responded if he had. But then, Jake had ignored all his old friends from school who still lived in Welcome. All but Justin. "Was Justin the one who kept up their friendship?"

Shandy nodded. "He never gave up, not even when Jake told him outright to leave him alone. He wanted to punish himself for Tiffany I think."

"By denying himself the comfort of friends." She nodded and thought about all that Jake had given up in penance. "I think he's punished himself enough."

All three of the other women nodded.

"Jake wanted more than conversation almost right away," she admitted. "But I insisted that he clear things with Theda first. Jake went to Theda to clear the air. They met in the park downtown and that's when things got really strange."

"But she had already smashed his windows," Shandy pointed out.

"And stolen your laptop," Mercy said with a slight shudder of revulsion.

"I shouldn't have told him to sort out his mess with Theda before we could, um..."

"I'd say spare us the details, but we all know that won't happen," Elle teased. "Have you slept with him yet?"

"No."

"Kissed him?" Mercy asked.

"Yes."

"Confided things? Because that's a big one in relationships. I miss that part of being with someone," Shandy admitted. "I wear my big girl panties every day, but at night I'd like to share my troubles." She shook her head and waved at Brianna to go on.

Elle gave Shandy a surprised look but said nothing in response to Shandy's vague admission.

"Yes, Jake and I have confided things," Brianna said after an awkward pause where Mercy shared a significant look with Elle and Shandy seemed lost in thought. "I think we trust each other that way. I know I trust Jake with my baggage. And he trusts me." After all, they shared the guilt of that night with Tiffany.

Shandy scooped Autumn up into her arms as if she needed a cuddle.

They all took seats at the kitchen table and suddenly Brianna saw her mother at the window. She rose to let Karen in.

"I had to come over here to say this." Her mom frowned with worry. "But I don't know if it's any help or just me being paranoid."

She settled herself at the table and ran her fingers through her hair in agitation. "But I like word games and puzzles and seeing that we can't find out who Theda really is, I wondered if there was a clue in the false name she chose." She looked from woman to woman, her brows lowered in a deep frown. "I just figured out that Theda Levi is an anagram for Evil Death. That's why she's so damned hard to find anything on. She hasn't stolen an identity, she made one up."

"What?" Four voices at once; all in shock.

Karen nodded and after checking that Dilly was nowhere near, repeated, "Evil Death."

Shandy hugged Autumn close, her eyes wide while the baby stirred sleepily.

Mercy stood and went from window to window closing the blinds. Elle stared wide-eyed at Karen.

Cold crept to the end of every one of Brianna's limbs. "I'll call Officer Branson," she said. "Right now." She doubted it would help, but maybe Theda had created other names too. She made the call. "It's a creepy choice for a name, don't you think?" She asked the officer after filling her in.

"It's another thing to look for," the officer responded briskly. "Another piece of her puzzle. Let me know when your security team shows up. I'll want the license plate number, make and model of their vehicle and their description."

"Will do. Thanks." Brianna ended the call and felt good about having extra security when she saw her mother's stricken face.

"Officer Branson didn't say if they're close to finding her?" Her mother asked.

Brianna shook her head. "If they don't have their hands on her there's nothing to report."

"Mommy, you hold Autumn," Dilly said clearly as she came to stand by Mercy. She wore a frown and her soft brown eyes held everyone's attention as they glared at Shandy. "You don't hold my sister," she said. "Only Mommy and Daddy and me."

Shandy smiled kindly at her. "I see. I'll pass her to your mommy then. Thank you for telling me."

A quick glance at Mercy told Brianna something had happened to bring moisture to her friend's gaze. "Dilly has been hearing everyone talk about me being Mommy," Mercy said with awe. "I guess my big girl wants to call me that, too."

Dilly gave one emphatic nod and suddenly Mercy was no longer Auntie, but Mommy and the room erupted into smiles and sighs. Once her little sister was settled in Mercy's arms again, Dilly went to play by the window.

Karen's eyes searched the group of women's faces. With the sixth-sense she was known for she zeroed in on Shandy. "And your ex has been around more than usual. What's happening there?"

Shandy widened her eyes in innocence. "He wants more time with Josh. He's growing so fast and Justin misses a lot by living in California."

"Do you think he wants Josh to move with him?" Karen asked. Brianna flashed her mom a grim expression for mentioning the delicate subject. It would kill Shandy if Josh opted for Justin over her.

"I'm not sure," Shandy muttered vaguely. "I can't see Justin doing that. He's never been cruel and he'd have a battle on his hands." Shandy's distress soured the room. Brianna couldn't comment because she didn't know Shandy's ex-husband. But, Jake did and she made a mental note to ask him what kind of man Justin was.

"I'll ask Jake for his opinion."

"Don't. He'll tell Justin that I'm thinking the worst and that'll only make things harder."

Karen rose and moved to run her hand comfortingly over Shandy's back. "He could be hanging around to try to reconcile. Have you considered that?"

"Absolutely not. He's never been one to change his mind once his course is set." Shandy gave Karen a determined look. "And neither am I." She moved her shoulders as if to loosen a burden. "He wants to spend Christmas in Welcome."

Elle frowned. "That's good though, right?"

When Shandy glared at her, Elle backtracked with a shake of the head. "I guess not. I shouldn't offer an opinion because I have no experience with men who come back. My exes left me and never wanted to try again."

"Stop talking about Justin wanting to try again, or come back. He doesn't want that. He doesn't want *me*." The breath Shandy drew in sounded shaky.

In the distance, dogs barked. A lot of them.

"I had no idea you could hear the dogs this clearly," Karen said. "It sounds like they're all barking at once." She turned her head, but the blinds had been closed. She got to her feet.

Dilly lifted the blind nearest her and pressed her face to the window. "There's black air outside. Maybe that's why Beau is here. He doesn't like it."

Dilly turned fearful eyes to Mercy. "Beau's scared!"

Brianna went to the door and opened it for a better look. Her heart leapt to her throat at what she saw. "Beau's running through the cedar hedge and there's smoke coming from Elle's place!" She grabbed her phone and called 9-1-1 with the bizarre thought that the dispatcher would probably know her voice by now.

Dilly started to wail. "Mommy, I'm scared."

"Get the children away from here," Elle said brusquely. "Go to town. It's been a dry summer and fire season is far from over. I'll get the garden hose. We'll stay here and try to wet down the roof if we can. The mobile will burn fast and if the trees catch, the fire will want this house, too."

But Mercy was already on the move with Autumn in her arms, reaching for the diaper bag, her purse, and ushering Dilly calmly but firmly toward the front of the house. "We'll go out this way, Dilly. Take your Hunny Bunny with you so we can sleep at Grammy's tonight if we have to."

"I'm going out there to see what's happening," Brianna said to no one in particular, but the 9-1-1 operator heard her.

"No, don't go near the fire, we have help on the way."

But Brianna was drawn outside, lured by the need to know how the fire started. *Was Theda back there right now?* Karen followed close behind with Elle and Shandy.

"Brianna, don't go back there. Theda could be waiting for you," Elle hissed the words.

Elle, good to her word, went for the garden hose. "Don't be a fool, Brianna. Stay clear."

But Brianna had to see. "I can't stay here doing nothing."

"Then the least you can do is crouch," Shandy said. "Stay down and be the smallest target you can be." Brianna and her mother took her advice and crouched low as they ran toward the cedars that separated the front from the back of the lot. For a flash, Brianna realized that these women had her back. They'd brave fire for her.

As she would for them.

While she moved, Karen used Shandy's phone to call Duncan and asked him to get the dogs to safety. Luckily a couple of the volunteers were still there. "Just get them loaded into the cars and we'll all wait for the fire department before we move the dogs. No, I'm staying with Brianna until this is settled." She listened for a moment. "Come over to Clay's to spray down the roof, that'll help." She disconnected and passed the phone back to Shandy. "He'll be over in a few minutes."

Brianna's adrenalin ran high, burbling and rushing over her muscles and through her veins. Her brain misfired with fear, but she kept panic at bay by reminding herself the building was empty and no lives were at stake.

At least not yet.

Chapter Twenty-six

AT THE STATION, THE next call came in at five-forty. Fire and paramedics required. Jake and Doug rolled out with the fire truck close behind. "The address is Clay Foster's," Jake said with a frown. Cold terror threatened to overwhelm him. "But it's not Clay's house, it must be the mobile out back." He radioed the fire rig and explained about the mobile home on the back half of the lot. "The house should be empty," he explained into the handset, fighting panic.

"Dispatch says there's a woman inside. There are witnesses."

Jake swore hard, his voice raw with fear. "Step on it. That could be Brianna." She was supposed to be with her mother and Duncan, safe at their place.

It was Doug's turn to swear. "Is this Theda's doing?"

"Likely." But after he said it, his detached, professional side shut down and Jake white-knuckled the now-quiet handset all the way out to Clay's. "Of course this is Theda."

The only difference with this vengeful act was she did it in daylight. But maybe it took this long for her to figure out where Brianna and he were staying. She probably thought they were lovers now. The idea must have put her over the edge and into a murderous rage.

Had she killed with fire before? Did she know what she was doing with accelerants or would she botch the job as so many did?

When they arrived at Clay's, the driveway was clear of vehicles. "It looks like Mercy got the children away," Jake said with relief.

Doug pulled to a stop a safe distance from the fiery mobile behind the fire rig. "They burn too damned fast," Jake yelled as he ran toward the heat and smoke, uncaring about Doug and the equipment.

He had to see, he had to get there in time.

He had to save her.

Black smoke billowed and flames licked the walls, black, and orange. Orange and black, the exterior starting to melt from the intense heat. The fire crew was busy soaking the trees, determined to contain the fire to this one building.

As Jake drew close, no one saw his approach. He thought he heard a scream from inside, but there'd be no air to scream with, would there? He jumped onto the front stoop and then wrenched open the door.

He saw a nightmare inside; a body, prone and unmoving on the floor near the kitchen table, clutching something close.

"Brianna!" He screamed while firemen pulled at his arms to prevent him from entering hell.

"There's nothing you can do, Jake. She's gone." The voice through the mask sounded alien; the words nonsensical. Strong hands tugged at his arms and he cried out her name again.

"We have to let the structure go and focus on keeping the fire from spreading. Jake, are you with me?" He felt a hard, determined shake.

"Yes, I understand." But all he wanted was to walk into the flames and lie down beside Brianna.

"Jake! Jake! I'm here!"

He turned at the sound of a woman's voice and saw her then, well back from the flames, flanked by her mother and Elle and Shandy. The pit bull Brianna loved so much paced back and forth in front of the group as if to keep them well out of harm's way.

And then Jake knew whose body he'd seen on the kitchen floor. *Theda.*

It was over. For her and for them.

"I'm okay," he said to the firefighter holding him and dashed toward the clutch of people watching the place go up in flames.

He grabbed Brianna and she grabbed him back. He slammed his lips onto hers, taking, teasing, loving. He ran his hands up and down her arms to be sure, absolutely certain that she was all right. "She didn't hurt you?"

"No, I'm fine I promise. We saw her, Jake. Through the window. I couldn't believe she'd stay in there, but she did. She had time to get out, I swear."

"She chose to die like that?"

"Yes."

They clung to each other, safe and glad and sorry all at the same time. The noise around them faded as the firefighters soaked the trees and what was left of the building.

LATER THAT NIGHT, IN Jake's living room, Brianna clung to Jake again, much as she had during those terrible moments after he'd been dragged away from the burning home. "When you ran to the door and wrenched it open I knew what you were doing."

"I thought you were in there. When I saw...I saw...her body in the kitchen..."

"Shh, it's all right. I'm here with you and we're both okay." He'd have died to get to her and bring her out to safety.

Jake Morrow would give his life for her and she didn't know how to handle the knowledge. So she kissed him and held him tight. The fire investigation was in the early stages, but it was clear what had happened. Theda had sprinkled gas or something like it around the living area and then dropped a match, setting the place ablaze.

An hour ago when word got out around town about the fire, Denise Jones came forward and admitted telling Theda about the home at the back of Clay's lot and that Elle was living there. As the school's administration clerk Denise had handled registering Elle's children so she knew about the second house on the property. She swore it had been innocent gossip, nothing more. Denise was known for spreading rumors her whole life so no one was surprised at her revelation, least of all Officer Branson.

It was no secret that Logan and Elle were away on a short honeymoon. It would have taken seconds for Theda to make the connection. Officer Branson said it was likely that when Theda saw Brianna's laptop and notebooks on the table and maybe even Jake's shaving gear in the bathroom, she lost control. Or maybe she'd planned murder all along. They'd never know now.

Theda had been clutching Brianna's laptop. No one could figure out why except that she'd been reading Brianna's book on the laptop she'd stolen the first time.

Jake relaxed in Brianna's embrace and his arms loosened around her. He lifted his head. "We've got past a lot together, Brianna. Can we please take the next step?" He nuzzled her neck and spoke into her ear, sending arousal on tippy-toe down her back.

"Yes, please," she murmured, fully engaged. She wanted him, always had and now he'd be hers. No more lying awake wondering what it would be like between them. No more watching him from a distance and hoping he'd look her way. No more mooning after Jake Morrow.

Finally, after fifteen years and more false starts than either of them could bear, it was time.

And it was right.

And full.

And love bloomed in the cracks and crevices of their abused hearts.

"I love you, Brianna. I have since I first saw you that day in the hall of Welcome High. You looked so startled when Tiffany singled you out. You picked up the end of your hair and chewed it when you realized she wasn't going to brush by you, that she'd actually stopped to talk with you. Your eyes were wary and I wondered why because I didn't know how mean Tiffany could be. She had me fooled."

"My wariness wasn't because of her, specifically. I was afraid of being noticed by anyone. All I wanted was to go through my days at school alone. And then, there you were, right in front of me and I wanted—oh, how I wanted—you to notice me. To see me. I was tongue-tied around you. Watched you whenever I could. That's why I felt so guilty about our kisses. I'd yearned for them." And now she'd had them.

And she was about to have all of Jake. "I love you, too."

"We're free now," he said with a beguiling, come-hither look. She molded her body to his and they fell together to the bed.

Somehow, he'd managed to coax her down the hall to his bedroom without her noticing. He was a sneaky one. "I love you," she repeated.

"Marry me and stay in Welcome. Don't leave me again," Jake asked in a tone husky with desire. "We've wasted enough years."

"We have, and yes, I'll stay in Welcome and marry you."

Jake dragged her beneath him and she felt his hip bones rub against hers. Felt his muscle and sinew, tight with pent-up tension. Felt his heart slamming near hers as he helped her wriggle out of her jeans and panties. Then she was naked from the waist down.

"This won't work," she said. "I want to feel your skin." She ran the arch of her foot up the denim on his leg and frowned at his fierce face. With a growl of frustration, he backed off the foot of the bed.

As he rose to full height Jake grinned a boyish smile and she knew his sons would beguile her and his daughters would always get their way. "You're going to give me children, right?"

He stopped disrobing long enough to flash her a look that the devil would admire. "As many as you want." His jeans hit the floor as he bent to yank off his socks.

"And pets? I want my own dog and cat," she said firmly, eyeing him hungrily. He was even better naked than she imagined. And she'd imagined a *lot*. She pulled off her sweater and bra.

Now they were both naked and he stood at the foot of the bed, hands on his hips. "What happened to Brianna the quiet one?" But his gaze roved over her as if the question was an afterthought.

"She fell in love. And that love means I'm changed. A changed woman."

He quirked an eyebrow at her statement. "I'm different, too. You make me a better man, Brianna. I miss the guy I used to be before that night. I had friends, buddies, and teammates. I had a mom and dad who were part of my day-to-day life. I shoved all of them away."

She leaned back on her elbows and his eyes flared interest. "But, right now, you're all mine. I'll share you when I've had my fill," she promised.

He laughed and crawled up the bed to settle his long body on top of hers. She felt the press of him against her cradle and melted in welcome. As he slid inside and filled her, she murmured, "I don't know if I'll ever have enough."

And then Jake took her to places she'd never been and gave her everything she'd ever craved.

And that's what she'd been doing for almost half her life; craving Jake.

Epilogue

DECEMBER 1

"Did you hear they found the camper van?" Sybil asked. Shandy sat with her friends as Clay's receptionist stood beside their table at the Welcome Bar and Grill. Her husband, Bud, stood with his wife, nodding and avid.

Clay cleared his throat and rose with baby Autumn in his arms. "Want to hold her, Sybil?"

"Of course." And Sybil and Bud, completely enthralled, forgot their juicy piece of gossip. While they cooed over the baby, Shandy surveyed her group of friends and marveled that they'd all found love and commitment after returning to Welcome.

She'd never left and wondered, slowly, deeply if she ever would. Once, she'd had a chance, but she'd made a different choice and now she lived with the choice she'd made. Happily, she told herself. All she ever wanted was here in Welcome.

And she had her son. There was nothing else she wanted.

Clay and Mercy shared a loving smile, content and happy to have a quiet Christmas season at home together. Come January they would leave for California for three months of filming and publicity tours Mercy had agreed to do. So far their plan to balance their lives was working well.

Elle and Logan, sitting on her other side, had just announced twins were on the way. A second set for Elle, but for Logan, these were his first children, and the couple couldn't be happier. Shandy felt a shaft of want when she looked at them. More children was a dream of hers that had been cut short when her husband had left.

That's how she thought of her marriage breakdown. Justin left. Simple and elegant. He claimed he didn't leave *her* and he certainly never left their son, Josh. She shook off the thoughts that were the beginning of an endless spiral into the blues.

This was supposed to be a happy evening, full of friends and children. Across from her sat Brianna and Jake Morrow, newlyweds who'd eloped. Brianna was a quiet, private person, so eloping made sense and Jake was so besotted he'd have agreed to a honeymoon on Mars if it meant having her.

Clay and Mercy's daughter Dilly sat with Shandy's son Josh. Their heads were together over a pair of coloring pages and crayons. Josh was so sweet with younger children, it hurt that he'd probably never have a baby sister or brother.

Of course, they all knew the van Theda Levi had borrowed from the Rhodes family had been found. Everyone had spent no small amount of time today dissecting the various notes she'd left behind in it. The notes were plastered on everyone's news feed and the locals had been completely engaged in the psychology of Theda's sick mind. She'd been deeply disturbed and had somehow decided that Brianna's thriller about a stalker being murdered by his victim was about her. In Theda's twisted thoughts, her arson was an attempt to thwart Brianna's revenge for Theda having Jake's love and devotion.

On Shandy's immediate right sat an empty chair. Her ex-husband Justin had texted that traffic was slower than usual due to the heavy rain. December was generally wet and dark. Very dark. The days were far too short and the nights too long and lonely.

Somehow, Justin had engineered an invitation to this early Christmas celebration for the friends and she had a feeling it was Jake's doing because he'd been avoiding her gaze since they'd sat down.

But Josh would be thrilled when their "surprise" guest showed up and who was she to ruin her son's Christmas? Besides, Justin would be staying at a hotel and not taking up space on her sofa.

"Did you hear about the bedbug infestation out on the highway?" Jake said around a smirk.

Shandy clenched her jaw. "No, I didn't." She watched as Jake slid his phone off the table and into his pocket. *Liar.* Luckily, Shandy owned a dry cleaning company and a small string of laundromats. "I'll call them to see if they need help with laundering their linens in time for their Christmas guests." She felt like a goalie blocking a shot. "There should be plenty of time to deal with the problem before Christmas."

She felt a movement beside her and the empty chair was suddenly filled with a man. The scent of man, the heat, the muscles, the profile of a man. Justin had arrived and like always had stolen her thoughts and her air.

"Buddy," he said quietly while everyone else waited for Josh to lift his head. "Pfft, Buddy. Look who's here for Christmas."

And with that, the jerk slung his arm across her shoulders as if he had the right. Before she could shrug him off, their son looked up and nothing, but nothing in this world would make her do anything to steal the joy from his eyes.

She allowed Justin to keep his arm where it was. The jerk. *Bedbugs.* How stupid did the Jays think she was? Jake and Justin had always pulled pranks.

Well, not this time.

No way would Shandy allow her ex-husband to ruin Christmas by staying with her. No way. Not a chance. *Na-unh.*

The End

If you enjoyed *Craving Jake* and have ever found a wonderful romance by reading reviews, please pay that joy forward by sharing a few words about how *Craving Jake* made you feel when you closed it.

A review doesn't have to be long, or a retelling of the plot, just a few words on how you felt when you finished. Did you sigh at the end? Feel happy?

The next book in my Return to Welcome series is *Claiming Shandy* and you've just read a bit about the story in the epilogue.

If you want to hear about exciting new releases and deals you can subscribe to Bonnie's Newsy Bits on my website. Readers can download a free e-book when they subscribe.

Over 40 romance titles are listed on my website at https://www.bonnieedwards.com/.

Don't miss out!

Visit the website below and you can sign up to receive emails whenever Bonnie Edwards publishes a new book. There's no charge and no obligation.

https://books2read.com/r/B-A-JXD-CRACB

BOOKS 2 READ

Connecting independent readers to independent writers.

Did you love *Craving Jake Return to Welcome Book 3*? Then you should read *Claiming Shandy Return to Welcome Book 4*[1] by Bonnie Edwards!

RETURN TO WELCOME BOOK 4

2

She thought her divorce was final...

Welcome WA, where rumor, gossip, and old grudges endure long past their best before date.

Justin Camden wants his life back. His wife back. His son back. And he's returned to Welcome to get them. Justin has a plan for the Christmas season and moving in with his ex and his boy is just the beginning.

Shandy Camden is stuck. Her big oaf of an ex-husband has finagled his way into her home for the entire month of December. He claims to want an old-fashioned family Christmas with their son.

---

1. https://books2read.com/u/mYyxWG

2. https://books2read.com/u/mYyxWG

She's forced to let Justin stay because refusing will break her son's heart.

Slowly, Shandy sees that her ex may have another agenda. But she doesn't believe in the magic of Christmas the way their son does. Helpless and forced to live with her ex, Shandy struggles to overcome her growing attraction to the only man who's ever left her. The only man she's ever loved. But Justin left once and if he leaves again, she'll never recover, and neither will their son...

When the truth comes out, Shandy and Justin may well have discovered that more than anything, Christmas is about love.

Warning: If you don't want to read a divorced man grovel, then this romance isn't for you.

About the Author

Bonnie Edwards has been published by Kensington Books, Harlequin Books, Carina Press, and more.

With over 40 titles to her credit, her romances have been translated into several languages. Her books are sold worldwide.

Learn about more exciting releases and get a **free** romance by subscribing to her newsletter, **Bonnie's Newsy Bits** through her website.

https://www.bonnieedwards.com/

Cheers and happy reading!

Bonnie Edwards

www.ingramcontent.com/pod-product-compliance
Lightning Source LLC
Chambersburg PA
CBHW031217020726

47499CB00002B/623